I0594608

N E ABSOLOM

The Dreamer's Wish

Book 1 of the Parasomnia Chronicles

Copyright © 2020 by N E Absolom

All rights reserved. No part of this publication may be reproduced, stored or transmitted in any form or by any means, electronic, mechanical, photocopying, recording, scanning, or otherwise without written permission from the publisher. It is illegal to copy this book, post it to a website, or distribute it by any other means without permission.

This novel is entirely a work of fiction. The names, characters and incidents portrayed in it are the work of the author's imagination. Any resemblance to actual persons, living or dead, events or localities is entirely coincidental.

N E Absolom asserts the moral right to be identified as the author of this work.

Second edition published 2021. Previously published in 2020 as "Somniloquy".

Second edition

ISBN: 978-0-6488668-4-8

This book was professionally typeset on Reedsy. Find out more at reedsy.com

To Sara and Steven,

We are separated by oceans,
or by time and the veil between worlds,
yet you endure, also, within these pages.

Sara, keep fighting.
Steven, I'll see you again one day.

CHAPTER 1

The Dreamer was stirring. Jehn paused his reading and watched the attendants scurry about their duties, their young faces lined with worry. *They should not be so burdened*, he thought. Worry was best reserved for those with nothing better to think about.

A light breeze rustled the leaves of the grove surrounding the courtyard. Smooth cream cobblestones radiated out in a concentric pattern, drawing the eye ever back to the central marble dais that gleamed in the bright sunlight. A single golden teardrop broke from its branch and danced upon the air. Jehn watched the leaf dip and fall before it settled on the ground, quivering slightly. He stared at it a moment, not wanting to break the spell.

'You have to be sure,' said the Dreamer, her youthful face unmarked by time. 'Be careful of your eyes.'

Jehn's gaze flicked to the dais where the Dreamer lay. She yet slept, her hands clasped loosely on her stomach, summer blonde hair carefully coiffed in place; but that would soon change. The Dream was approaching its end.

A sandy-haired young man—little more than a boy, really, as was the case with all the Dreamer's attendants—scribbled the spoken words into his journal, catching Jehn's eye. Jehn inclined his head, but he wasn't really paying attention to the boy. Instead, Jehn's thoughts drifted, as they often did, to what the Dreamer's words might mean.

Each attendant carried a journal when they were on duty. One could not predict when the Dreamer might speak, so the attendants were always ready. Their journals were dated and recorded into a great archive. Complementing this archive were the works of scholars past and present, who wrote the supporting narrative around the Dreamer's words: what was happening in the world of Palantia, what changes eventuated after words were spoken, theories and musings on their meaning or use as a tool to guide Palantians' lives for enrichment and advancement.

Jehn was such a scholar. He spent his days studying the words transcribed by attendants throughout the centuries. It was a simple life, uncomplicated by the politics and intrigue of the cities, but not so mundane as to invoke boredom. Jehn enjoyed the clarity that came with routine. When he found his thoughts turning to his old life, a stretch spent nose-deep in the historical texts was usually enough to regain his focus.

The Dreamer's words were such a fascinating subject. Much of what was recorded could be dismissed as a natural by-product of Dreaming, of simple subconscious ramblings, but every now and then, the Dreamer's words had a special weight to them. They felt portentous. Was this such a time? But one could not recognise a portent until after the fact, and so there was little else to do but ponder, study, and hope that if something did come to pass, it would not be a catastrophe. Jehn was pragmatic in that way; a remnant of his former life.

But I digress, he thought, chuckling inwardly at the ease with which his thoughts phrased themselves so academically. Jehn not only studied the words and histories of the Dreamers, he was also a prolific writer. Essays, lectures, dissertations, theories; Jehn was as verbose on the page as in his own head. He was passionate about his subject and enjoyed explaining his thoughts to any who would listen. Right now, however, he was uneasy.

The Dreamer was more than a physical presence and source of veiled wisdom. From their sleeping imaginations, Dreamers brought forth new regions to explore and strange new creatures to discover. They sowed innovation, invention, and philosophy. Through the manifestation of their Dreamings, the world of Palantia was built and shaped. Palantia needed a Dreamer as its anchor. Without one, it would drift from reality and cease to be.

Jehn laid the tome he was reading upon the wooden bench beside him and looked up at the sky. The golden aspen leaves shivered, the sound almost resembling a whispered voice. The early afternoon sky was clear in the gap between the circle of trees, and Jehn watched a handful of tiny striped finches rush after a cloud of gnats, predators swirling amongst their prey. The scholar stretched his long fingers and intertwined them behind his head, mussing the auburn strands of his ponytail. He leaned back against the bench, wincing slightly at the crack and pop of his stiff joints, and sighed.

It had been a thousand years since the current Dream began, and Jehn knew time was running out. He had uncovered long-forgotten knowledge—the signs of the Awakening—and soon, a new Dreamer must be found.

Lately, the attendants had mentioned the Dreamer's restlessness. Jehn had seen it himself just two days before. The Dreamer's normally still repose was broken by bouts of tossing and turning, coupled with clenched fists and a furrowed brow.

Jehn was troubled. This was not as the ancient texts suggested. This seemed far more intense—violent, even—compared with the gentle Awakening recorded in the historical journals of the distant past. A sense of urgency compelled him. He'd met with the Elders yesterday to raise his concerns. The Elders were famous for their ability to discuss any matter until it was done to death, so it was to his surprise they had agreed with his concerns with very little fuss or bluster. Less surprising was that the Elders couldn't agree upon a course of action. He'd left them arguing about the matter after several hours.

The old Jehn wouldn't have stood for that. The old Jehn was impulsive, lacked patience, and was quick to anger. *No. You stay right there in the past, old self. This needs a measured approach.*

He'd returned to the texts in search of further insight, but uncovered nothing that explained why this Awakening would be different. Frustrated—yet intrigued nonetheless—Jehn soon found himself itching to take matters into his own hands. Yes, the Dreamer could sleep for another year or more, but maybe not. Surely, having a replacement trained and at the ready would be advantageous. The Elders had been known to take days or weeks to decide on trivial matters, let alone something of such importance. What else could Jehn do? *Someone needed to do something.* It may as well be him, a man with the means and motivation.

* * *

From the shadows of the surrounding trees, a shrouded figure watched the Dreamer sleep. It went unnoticed among the dappling of sunlight through the canopy, a trick of light and shadow. The creature shifted its form to match the moving light and melted into the dark gaps between, lying in wait close by. The hours passed, but it was patient, waiting until the attendants changed shift. The first one was leaving now, nodding in acknowledgement to his peer, a dark-haired girl of around fourteen. The girl carried a small amphora, its mouth stoppered with a large cork. The attendant walked with extra care, her eyes fixed on the vessel.

Now.

Beneath the inky blackness of its shredded robe, the figure's green eyes flickered in the light, pupils thinning and elongating into vertical slits. A murmured word, guttural and thick, emitted from the crack of its mouth: 'Gathak.' It gestured, thin fingers twisting and crabbing. 'Nyatak.'

The Dreamer's back arched with a violent crack, and a strangled cry erupted from her sleeping lips. The attendant jumped in surprise and dropped the amphora. It smashed into pieces, its amber fluid seeping into the thirsty ground. The girl cried out.

Without hesitation, the figure in the shadows pursed its lips and took a deep breath. A tiny, faint thread rose from the Dreamer's temple and snaked its way toward the trees. As the thread touched the creature's lips, a smile of sadistic pleasure played across its dark face. It took in the thread with a long, sensuous breath, and let out an almost imperceptible sigh.

Merely a minute later, a group of attendants ran into the courtyard. They stood staring as the Dreamer's body bucked and twisted on the sleeping dais. 'What's wrong with her?'

they asked, but the girl could only shake her head, unable to proffer any kind of answer.

Like a lost thought, the mysterious figure disappeared into the forest.

CHAPTER 2

S ara's foot slipped as she stepped off the bus. Her sneaker skidded on the last step, and she flailed for the handrail, avoiding an embarrassing tumble at the very last moment. With not a care for her fate, the bus sped away, belching a dark cloud of smoke from its exhaust as it rounded the street. She wrinkled her nose at the smell. *Gross.*

It was a Wednesday, and winter was giving way to longer days. Sara was glad for that. It meant more time in the garden; though that also meant days in the office, where she worked doing general IT support, would be harder to endure, when the sun was bright and inviting outside the sterile glass and steel windows of the office building.

Sara had been doing jobs like that for nearly two decades, bouncing around from one workplace to another, never staying too long. This latest one, she'd been at three years. Most of the time, she helped her colleagues with their documents and spreadsheets, reset forgotten passwords, and replaced broken keyboards. The role didn't really suit her, as she had to deal with people far more than she would have liked, but it paid the bills and the work was usually easy. The stereotype about IT people was beneficial for her; she was socially awkward and made weird jokes that nobody understood, and so they generally left her alone.

Alone is just fine, she told herself, firmly. *I've managed well enough that way for a good long while. Anyway, I have plenty going on in my own head to keep me company.*

She hiked her backpack up onto her shoulders and sighed. It was time to face The Hill.

It was a horrible hill. *Unnecessarily steep*, she thought, which was enough of a description. Sara wasn't a fan of exertion in the slightest. Muttering expletives under her breath, she grumbled and puffed the whole way. *At least the weather is on my side*. The rain and wind were staying well away. Though, as the local saying went, *if you don't like the weather here, wait five minutes.*

Sara crested the hill and stopped to catch her breath. Her ashy blonde hair stuck to the back of her neck despite the cool air, and she ran her fingers through the damp strands. Here was a good place to pause. Nestled between the tightly packed houses was a patch of bushland that had been spared the fate of urban sprawl. The lot was too small for a house, so the parcel of land had been left to its own devices. Sara loved it.

It was a tangled little paradise of soft wild grass, with trees that grew thick and close, throwing mysterious shadows every which way. In summer, native wildflowers bloomed and gave off a delicate fragrance. You could only catch a waft if you stood in just the right spot.

Sara liked to imagine that the little wild place was a secret doorway to another world—a fanciful musing, given how built-up and industrialised the surrounding area was, but she enjoyed the fantasy anyway.

A tiny blue bird—a superb fairy wren, Sara recognised,

being somewhat of a bird fancier—hopped boldly from the bushes and chirruped. Swift on his heels came a little harem of lady wrens clad in muted shades of brown and tan, but no less beautiful and dainty. Sara smiled as she watched the small flock flit around on the ground, picking at grass for tiny insects. Fairy wrens were her favourite bird, especially the blue males with their iridescent feathers and dashing black markings.

'If ever a bird was a magical creature, it would be you,' she said to the wren and gave a whistle, trying to imitate the bird's musical chirp. The wren cocked its head and eyed her, but offered no reply. 'Well then, time to go,' she said to the silent wren and his lady friends. Sara hefted her backpack, turned into her street, and trudged the short stretch to home.

Reaching her driveway, she leaned on the heavy concrete letter box, trying to slow her puffing breath. That last two hundred or so yards from the small wild place to her house were the worst. Living high on a hill had its advantages, but in Sara's opinion, arriving home with an elevated heart rate was not one of them.

The letter box contained just the usual junk mail and a pair of envelopes that were almost definitely bills. Sara had hoped for something exciting, but the catalogues and brochures would have to do. If nothing else, they'd give her something to flick through while watching TV. *I really should put up one of those 'no junk mail' signs,* she thought, knowing it was one of those things she'd never get around to. One day, maybe.

With the bundle of paper under her arm, Sara fished her house keys out of her backpack. She fumbled the key into the lock, almost dropping her mail as she pushed her way into the small tiled foyer. The house was silent except for the usual hum and tick of the old refrigerator. Another thing for 'one day.'

She kicked her shoes off, abandoning them in the corner to hold company with a dust bunny and a dead spider. Sara wrinkled her nose in disgust—mostly at herself for not having gotten around to vacuuming yet.

As she climbed the stairs, her socked feet sinking into the soft carpet, she wondered where Sam was. The fluffy black tom cat's particular custom was to wait at the front door for when she came home. He liked to wind around her legs, and she was certain it was a deliberate attempt to trip her. Maybe he was envious of her height.

Sara trailed her hand along the staircase wall, her fingers bumping on the dents and divots made by various mishaps over the years—this one from the movers nearly dropping her heavy blackwood wardrobe, that one from Sam knocking a vase off the riser and having it bounce off the wall before shattering on the foyer tiles below.

'Sam! Where are you, mister?'

Perhaps in the lounge. Sam often slept in the sunbeams that fanned across the floor. The house was blessed with floor-to-ceiling windows that collected the all-day sun, trapping the light and warmth to make the perfect sun-bathing environment for a cat. Sam slept a lot these days. He was eighteen years old and arthritic, but still an absolute gourmet and an expert snuggler. Sara felt a twinge of concern.

She stepped onto the landing and dropped her backpack. 'Sam?' She clicked her fingers, but he did not respond. Heart in her throat, she padded down the hallway and into the lounge room.

In the last long beam of the day, there he lay, eyes closed and fur rusty from the sun. He was a perfect statue, a miniature panther in repose. Sara's breath hitched in her throat.

'Oh, Sam, my little Sammy.' She ran her hand across his still form. Despite the sun, he felt cold, and Sara knew he'd been gone for some time. Something broke inside her, and as she lay on the floor curled around the cat's small body, her chest heaved in violent sobs, tears streaming down her cheeks to mingle in his soft fur.

Sam had always been there. For half of her lifetime—most of her adult life—the cat had been her constant. He'd been a companion during the ups and downs of a solitary life, one who didn't judge or criticise, who just sat on her lap and purred while she cried, or laughed, or ranted to the air. And now, he was gone. Eighteen years was a good life for a cat. But it still wasn't long enough.

What was life without her best friend?

Time paused then, slowing down as it does in times of shock and grief. Afterwards, Sara couldn't recall the exact number of minutes she'd laid on the floor with Sam, but she remembered the sudden rush to consciousness when time sped back up.

There was a diffusion of light in the air above. Sara didn't notice it at first, but it gradually caught her eye. Through a haze of tears, she saw the misty outline of a cat. With a short intake of breath, she glanced down at Sam's lifeless body in confusion, then raised her gaze to the feline apparition. 'Sam?'

The ghostly cat shimmered like sunlight on water, and a gentle sound echoed out towards Sara. The sweet, melodic hum calmed her at once. Sara looked closer at the cat and realised it was much smaller than Sam and distinctly feminine in feature. It was an exquisite little creature. Sharp triangle ears tapered to a tufted tip, with delicate hairs wisping within.

The cat's tail was voluminously fluffy, and it swayed gently in a mesmerising rhythm.

The constant scintillation made it almost impossible to discern the cat's colouring, but Sara could pick out speckles of honey and chocolate. For want of a better term, Sara decided on tortoiseshell. The shimmering cat's whiskers were much longer than her small body warranted. A cat's whiskers were designed to guide the animal through small spaces, and were usually a fraction longer than its body-width. But this cat's whiskers stretched out and out, lengthening and then tapering into nothingness. They were darker than black; they *stole* the light from around it, which created an odd dissonance against the shimmering fur.

And those enchanting eyes! While Sara was studying her, the ghost cat continued humming, eyes closed in a serene expression. Now, the cat opened her eyes slowly, languorously, as if she had all the time in the world. Perhaps she did. This cat's eyes were unlike those of a normal cat, not green or yellow or even blue. This cat's eyes were amethyst.

Sara stared at the cat, unsure what to do. The cat stared back. Sara hesitated. Dare she? She reached her hand out to touch the little feline.

A small flash of light, a sudden silence, and then all Sara saw before her was empty air. The strange cat was gone. Sara withdrew her hand in confusion. Sam's body remained on the lounge room floor, and she stroked his cool fur absently as the tears dried upon her cheek.

* * *

Sara closed the front door and leaned hard against it, staring through the glass panel at the vet nurse making her way down the steep driveway, carefully carrying the black plastic bag that held Sam. Sara's heart felt broken into a million pieces, but the rational part of her trusted that Sam would be handled with the utmost care. In a week, his remains would be ready to collect from the pet crematorium. Sara would take the small velvet bag and ponder how such a big life could be reduced to such a tiny package. The bag would sit on a special shelf and gather dust and memories.

Sara returned to the empty lounge room to sit on the floor where Sam had died. She touched the spot on the carpet where he'd lay and gave a sad smile. *What do I do now?* Sam had been with her since he was just a tiny kitten. She had adopted him for a shelter when she turned twenty; an incredible, life-changing gift to herself that she could not have fathomed at the time. *Who am I without him?* She stared out the window, surveying the street below. The rows of modern houses were stacked together like blocks, packed in close with little room for more than a strip of lawn between them. Sara found it depressing. Urban sprawl everywhere. Nature repressed.

The sky was darkening as the day approached its end. The lights across the town below were starting to flicker on, and the last vestiges of sunlight streaked the sky purple and orange above the grey hills in the west.

Sara had never felt so alone.

She'd been single most of her life, with just a short dalliance here and there. But she'd never met that special, right person, and so marrying or settling down had never been an option. It wasn't that she didn't want to; she just lacked that easy knack so many others seemed to have with making human connections. Sara could talk at length to any animal she might meet, but people were another story. People were hard. She really didn't enjoy being around them for long. It seemed to Sara they were judging her on her appearance, or choice of clothing, or habits or interests—or especially on how she tended to ramble when she was nervous.

Animals were easy. They never laughed at you if you were awkward, they never looked at you like you were stupid; they never judged. Cats were her favourite. She admired them for their independence and intelligence, and how every cat was different—she'd never met one the same as another. Cats were always interesting; there was something magical about them. They were mysterious, but could always let you know if they wanted something, and their purrs were a healing balm like no other. Cats were the best kinds of people.

Sara wandered into the kitchen to put the kettle on. *Tea is always a good idea.* Emotionally drained, she dropped onto a chair. Her thoughts turned to the strange cat apparition. As much as she'd hoped, she knew it wasn't Sam's soul saying a final farewell. *A different kind of cat entirely*, Sara thought. She couldn't recall reading or hearing about anything like it. Sara was fascinated with magic and the fae. Since she was a child, she had devoured any literature she could find on the subject.

She cast her eye to the bookshelf in the corner. Books of all sorts stuffed the shelves, which bowed from the weight of their load: fantasy novels upon whose covers knights and adventurers did battle or quested for glory and riches, books about herbs and natural healing, tomes of modern witchcraft and paganism, but more than anything, volume after volume of faerie myths and legends. She had studied them, and knew them well. Indeed, Sara considered herself somewhat an expert on faery lore, and held to the belief that the fae still existed in this world, despite human civilisation encroaching into their domain.

In Sara's opinion, most people lived shallow surface lives with no real thought to the mysteries of the universe, and perhaps that was another reason she found it difficult to relate to others. Sara liked to dream and wish and wonder about what was, is, and might be. Many people found that a childish waste of time. *Many people are stupid.*

She sipped at the steaming mug of tea and closed her eyes, letting her mind drift, glad for a moment's release from the numbness of her grief. After a while, she realised she was humming. It wasn't any song she'd heard before, but the tune felt somehow familiar. The melody was sweet and soothing. Sara opened her mouth and sang the tune wordlessly. She liked the way it sounded, echoing from her throat and into the empty room. As she repeated the refrain, a soft harmony joined her.

At once, the song burst forth from her, all her emotions entwined within the music. The harmony rose and fell in cadence, and Sara was aware of a thrumming sensation, vibrating throughout her body. Her eyes snapped open in surprise, and there was the ghost cat, shimmering and sparkling, watching Sara intently whilst softly humming in tune.

The two continued their song for several more moments before fading to an end. 'Who are you?' said Sara.

The cat winked and was gone again in a flash. Sara chuckled wryly. *Is this my life now? Singing in an empty house with a magical disappearing cat?* She felt vindicated. She'd always believed there was more to the world, more than the mundane and everyday. She felt the magic in small things: the whisper of grasses in an untended yard, the cool sharpness of winter stars, the thrum of nature's heartbeat. She had seen things once or twice. Shadows and glimmers that darted out of sight, the sense of a presence beyond her own. Memory had softened with time, but the feeling remained.

Well, this time there was no explaining it away as a trick of the light or a poor memory. This cat, whatever it may be, was real. And it was magic.

'See you soon, faery kitty,' Sara said to the deserted room as she finished her tea. Perhaps next time the cat visited, the creature would make her intentions a little clearer instead of vanishing the instant Sara spoke. But you never knew with cats. *The word 'fickle' springs to mind.*

Sara set the empty mug on the bench and stared out the kitchen window, torn between her grief and a new sense of wonder.

CHAPTER 3

Jehn sat at his kitchen table, picking at the leftover bread from his evening meal. It had been a tasty soup, made with fresh vegetables and a thick meaty broth. He unconsciously checked for any leavings, but the wooden bowl was scraped clean. *How long?* he wondered, impatience biting at his nerves. He rubbed his face wearily, knowing sleep would not be quick to arrive tonight. Not that it was at the best of times. Jehn was plagued with insomnia. Unresolved guilt, perhaps. *Think about that later. The wee hours of the morning, for example.*

With soft whisperings and a gentle song, he'd sent the hummingcat to seek out a new Dreamer Candidate. They shared a bond, the scholar and the cat, one born from strife and forged over the years of their unshakeable friendship. Hummingcats were usually solitary creatures, living their lives with no ties or obligations. They travelled freely and were well-respected throughout Palantia, but most people went their whole lives without seeing one. Jehn treasured his bond with this particular cat, knowing it was rare beyond measure. The hummingcat genuinely enjoyed his company as much as Jehn did hers.

He had called and she had answered, glad to hop through for

a scouting mission. *Be patient,* he told himself. Time worked differently between the two worlds; it was hard to judge how long she had even been gone. A matter of an hour or so here, but there? It could be days, or only minutes. There was nothing else to do but wait.

The time differential was the subject of Jehn's latest dissertation. It was one of the great mysteries of Palantia's existence and a common discussion topic among the scholars. Whilst everyone had their own ideas, the most widespread theory was that both worlds existed along a similar timeline; one was linear, whereas the other took an irregular, rambling path. The latter turned this way and that, doubled back on itself and looped around, never staying the straight line. No one was quite sure which world was on what path, however. Jehn's paper discussed why this might be. He knew from his own harrowing experience that there were rules around mortals being privy to this information. He thought that it had to do with the Dreamer always being from the human world. He theorised that only potential Dreamers could set foot in Palantia, and only certain fae could reach the human world. He wondered if there would ever be a way to measure such a thing.

He'd touched the other side once, had seen a glimpse. Exotic buildings and strange contraptions tantalised just beyond his reach. He'd lost himself then. Gone mad for a time. A man obsessed. He'd broken the rules and there had been consequences. *No. Don't remember.*

A knock at the door jolted Jehn back to the present. He hadn't expected to be disturbed this evening, as the Elders would still be arguing and wouldn't be finished for some time yet. *Who could it be at this hour?*

Jehn pushed back his chair and stood up from the table, brushing crumbs off his clothes as he hastened to the door. The incessant knocking continued, and he rolled his eyes in annoyance. Whoever it was, they were very insistent.

'Yes, yes, I'm coming!'

He wrested the heavy oak door open. A Dreamer attendant stood on the threshold, chest heaving with exertion, sweat beading his brow. Jehn stared at the boy for a moment, sifting through his brain for the attendant's name. Remembering, he said, 'Yes, Senna, what is so urgent that has you beating down my door in the middle of the night?'

The attendant paused to catch his breath, and reached for Jehn's sleeve, tugging him forward. 'It's the Dreamer, something's wrong! You must come. Hurry!'

Without hesitation, Jehn darted outside, pulling the door closed in one smooth motion. He locked it with a key on a leather thong attached to his wrist.

'Let's go,' he said, marching down the cobblestone path to the main street, the attendant on his heels.

The street was thick with people rushing towards the Dreamer's grove, faces grave and pinched with concern. Jehn increased his pace.

The pair arrived among a jostling throng. Senna pushed through the crowd, dragging Jehn behind him. Attendants circled the dais, blocking the Dreamer from view. The circle opened to let the two pass, then formed up to close the gap, preventing the crowd from seeing what lay beyond.

Jehn's mouth dropped open. The Dreamer's face was stricken in contortions of agony and fear, hands clenching into fists and opening again, her fingers stretched to a painful extent. Sweat poured from her brow and the attendants mopped it away with soft white cloths.

Jehn's voice was hoarse and thick with confusion, 'What happened?'

Despite his suspicions, nothing had prepared him to see the Dreamer in such a state. Jehn stood in shock, his mind whirling. He was now convinced this was more than the onset of waking. The Dreamer was suffering intense pain. If the historical texts were to be believed, this was very serious. Because of the Dreamer's link with the world, strong negative emotions could manifest in treacherous ways. This was wholly dependent on the Dreamer, and impossible to predict, but Jehn had read of effects as benign as changeable weather patterns, to one account that seemed to suggest a large-scale continental shift. The danger lay in the unpredictability, and Jehn's heart began to race.

'You were there before, everything was fine!' said Senna. 'The Dreamer stirred and spoke the words and then settled back to sleep. She seemed normal! But apparently some time tonight, she had some kind of spasm, cried out, and began thrashing about. My friend, Keir, saw it happen when she came to provide the sustenance. I thought you might have some insight—you study the histories, and you wrote that paper last month. Is it the Awakening?'

Jehn looked into Senna's eyes, his expression grim. 'No, Senna, the Awakening should be a peaceful transition. Whilst the Dreamer's prior agitation seems a precursor to the Awakening—and indeed, my recent discovery suggests so—I fear this most recent disturbance is something else.'

'Something else? Like what? We need to do something! In class only a fortnight gone, Master Piranus told us that if the Dreamer dies, so does all of Palantia!' Senna's eyes were wide in dismay.

'Master Piranus has always been an outrageous doom merchant,' said Jehn, shaking his head, his mouth set in a grim line, 'I'll be sure to have words with him. He should not be unduly alarming his students in such a way. Come, Senna, I need to speak with the Elders again. They must surely listen now. I'd best tell them what I've done—'

'What do you mean? What is it you've done?' The attendant gripped Jehn's arm, his young face a litany of conflicting emotions.

'I'll explain on the way.'

CHAPTER 4

A week passed. Sara stood in the garden, the sun warming her back. She'd thought of the strange cat's last visit often, even as her life slipped back into its usual banality. That first weekend without Sam had been hard—harder still when his cremains came in to the vet surgery for collection—and her emotions had threatened to overwhelm her at every turn. But rather than face up to this new reality, she spent the time pottering around the house, doing chores and running a few errands. These distractions took her away from dealing with her feelings. Sara was very good at that. *Next level conflict avoidance.*

Today's strategy was tending to her garden. Sara felt at peace amid the life and growth, with its backdrop of untouched bushland spread upon the hill behind her house. Despite living in a large town, Sara's home was high above the busy streets, and the bush reserve behind meant no one would ever live there, ensuring the backyard was always a haven from people. Sara considered it a paradise in suburbia.

Created all from scratch, entirely by herself, the garden was a true labour of Sara's love. Over the years, she'd built the beds, learned how to compost and improve the soil, weeded, sown, pruned, and coaxed every bush, vine, and tree to thrive. It was her greatest pride in a life most ordinary. The garden was her centre. She stood within it now, gently touching the newly sprouted beans and whispering encouragement for them to grow big and strong.

The garden was mostly herbs and vegetables with several fruit trees and raspberry canes. Other plants served as companions, or as sacrifices to lure pests away. The onset of spring meant a profusion of growth everywhere she looked. Bees and hoverflies zipped from plant to plant, seeking out the flowers that had begun to open. Sara looked forward to the daily journey of growth. It was one of those small joys to visit each day and see the fruits and vegetables swelling ever larger, progressing their way to harvest time.

Sara watched a particularly fat bumblebee meandering around the garden, legs laden with pollen. It dipped and lifted, struggling with its load. The little creature moved from flower to flower, efficiently extracting the golden dust. 'Little bee, bumbling around,' Sara sang, 'bumbling up and bumbling down.'

She had a soft spot for bumblebees. One of her favourite fancies was to imagine them the steeds of tiny faery creatures who rode upon them like miniature horses, racing up and down the garden when she wasn't looking. A good fantasy. An even better distraction.

Don't forget to tell the bees.

Her mother's voice, a memory in her head, but insistent. It had been a long time since she'd heard that story. How did it go again?

When of the household one should die,
those left behind should quickly fly—
Tarry not, must tell the hive

of he who passed, no more to thrive.
If thy neglects this grave behest,
thy grief will grow, shall gift no rest.
Let know the bees or love will spurn.
Away, never return.

It seemed a little overdue to do this now, but once the idea was formed, Sara found it difficult to ignore. She had a tendency to listen to small instincts. Perhaps it was nothing more than superstition, but Sara did not like to test fate, just in case.

She sat down on a pile of stone pavers, next to a lavender bush bedecked with heady blooms. Several honeybees buzzed amongst the purple flowers. *How to begin?* 'Um. Hello, bees. I'm sorry I only remembered to do this now, I hope you understand. It's been really hard. So, ah,' she paused, the sadness bubbling to the surface. *So much for avoiding this.* 'It's Sam. He… he's no longer with us. He's gone.' The words choked out, 'He's dead, and I'm all alone. I have no one! What am I going to do? Please don't leave, bees. I need you for my garden. I want you to stay and be happy. Please stay.'

The sun beat down upon Sara's bowed head. The bees continued their busy work, unperturbed by the gulping, sobbing human in their midst. Perhaps the plea had been heard. Perhaps not. Nevertheless, the dam had finally broken.

A wattlebird called in the tree behind her, the guttural noise pulling her back to now. Sara smiled sadly. *No more tears.* She clicked her tongue and made a swallowing sound in her throat, attempting to return the bird's call. It was a good enough imitation for the bird to respond in kind. They spent a few minutes calling back and forth to each other. The small connection with another creature lifted her spirits, just a little.

Sara clapped her hands to loosen the damp soil clinging from her purple gardening gloves. Her thoughts returned to the mysterious cat. Where had she come from? What did she want? Perhaps she was just curious, in the manner of all cats. Sara had an affinity for animals of all sorts. She always tried to communicate with them, either by speaking in her language, or imitating theirs. Whether they understood her or not, she enjoyed the interaction and she was sure they did as well.

She picked up her trowel and shoved the handle in her back pocket, then carefully reset the bird-netting over the garden bed to protect it from opportunistic foragers. Pulling off her gloves, Sara took a final turn around the garden. Perhaps the magical cat would stop by tomorrow, and if she did, Sara would do her best to speak to her.

CHAPTER 5

A cacophony of voices rose from within the chamber. The Elders' words overlapped and ran together while attendants stood or paced nervously nearby. Jehn glanced to his side; Senna sat in silence, staring down at his hands which were clasped firmly in his lap. The young man had taken Jehn's hurried explanation of his suspicions stoically, which impressed the older scholar. *He has a sensible head; that will be useful to keep the other attendants calm when things invariably get worse.*

The Elders continued their heated discussion, and Jehn's frustration at the lack of action increased until finally he decided enough was enough. The Dreamer's violent seizure had now calmed to twitches and grimaces, but nevertheless, the gravity of the situation could not be ignored.

Jehn glanced at Senna, who nodded in tacit agreement. The scholar rose to his feet, straightening his tunic. 'I've sent for a new Candidate.' His voice rang out strong and clear, silencing the Elders' furious shouting. They turned to him as one, faces drawn in varying degrees of shock and confusion.

'You've done what?'

'You have no such authority!'

'You overstep, scholar!'

Jehn ignored the clamour. 'Many of you now know that the Dreamer's Awakening is due. My research tells me this should be a slow and gentle process, in order that a new Dreamer can be trained and instated parallel to the other's waking. This gives Palantia continuity. It allows a new Dreamer to adjust to the transition and for the current one to pass on their experience. However, there is something greater—more sinister—at play here. I believe we may be in grave danger if we do not act quickly. While we await the arrival of the Candidate, we must send a group to speak to the Court about the Dreamer's affliction.'

The Court was the democratic representative of Palantia. Members of the Aes-Sidhe, the first race of Palantia, sat in session in the city of Thalanthas and adjudicated disputes amongst the world's citizens. Such matters were rare in Palantia, but on those occasions where the parties could not come to a compromise, the Court could be relied upon for a wise and just decision.

Thalanthas, known colloquially as the Great City, was a thriving metropolis in contrast to the other towns and villages scattered across the Western Continent of Palantia, and so it was also a place where all manner of people gathered to share news and discoveries. When the Court was not resolving civil issues, its chambers were open to receive petitioners and those with information to be shared among the larger population. The Great City's streets and public houses were filled with a concentration of both the well-informed and the adventurous. If anyone knew what was happening to the Dreamer, it was likely they would be there.

An Elder stepped forward. The man's beard was long and beaded intricately with feathers and bones intertwined amongst the snowy hair. Jehn recognised him as Finnian Braydan, one of the more senior members of the Elders' circle. Jehn had met with him several times before on scholarly matters—clarifications about ancient language and the meanings of words long lost to history. The man was as insufferable as he was knowledgeable.

'Oh-ho, must we now? And just who do you propose will form this group, young man? Who shall take this message to the Court and present it there? And what, indeed, should the message be? We do not know exactly what is happening with the Dreamer. Perhaps this is simply the Awakening and you are mistaken as to an outside influence.' Finnian stroked his beard. The old man's fingers were long and fine, with carefully manicured nails—the fingers of someone who'd never done a day's hard labour in his entire privileged life. 'These are important matters for discussion, young man, and I'll remind you to respect your betters and leave such decision-making to those with cooler, wiser heads!'

Jehn prickled at the condescension, 'You can discuss all you like. The Council needs to be informed that the Dreamer is under attack. If you can think of no one better, I will go.'

Senna rose from his chair, and stood, shuffling his feet. His young face was determined, 'And I.'

Jehn looked sharply at the attendant, but before he was able to protest, Finnian continued, 'Please understand.' He spread his hands as if in supplication, but the gesture was anything but. 'A journey such as this needs the diplomacy, the sagacity of an Elder. Perhaps even a delegation.' The other Elders nodded and murmured in agreement. 'A mere scholar and attendant are just not appropriate choices for such an important undertaking. And let us not forget the danger inherent in the journey this would necessitate. It will take time to assemble the appropriate protection. Therefore, you see, *plentyn*, we simply cannot send someone now. We must discuss the matter until we come to the right course of action. Then we will proceed. Perhaps you may join the party if you so desire; however, for now you should return to your studies and duties.' Finnian turned away, clearly done with the conversation.

Jehn's irritation heightened. 'I can only hope you live to regret this misguided folly, Finnian Braydan,' he said. 'So unless you are volunteering your services, or will put forth your chosen… diplomat… we will be on our way.' *Fools, every one.* He sniffed in disdain, mouth twitching as he stared down the Elders.

Finnian regarded Jehn in silence, shaking his head in disbelief at the younger man's outburst.

Receiving no further response, Jehn turned to Senna. 'Gather your things and say your farewells. Meet me at the well at dawn.' He turned on his heel and stormed from the chamber.

* * *

The guild district was conveniently situated in the centre of town and was invariably a hub of activity. Jehn moved briskly, unperturbed by the bustle at such a late hour. His anger and urgency kept pace. *"A mere scholar." By the gods, if they only knew.*

The guilds operated at all times of the day and night, so business was always good. No matter the task required, there would be someone awake and ready to assist, if the price was right.

Jehn muttered an apology as he pushed past a couple inspecting leather goods at an open-air stall. The two barely noticed him, intent on assessing the quality of tanning techniques and suppleness of hides.

The air was cooling as late evening set in. Jehn eased out of the main forum and veered into an alley. He preferred to keep his business his own, and besides, it would not pay to be accosted by someone asking questions about the Dreamer. Jehn was a terrible liar. *Best to slip in the back.*

Hastening down the darkened lane, he stepped up to the lintel of a plain, nondescript building. A thin line of light streaked from beneath the door, and the sweet smell of smoke tickled his nostrils. This entrance was usually reserved for deliveries, but to those in the know, it was a discreet way to come and go without unnecessary attention.

The scholar rapped thrice in quick succession, paused, and knocked once more. A panel slid back, and a tanned face peered out. Jehn stepped forward letting the light hit his face. The panel slammed back and the door opened, a hand beckoning him within.

Easing past the threshold, Jehn took a quick glance over his shoulder at the alley behind. Seeing no one, he stepped inside.

* * *

Jehn strode down the dark hallway past the storeroom and kitchen, out to the tavern's main hall. The hall was well-lit by a multitude of oil lanterns and candles in sconces—the former hung from the rafters, while the latter were spaced close together on every wall of the room. White haze from smoking censers diminished Jehn's visibility to little more than a few feet ahead.

The scholar picked his way past the many small tables dotted about the place, nodding at people here and there as he passed by, but his expression made it clear he would not be stopping. Those seated were participating in the usual after-dark tavern affairs of drinking, smoking, gambling, and lying to each other about their adventures. On another night, Jehn may have joined them.

Instead, he made a beeline to the bar. A stout, wide-shouldered man stood behind it, drying a tankard with a pristine white cloth. He worked methodically, pushing the cloth inside to sop up the tiny drops of water until he was satisfied enough with his ministrations to return the vessel to a shelf behind him.

The barman looked up as Jehn approached and unleashed a hearty grin. 'Ah, Jehn, my fine fellow! I did not see you come in! What will it be this evening?'

Jehn leaned on the bar. It was crafted from walnut and made smooth from many years of use. 'I apologise, my friend. I came in the back. And I am not drinking tonight.'

The barman eyed him with interest, 'No? Then what brings you to the Balanced Scale?'

So, word has not yet reached this far into town. This was indeed a boon. Once the townsfolk heard about the incident at the Dreamer's grove, tensions would rise, and the town could be faced with an outright panic by the most fearful citizens.

'Is he here?' said Jehn, evading the barman's interest.

The fellow waved towards the darkest corner of the tavern. Jehn's eyes followed the barman's pointing finger, and amidst the haze, he could just make out a cloaked figure sitting alone.

31

'My thanks.'

As Jehn approached, the man pulled back his cowl. The other's hair was raven black with streaks of silver shot through, like a handful of stars against the night. The barest hint of a tapered ear betrayed his heritage. Jehn moved to face the robed figure. Their eyes met, and the other gestured at the stool opposite, offering Jehn a seat. Jehn obliged, nodding in thanks.

The man's skin was tanned and leathered from many years in the outdoors, yet it retained a fineness of feature. His sharp, angular face was lined with age, but his eyes—the singularly large irises shaded dark forest green with flecks of gold—sparkled with intelligence and curiosity. 'Well met, scholar,' he said in a rich, sonorous voice, 'I wondered how long it would take for you to appear.' The man raised an eyebrow and pushed a full tankard towards the scholar, setting free a trickle of foam from the ale's frothy head.

He then took a long pull from his own mug, eyeing Jehn as he did so. The man's stare was unwavering. To another it may have been unnerving, but Jehn simply smiled and shrugged. 'I should have guessed you would hear what none in town yet has. And that I would come to find you. One day you must tell me who your spy is.'

'Spies,' the other corrected, with a wry smile, 'and that is a day I hazard will never come!'

The two men laughed; the tension dissipated. Jehn took the mug of ale and raised it to his lips. The brim was ice-cold. Jehn looked around the room at the patrons enjoying their evening's activities and felt a sudden weight of responsibility upon his shoulders. He knew the choice had been his, but really, who else would have taken on this burden in his stead?

Jehn was a scholar, that was true, but he hadn't always been. In his distant past, Jehn had been a wanderer, a man with no home who travelled as the wind took him. He had answered the call to adventure wherever he had found it, though that path had not always been a righteous one. *More often than not, is a nearer truth.*

He returned from his self-reflection and leaned forward, 'I need your help, my friend. You know well enough that I am not prone to dramatics; however, in this case…'

'Out with it.' The lines around the man's eyes deepened as he teased, 'Tell me your trifling concern.'

'A small thing, then,' said Jehn. 'The future of Palantia's existence.'

The dark-haired man gazed intently into Jehn's eyes, seeking any sign of humour and finding none. He reached across the table and clasped Jehn's hands with his own. 'You shall have it, *mo chara.* You well know I can never resist an opportunity to be heroic!' He laughed heartily, and Jehn could not help but chuckle in return.

'How much do you know?' asked the scholar, wondering who was feeding the other his information.

'As much as you, I'd warrant. The Dreamer seems to be Awakening. But rumours persist there is more to it. Tell me, Jehn, what do you think is going on?'

Jehn took a deep breath and let it out slowly. He tilted back his mug and drained the ale to the last drop. 'We'll need another round, Thorn, my old friend. This will take some time.'

CHAPTER 6

I t was well past midnight when Jehn returned home, shouldering a large pack stuffed with travel supplies—rations, flint and steel, waterskin, healer's kit, a knife; the usual gear for any trip. *Clothes for the Court, too.*

Much of the evening was spent in discussions with Thorn, filling his friend in on his suspicions and planning their approach. Despite his annoyance at the Elders, Jehn conceded they were right about some degree of diplomacy being needed. Thorn offered to send a messenger bird with an introduction and brief explanation as to the nature of Jehn's concerns. If the Dreamer was under some kind of attack—as Jehn suspected—the scholar's petition would be expedited. No doubt, the Court would begin immediate preparations for the appropriate response.

Jehn knew he should retire and try to snatch a few hours of sleep, but his mind was racing. He set the pack on the floor beside the door and moved into the kitchen, retrieving a heel of bread and a small piece of cheese from the pantry. Resting an elbow on the table, he cradled his head in his hand, picking at the food and staring vacantly at a spot before him. Behind his calm visage, his thoughts swirled. He scratched a note on a roll of parchment on the table beside his plate, jotting down a few ideas for what he would say in his petition to the Court. *I need to be clear and concise, and effectively communicate the urgency of obtaining assistance.*

Jehn sighed and laid the pen upon the parchment. *Was I too hasty? Too forceful? But no, they could've taken another week before they even decided to send a delegation!* The scholar dragged his fingers through his russet hair. *I wanted to go,* he finally admitted. *Wanted to be there when my claims were validated.* He shook his head wryly. *Wanted to be the hero.*

The journey would start at dawn. Thorn estimated they'd need a week to arrive at their destination. The first stage would see them travel through the town outskirts of farms and rolling hills before passing to lightly forested land, which would soon grow thick and dark.

Those deep forests—the 'Shadowing, as they were known—were inhabited by all manner of strange and sometimes deadly creatures. It was a place that few people ventured to travel, except for those with a taste for the unknown. *Or fools with something to prove.*

Jehn's thoughts drifted to the first time he'd been such a fool.

Jehn had left the farm after another scene of shouting and crying on the parts of both Mother and Father. They could not forgive him for what he'd done, and in truth, he didn't think he could forgive himself either. The young man left everything behind and took to the road. It was lonely, but he needed that. His anger dissipated as the days passed, but the guilt remained.

Jehn stopped at small towns and worked for his keep at the local taverns, which were always a fine place to pick up news or gossip. And stories. Oh, the stories! Never a night went by without a traveller or adventurer stopping by for a drink or several. Jehn cleaned the tables, mopped spills, and tidied away cups and bowls, all the while lingering to listen.

The tales of the 'Shadowing were his favourite. He'd hazard any chance he had to hang around close to the men and women recounting their tales. Many times, he felt the sting of a switch on the backs of his legs when the tavern owner caught him idling in rapt attention instead of working.

The pain brought him back to the moment, but he would soon drift again to the storyteller's table. Jehn had always craved adventure, and each story stoked the wanderlust in him, until finally he declared he would see this wondrous place for himself. He'd wander alone, not tied down by his guilt, and would find peace in the adventure.

I was so naive. So arrogant! Even after all that happened, I didn't learn...

Despite—or perhaps because of—the protestations of most everyone he talked to, Jehn had packed up what few possessions he had and set off alone to the boundary of the 'Shadowing. He was woefully ill-prepared and over-equipped with the brash overconfidence of youth. Even tempered by his own past experience with the changeability of Palantia's environment, Jehn dismissed what he'd been told as exciting exaggerations, inflated to make for a better tale.

Entering the dark forest was exhilarating. The young man felt more alive than he had in months, and the thrill of the unknown made his heart soar. Every new sight, smell, or sound was blood-tingling, and Jehn couldn't help but grin as he explored beyond the boundary.

The initial few hours were safely uneventful, and although he'd heard the grunts and squeals of unseen creatures and spied the occasional strangely-coloured bird fly overhead, Jehn had yet to encounter anything remotely like the terrors in the tavern stories. Supremely self-confident, he strode through the forest, convinced it was all a big lie to keep youngsters like himself at home so that they could be put to work in boring, menial jobs. Absorbed in his own convictions, the young Jehn failed to notice the utter stillness that had overcome the shadowy forest.

Soon, though, the silence became so complete it created a numbness in the ears. The absence of sound was deafening, and Jehn shook his head to try to clear the strange feeling. He felt a sinking sensation. He looked down and, to his horror, saw the sandy ground was snaking over his boots and up his pant legs. The individual grains of sand glittered with an oddly dull shine, first refracting then absorbing the light. *Quietsand!* He'd been warned of the stuff but hadn't believed; now Jehn was in big trouble.

The sand wended its way past his knees to his mid-thigh, and he could feel it slowly and inexorably drawing him downward. He cast about desperately for something to grab hold of. A thin branch dangled tantalisingly out of reach above him. He stretched in vain, almost hysterical with panic, unable to reach salvation. The sand was at his waist now; his attempts to extricate himself had only hastened its motion. He cried out then in fear, terrified at how powerless he was.

He heard movement in the trees to his left and whipped his head around in an effort to see who or what it was. Hope rose—had someone heard his plea?—but a black shape pushed from between two close-together swamp oaks, and his stomach dropped as he counted one, two, *four* sets of jointed legs attached to a hairy body, the length of which rivalled his own. It was no saviour, but instead a monstrous arachnid, its abdomen resembling that of a giant spider, but with a head that was sharp and whiskered like a wild feline. The creature spotted him, and its catlike muzzle split with a sharp hiss, saliva dripping from its maw. It scuttled forward to him at a speed that belied its great size.

Jehn's attempts to escape became frenzied, and he shouted in fear as he twisted and turned, trying to claw his way to solid ground. He half-waded, half-dragged himself across the quietsand as the giant spider darted towards him, a set of red mandibles below its mouth clicking viciously in anticipation of an unexpected meal. He squeezed his eyes shut as it drew within striking distance. A second later, he felt a thick, wet substance hit his back, and then he was being pulled out of the quietsand and back towards the creature. Opening his eyes in terror, Jehn realised the beast had spat a fat globule of webbing at him and was using it like a fishing line to bring him to shore. His thrashing began anew, trying every which way to escape this new peril.

As the beast loomed above him, fangs glistening, he heard an ululating cry, and something struck the spider from behind. A silver blade thrust through the creature's skull, piercing all the way through to the hilt. The sword's tip peeked from between the beast's jaws, greenish-black ichor tarnishing its sheen. The sword disappeared as it was pulled backwards, and the spider collapsed. Jehn quickly rolled to one side, narrowly avoiding being crushed by its loathsome bulk. His chest heaved as he drew in breath after ragged breath, heartbeat racing.

A shadow passed over him, and he opened his eyes to a tall, dark-haired man, dressed in dark leather with a forest-green travelling cloak. The man reached his hand down, and Jehn took it. The stranger pulled the young man to his feet, and without missing a beat, quipped, 'My, my, just look what the cat-spitter has dragged in!' He let out a bark of laughter and slapped Jehn across the shoulders. 'Lucky I came along, eh?'

Lucky, indeed. If Thorn had not appeared right at that moment, Jehn would surely have met his demise. The man encouraged Jehn to continue his adventure, despite his newfound reservations. 'Experience is not something you gain overnight,' said Thorn, 'and forgive me if I've misjudged you, but you don't strike me as a man to cut and run after one little misadventure! Be bold, be brave, but always be prepared. Only then will you find the mettle necessary to make the 'Shadowing your playground.'

With promises to keep the younger man safe and teach him some of the skills needed to pass safely through the 'Shadowing, Thorn's charisma won out. Jehn's respect for the forest grew, and he no longer doubted the veracity of even the tallest tales he'd heard during his days as a tavern boy.

The pair travelled together for the better part of a week. Thorn taught the young Jehn signs to watch out for that indicated environmental hazards, such as the quietsand or blightfire—a strangling vine that blistered the skin at the merest touch and continued to burn until an antidote was administered. Thorn detailed the more dangerous creatures he'd encountered previously, and taught Jehn to identify their tracks and calls. The Aes-Sidhe also showed Jehn how to forage for food. 'Should you ever return here with such a distinct lack of provisions again!' said Thorn, laughing affectionately.

By the end of their adventure, Jehn was more credulous of the stories he'd been told back home and far less ignorant of the dangers the 'Shadowing could present, even to the most experienced of explorers. Thorn brought him to the boundary then, returning Jehn to a place not far from his original entrance point. The Aes-Sidhe set the young man on his way, but not before extracting a promise to only return alone if he was much better prepared. Jehn agreed, filled with an excitement that all but guaranteed he would be back again, and soon.

A soft humming roused the scholar from his memories. A point of light appeared in the air before him, coalescing into a shimmery feline shape. Jehn breathed a sigh of relief at the hummingcat's return. The cat solidified into her natural form and poised on the table in front of the scholar, swishing her majestic tail.

She hummed a trilling melody and Jehn hummed back, his tone much deeper, playing counterpoint to the sweet sound of the cat.

'What did you find?' Jehn asked in earnest.

The hummingcat began to sing. The lilting notes conjured images in Jehn's mind as the cat showed him her discovery. Jehn felt a wave of relief wash over him. There was hope.

* * *

Dawn was approaching, the sun's arrival evident in a brightening of the eastern sky. The light chased away the last purple tinges of the previous night. It would be a clear day, one perfect for travelling.

Jehn was in high spirits with the news brought by the hummingcat. A potential Dreamer had been located, and with luck, they would be deemed suitable for the transition once the Awakening began. It was one less thing to worry about, and he could focus instead on reaching the Court quickly and safely.

Despite his reservations, he knew that cutting through the forests of the 'Shadowing would make for the shortest path. The forest was a rich and bountiful source of fruiting plants, and so the party could limit what supplies they need bring with them. This would make their travel light and fast.

Once on the other side, it was but a few days' journey to reach the Court. Both Thorn's introduction and news of the Dreamer's affliction would surely have reached Thalanthas by such time. If all went well, they would gain admittance early and be provided an audience soon after.

He took a final look around the living area, then hitched the pack onto his shoulders, strapping a cord around his waist to balance the load between his upper and lower back. Now in his fourth decade, Jehn was regretfully conscious of the increased regularity of aches and pains in places he'd not experienced before. Headaches, back twinges, and the occasional unsteady knees were now a part of life, and despite keeping fit and healthy, time marched on for everyone, with Jehn being no exception.

He opened the door and stepped outside, turning the key in the lock with a quick snap. Moving smoothly out onto the street, the scholar headed to the rendezvous.

CHAPTER 7

T he bus doors flung open, and Sara spilled out on to the footpath, her brow pulled downward in a severe frown. She was in a foul mood. Work today had been horrendous. *I shouldn't have said anything! Why didn't I just keep my big mouth shut?*

Today had been the monthly whole of office staff meeting. All the managers and employees were corralled into a stuffy, windowless conference room, and made to endure that timeless tribulation of workplaces everywhere: a planning day. Sara was not normally one to make a contribution in any kind of meeting, but she'd been feeling confident after her experience with the mysterious cat the week prior. Knowing the creature existed and may one day visit her again filled Sara with joy, and that joy overflowed into an uncharacteristic positivity.

The meeting had been dragging on as they usually did, but rather than doodling in her notebook and pretending to pay attention, Sara had been listening closely and decided to pipe up with a comment. The discussion—on standardising data back-up procedures—had been going round and round in circles with no resolution, so Sara thought she'd make what seemed a common-sense suggestion. 'What about if we refer back to the document that Dan prepared last year? He did all that work on business continuity, so maybe we could apply it here too.'

Unfortunately, the person leading the discussion was someone Sara should've known not to cross. Robert was a senior manager who had taken a dislike to Sara from the very beginning of her employment. He didn't appreciate her odd sense of humour, or her lack of interest in playing office politics. After several clashes early on, Sara had learned the easiest way to deal with Robert was to let him go off on his tangents and not question him, particularly not in front of anyone where he might feel his authority was being challenged. Robert was well known for his unpredictable temper, and anything might set him off. Today, it had been Sara's innocent remark.

Robert had whipped around to face her, his eyes bulging in fury as he shouted at her, 'No, no, no, no, NO, SARA! Dan's document is not at all relevant to this discussion! This is an entirely different situation, and you'd know that if you'd shown any interest in this matter previously. In future, I'd ask you not to interrupt when you have nothing useful to say.'

Sara hated conflict and found it incredibly difficult to stand up to bullying behaviour. Unable to respond to the verbal assault in a calm, professional manner without betraying her emotions, she simply sat in silence, face flushed beetroot red. Dan met her eye from across the conference table, but his faced betrayed no emotion. He, like the rest of her colleagues, awkwardly ignored Robert's conduct, and continued the discussion. Inwardly, Sara fumed that Robert could get away with this sort of behaviour, time and again, and no one did anything. She was furious at herself for not confronting him. The meeting had finally wrapped up mid-afternoon, and everyone else had gone about their day like it was nothing, but Sara remained affected all the way home. She couldn't stop thinking about the stupid little man, and how it seemed completely acceptable for him to speak to her in such a way. *Stupid jerk. Those meetings wouldn't be so long and boring if he didn't carry on like an idiot the whole time.*

The hill seemed steeper than usual as she dragged herself up its height, replaying the meeting over and over in her head. Sara struggled to just let things like that go. She knew rationally that the situation said more about that manager than herself, and it was unlikely anyone perceived her poorly, but her emotions were running high. She imagined the scene again, this time fantasising about having the perfect comeback to his ridiculous rant. She saw herself standing proud over him, his buggy eyes blinking frantically while she methodically counted down on her fingers the many ways he was incompetent. But of course, that would never happen. Sara was too much of a coward. Angry tears threatened in the corner of her eyes.

She struggled up the street, so consumed she barely noticed the small wild place as she passed by, until a blue wren hopped onto the path and piped a note at her. Sara stopped at once. The tiny bird's iridescent blue and black feathers caught the sunlight, glinting. Sara couldn't help but smile at the small joy being offered. It was difficult to hold on to anger with such a proud little display right in front of her.

Sara chirped back and said, 'Good greetings, little sir!'

The wren hopped back and forth upon the path then flitted away to the grass. Its harem of females joined it and, as one, they all turned to face Sara. She blinked in surprise. Sara was by no means an expert, but she knew normal wren behaviour didn't customarily involve the birds watching people with such measured interest. The occasional individual might be more curious than its mates, but nothing at all like this.

Seeing no other reason for their interest, she ventured hesitantly, 'Can I help you?'

The wrens proffered no response. The male piped at her once more, and the group hopped away into the bushes without a second glance her way.

* * *

Still smarting from the day's earlier rebuke, Sara fled into her imagination, revelling in whimsical notions of other worlds which teemed with magic and creatures thought lost to myth.

When Sara was a child, her every birthday wish was to meet a real, live unicorn one day. Sara loved all the strange and wonderful creatures from mythology, but the unicorn was special. The wisdom and grace of the beast filled her with wonder and hope. Her childhood overflowed with unicorn toys and trinkets, so that she could feel a measure of closeness to the magical creatures.

Even as a she grew into a teenager, when the innocence of her childhood started to drift away and she'd first started to feel the painful reality of the world, Sara clung to the fantasy of the unicorn. When her parents were fighting, or when her school friends ousted her, or when her first boyfriend cheated... the dream of unicorns was always there to escape to.

She'd imagine hiking in the hills and stumbling upon a rainforest glade, full of greenery and ferns that towered above her head. She'd step quietly inside, and within, she'd find a unicorn at rest, coat like snow with flowers tangled in its mane. It would meet her gaze with eyes containing the ocean's depths, and she would see peace and acceptance. Her real life would be forgotten, and time would hold no meaning as they rode together through the glade.

In her adult life, Sara held on to the feelings evoked by that fantasy, but her belief in the existence of unicorns was tempered by a cynical understanding of the world she lived in. She believed they were real, but thought they no longer lived in this world. *How could they?* There would be no unicorns left here as humans spread and destroyed any places they may have once roamed. Only small places of magic were left, or habitats remote and wild that Sara might never see.

And yet, she remained hopeful that unicorns still existed somewhere far away, beyond the reach of most. It was an unusual belief for an adult these days, but she was not ashamed by it. Sara thought it was something to be proud of. *Magic is real, and that cat proves it. So why couldn't there be unicorns, too?*

Putting her musings aside, she cleaned up from dinner and headed upstairs to bed. That night, Sara dreamed of running with unicorns, the sunlight dappling the forest floor and sparkling off the hooves and horns of the magical beasts as they jostled and leapt around her.

CHAPTER 8

J ehn stepped into the square, his eyes watering from the cool dawn air. He blinked and scanned the area, his gaze falling upon Senna, who was standing against the well, having traded his attendant's robes for sensible travelling clothes. The boy's tunic and leggings were freshly pressed, but his knee-high hide boots bore the scuffs and stains of regular wear. Senna's pack rested on the ground at his feet, and he picked at his fingernails while he waited. A nervous habit he couldn't seem to quit.

Jehn was surprised to see him, half-expecting the attendant to have changed his mind once the heat of the moment had passed. 'Well met, Senna.'

Senna thrust his hands in his pockets and nodded a greeting at the scholar. 'Good morning, Jehn.'

'I must admit,' said Jehn, 'I was not sure you'd be here, and you may have a change of heart soon enough.'

'I mean no disrespect, but I won't,' said Senna, his gaze steady, 'I couldn't just stand by and leave you unsupported against Elder Finnian. I knew you were too stubborn to back down.' The attendant's gaze wavered, but he continued, 'You would've gone by yourself, regardless. I don't think that's a good idea, and besides, the Dreamer's welfare is just as much my responsibility as yours. More so, actually.'

Jehn nodded. *I doubt this is worth arguing about, he thought. I see myself in this one, just as stubborn.* 'Very well, Senna,' he said. 'I can see you are a man of conviction, and I respect your sense of duty. However, I never intended to go on this journey alone. I have it on good authority our company is the best in the business.'

The attendant's brow furrowed. 'There's no one else here.'

'Patience. They will be here soon enough.'

Lo and behold, a small group rounded the corner of the square. The dark-haired man from the tavern led the way, his navy travelling cloak billowing with the quickness of his pace. Two others followed in his wake.

The first was an athletic woman clad in light leather armour, shaded in ruddy browns and reds. She was taller than most men, and her chocolate brown hair was braided and pinned close to her head. The woman bore a longbow and quiver on her back, with a silver sword strapped at her waist. A glint of steel flickered from the top of her boot as she strode behind the leader, carrying herself with an obvious strength despite her lithe form.

The woman was accompanied by a man even taller than herself. The fellow was broad of chest, with muscular arms bare to the shoulder. He wore soft hide pants and a boiled leather vest that was moulded to his body; the vest was dotted with metal studs and rivets. Across his chest was a brace of throwing knives, and he bore a heavy axe on his back, strapped lengthways with the handle jutting above his left shoulder. Despite his giant stature, he moved with an easy grace.

The trio drew abreast with Jehn and Senna, and the dark-haired man stepped forward. 'Well met, scholar,' he said, reaching for Jehn's proffered hand and grasping it firmly. 'May I present you Belina and Ander Findomar. This lovely couple will be our escort for this adventure.'

'Not too much of an adventure, I hope,' said Jehn, his mouth tugging upwards in a wry smile. *Though, to be honest, a little excitement will clear the cobwebs.* 'Well met, Belina, Ander. I am Jehn.'

The woman dipped her head in a polite nod, but the man lunged forward, enveloping Jehn in his massive arms. 'We shall be fast friends!' said Ander, lifting the scholar off his feet with the ferocity of the embrace. 'I know this to be true!'

He released his hold and slapped Jehn's shoulder, grinning like an excited child. Jehn staggered under the blow and was almost knocked to the ground. He met Belina's gaze, who shook her head with barely restrained mirth.

Thorn let out a barking laugh at the scholar's stunned expression. 'Apologies, *mo chara*,' he said, eyes twinkling with good humour. 'Ander's greetings should come with a warning.'

'Now now, little Thorn in my side,' said Ander, 'You would have it no other way, and that I also know to be true!' His arm swept low is a mocking bow, but the gesture was brought to a swift halt by a resounding smack to the back of his head by Belina.

'You go too far, Ander!' she scolded, frowning, 'Forgive him, my lord, he finds himself hilarious but is severely lacking in diplomacy!'

The dark-haired man grinned, pushing a lock of raven hair away from his face and tucking it behind one ear. 'I can't recall how many times I've asked you to dispense with the formalities, Belina. "Thorn" is just fine.'

He grinned at Ander, who was staring at his feet in embarrassment, properly chastised. 'Fear not, *am Mathan Mòr*, you know well I am not one to take offense at a jest between friends.'

Turning now to Senna, who had been watching proceedings in stunned silence, he said, 'Anwyl Orinthorn, at your service. And you are?'

Senna's jaw dropped open in surprise and he stammered, 'A-anwyl... Orinthorn...? Lord of the Fir'Dannan? That Anwyl Orinthorn?'

'None other!' said Thorn, with a flourish of his cloak, 'but call me Thorn. Or Whitethorn if you must. Either is fine. But definitely not lord, nor highness. Nor anything of the like, actually. I left that life a long time ago.' He paused. 'But you didn't tell me your name.'

The boy briskly straightened his tunic in an effort to regain his composure. 'It's Senna Breen. Very nice to meet you, my lor—uh, sir.'

'That will have to do, I suppose,' said Thorn, trying with little success to hold back his smile. 'It is a pleasure to meet you, Senna.' He turned then to face the others. 'Are we ready? Should we away? Whilst I do love a chat, and a chance to meet new people, the Dreamer needs us, and we'd best not tarry.' He tipped his chin at the Findomars. 'I've given them the background, and though our big man Ander here seems a merry chap, he and Belina are well-apprised of the seriousness of our quest.'

'It appears we are in good hands,' said Jehn, 'and furthermore, I've received glad tidings this evening past, so it seems our journey is blessed with good fortune.'

'Oho!' said Thorn. 'An excellent way to start us off!'

'What tidings, Jehn?' said Senna.

'It seems a Dreamer Candidate has been located,' said Jehn.

'That's very good news!'

Jehn nodded, gesturing to Senna to pick up his pack. 'It is indeed, and takes a little pressure off our quest. However, we should not be complacent. As you know, a Candidate is just that, and will need to be deemed suitable.'

'That's true, Jehn,' said Senna, pulling the pack's straps over his shoulders. 'But it's a good sign, and we can now focus on getting the Dreamer the help she needs. I think it means good things for all of us.'

'I think you are right, my friend,' said Jehn. And with that, the party were off just as the sun poured its first golden rays into the dawning sky.

CHAPTER 9

Sara awoke with a start, bolting upright in panic. Filled with dread, she turned the digital alarm clock so she could see its face—it was always too bright at night, and bothered her eyes—and as she feared, it was late. Very late. The night's wondrous dreamings were forgotten in a flash as she leapt out of bed in horror. Throwing on some clothes, she dragged a brush through her hair. *Late to work again! Oh man, why can't I get it together and wake up at a reasonable hour like normal people?* She sprinted around the house, rushing to complete those morning tasks she couldn't avoid.

Sara's mother had always teased her gently about her lack of punctuality. 'You were late being born,' she would say, not unkindly, 'you'll be late ever after.' Despite the humour in that, it really did seem to be true. No matter how prepared she thought she was, Sara would always end up losing herself in unnecessary time-wasting. 'I'll just put this away' or 'I'll just do that quickly'—and suddenly she was rushing out the door, only to arrive well past the appointed time. It was yet another thing that added to her awkwardness around people, because most people were perfectly able to be on time for things.

Grabbing her house keys, Sara flew out the door, jogging down the street to the bus stop. The sky was grey and heavy with rain clouds, and she prayed to any gods who'd listen that the downpour hold out until she was at least on the bus. Those prayers fell on deaf ears, however—or perhaps instead were heard by a mischievous deity—and the heavens promptly opened, letting loose their contents in a torrent of thick, freezing rain. Sara was drenched in an instant. Flinging up her hands to the sky, she let out a cry of frustration. But the rain, not being possessed of any empathy, refused to relent.

As Sara stood on the street, soaked through and shouting at the sky like a lunatic, the mysterious cat materialised in a flash of bright light and the crack of a thunderclap. Sara cried out in surprise and leapt back at this dramatic arrival. The creature's form had lost its haziness, and now had a solid appearance. Despite the surrounding deluge, the cat was perfectly dry. The heavy droplets disappeared before hitting the cat's luxurious coat. *Of course a magical cat could avoid getting wet whenever it wanted.*

The cat's long, elegant tail quivered, and Sara could spy tiny sparks flicking forth with each shake. Sara crouched down, ignoring the torrential rain, until she was at eye level with the cat. She hummed a tentative note. The cat let out a long, throbbing purr and raised her lovely head, staring steadily into Sara's water-laden eyes. Sara felt a connection deep in her soul, and she stayed perfectly still, not even caring that the pouring rain was making rivulets down the back of her neck. The cat leaned forward and rubbed her soft face against Sara's. The sensation of warm, dry fur and tickly electric whiskers against her chilly cheek was remarkable, and filled her with a joy beyond that of any experience.

The cat thrummed a staccato of notes and the air about sizzled with energy. The mystical field that surrounded the cat and protected her from the rain extended to protect Sara as well. She could see the drops falling, but they did not land.

The magical cat continued her lilting song, and at once, there was a pressure from all sides. Sara's ears felt about to pop, so she instinctively took a deep breath. The air shimmered before her eyes, and lights began dancing all around her. Colours swirled, and all at once, the world was upside down. Sara felt her stomach rise. She squeezed her eyes shut lest she embarrass herself and offer up a reappearance of last night's dinner.

Finally, the crushing heavy sensation lifted, and the cat fell silent. Tentatively, Sara opened one eye, then the other. To her amazement, she found she was crouched on soft ground, her hands prickling from the tiny ferns that thrust from the earth around her. The air was moist and cool, and so sweet! She breathed in long and deep, revelling in the scent of the ancient forest. Gone were the slick footpath and flooded suburban road. Trees and greenery stretched out into the distance, as far as the eye could see.

A sunbeam cut through the canopy to light up the small glade. The clearing was clad in wildflowers of every shape and colour imaginable, their fragrance soft and heart-warming as it wafted to her on the gentlest of breezes. She raised herself to her knees and stared around in wonder.

'Ahem,' a resonant voice behind her said.

And there, more majestic and glorious than anything Sara had ever dreamed, was a unicorn.

* * *

Sara's mind raced to reconcile what she was seeing. Her heart fluttered as she struggled to pull herself together before she made a fool of herself in front of the noble creature. Her eyes roamed over his beautiful form; his uncloven hooves were silver and wrought through with coruscations of twinkling light, giving the illusion of movement within. Fluffy fetlocks feathered his heels, and his limbs were strong and fine, the muscles smoothly defined beneath his flawless white hide. The unicorn's tail flicked now and then, and she saw that it was not at all the leonine appendage often represented in heraldry in her world, nor the fall of a horse, but instead thick and magnificent, with waves and curls. The tail was white, but with tinges of lilac, and the unicorn's double mane was decorated with tiny gems that glinted in the light.

Sara's eyes moved to the unicorn's face. Thrusting from the centre of its forehead was a spiralled horn some two feet long or more, glimmering with opalescence. The beast's eyes were darkest indigo and filled with pinpoints of light, like miniature stars. Black lashes, thick and long, outlined the old, wise eyes.

'Staring is rather rude, you know,' said the unicorn. 'Didn't your mother ever teach you that?'

Sara's eyes widened, and her entire face flushed bright red as she found herself utterly speechless. The magical cat sat at her feet, purring in a satisfied manner; she would be no help at all.

The unicorn tossed his head in irritation, 'Well don't just stand there, at least introduce yourself.'

'Um, uh, Sara. My name is Sara. I'm a human.'

'Yes, I know you are a human. I'm not an idiot.' The unicorn rolled his eyes.

Sara could only blink in stunned silence. This was a unicorn.

A unicorn! But he was not at all what she expected. *He's... kind of a jerk!*

The unicorn rounded on the cat and stamped a hoof. 'Is this really the best you could do?' The little creature began grooming her long whiskers. 'Don't ignore me,' said the unicorn, but the cat continued her ablutions, offering no indication that she would engage with the exasperated unicorn.

The unicorn sighed. It was a long, drawn-out huff, and really quite insulting. 'Well, Sara,' he said, 'I expect you will have to do. My name is Terentius Aodhfin, and you have been brought here to Palantia on a matter of great importance. I will be your guide and mentor, and by my horn, I will do my utmost to ensure you not ruin everything.'

He wheeled about and trotted away, heading towards the far side of the grove, mane and tail lifting on the breeze. He twisted his head around to glare back at her. 'Are you coming? Or are you just going to crouch there in the dirt for the rest of the day?'

Completely gobsmacked, Sara nevertheless managed to gather herself enough to rise to her feet. She realised her mouth was hanging open, and she closed it with an audible snap. Blinking a few times, she shook her head in astonishment and trudged off after the unicorn. Trilling happily to herself, the cat watched for a moment, and then, with a spark and a single short note, she was gone.

CHAPTER 10

I n the Dreamer's grove, the day grew warm and pleasant. The Dreamer had returned to her usual state of calm slumber, the previous day's violent episode finally over. Now only occasional hand twitches betrayed any disquiet: motions far removed from yesterday's clenching fists and strained tendons. The Dreamer seemed at peace.

The attendants remained watchful in case of a relapse. They cast nervous glances at each other from time to time, but it seemed the disturbance had passed.

'Ask for forgiveness for the forgetfulness,' the Dreamer murmured, releasing a long sonorous breath.

An attendant transcribed the Dreamer's words. He passed his notebook to another attendant, who tucked it under her arm and scurried off.

Hidden in the shadows beyond the grove, the Sluagh's smile was sharp with malicious intent. It ached to taste the Dreamer's essence again. Every fibre, every taut sinew of its whole being yearned to move forward, to slink just close enough. But it showed restraint: the creature was not a slave to its baser instincts. It was clever and patient, and in time the attendants would relax their vigil. Then the Sluagh would strike.

The Sluagh race were well-respected by all the denizens of Palantia, but especially the Aes-Sidhe. The Aes-Sidhe were among the foremost of the elder races—unicorns being another—but the Sluagh were beloved for their kind and caring natures. Since history's record, Sluagh were the curators of the lifeblood of Palantia: The Dreams of the Dreamers.

Most Sluagh were Seelie: good and helpful fae tasked by the Aes-Sidhe to travel between Palantia and the human world. Sluagh observed human sleepers and extracted their dreams and nightmares. Sluagh were able to convert these nocturnal fancies into the energy the Dreamer needed for their millennium of sleep and imagination.

Sluagh were shy, quiet creatures who carried out their duties undetected by their human subjects. They took their work seriously and without reservation. Whilst a Dreamer's mind was a rich and fertile ground, without the Sluagh to provide a supply of sustenance, the Dreamer's imagination would eventually stagnate. Palantia would suffer without an influx of change and creation over the thousand-year span of a Dreamer's sleep.

Like most fae, Sluagh were long-lived. They carried out their responsibility for many decades, even centuries. New Sluagh were born from a dewdrop of dream essence, and so, it was said, possessed human characteristics as well as those of their fae brethren. They were creatures of both worlds and could freely move between—an ability forbidden to the vast majority of Palantians.

This Sluagh was young, but headstrong and ambitious. After a few decades spent toiling amongst the humans to bring forth the essence that fed the Dreamer, it had grown dissatisfied with its dutiful life. It craved a different life, one free of the shackles of obligation. Sick of the time it saw being wasted, the Sluagh callously abandoned its responsibility to Palantia and the Dreamer for another more selfish agenda.

The Sluagh had discovered it could do more than simply extract dreams. One night, while staring down at a sleeping human, the Sluagh felt nothing but disgust. It saw the human as something contemptible, a slug with little purpose but to feed something greater. A malevolent flame flickered within the Sluagh's heart.

Brimming with hateful intent, the Sluagh stoked this anger, letting it build and burn until it gestated into a sinister power. Through surreptitious experimentation, the Sluagh learned to create and sow a nightmare of almost limitless terror. Perhaps it was not the first among its race to discover this ability, but instead of staying true to its Seelie nature, a darkness awoke within the Sluagh.

The energy produced from generating such fear proved to be both delicious and addictive. The Sluagh laboured in secrecy, refining its technique first on animals and lesser beings before seeking the greater prey of Palantia's intelligent denizens: the fae and other races.

As time passed, the Sluagh grew ever more proud and sly, and desired to taste real power.

And the most powerful being in this world was the Dreamer.

That first taste had been almost excruciating. But while its skin itched at the thought of a second savouring, the Sluagh would wait.

CHAPTER 11

The day's travel had been pleasant despite the circumstances of their journey, and the weather had remained fine and clear. Jehn checked over his shoulder to see how Senna was faring. The young man appeared to be enjoying himself, looking around with interest as they passed out of the main town, its outskirts, and finally the outlying farms and homesteads.

Jehn was quietly impressed. He had assumed Senna to be inexperienced with the requirements of such a trek, but the attendant had revealed otherwise. 'My parents are from Hunter's Dale, which borders the lower passes of the Western Reaches,' said Senna. 'We often took trips to the mountains and other local picnic spots. My elder sister, Delma, detested it, but I have always loved the outdoors.'

'Why did you become an attendant then?' asked Ander, bluntly. 'You'd be stuck inside writing all day!' He rolled his eyes in exaggerated boredom. 'I couldn't bear it!'

Senna laughed. 'I've always had a love of knowledge, as well. The best education can be gained within the Dreamer's grove—unless you are an Aes-Sidhe, of course.' He chanced a quick look at Thorn, but the man did not appear to have heard.

'The University of Thalanthas is only available for members of the elder race,' Jehn explained, noticing Ander's puzzled expression.

'Never mind though,' Senna continued, 'I have learnt much, and will further my studies once my attendant tenure ends. I have already received teaching in philosophy, history and economics. Part of the training for all Dreamer's attendants requires a rudimentary knowledge of medicine as well. And I've been studying the history of Palantia in my free time. I hope to be a scholar, like you, Jehn.'

Jehn smiled wryly. 'Perhaps not quite like me,' he said, 'I'm not the most popular among our residents.'

'Oh ho!' Ander rubbed his hands together. 'That sounds like a story worth hearing!'

'Another time, maybe,' Jehn replied. He quickened his pace with absolutely no subtlety, hoping to catch up with Thorn at the head of the party and avoid Ander's curiosity.

Ander's eyes narrowed and his mouth twitched playfully. 'I'll have it out of you soon enough,' he called to Jehn's retreating back. 'No one can resist my charms! Just ask my wife.' His booming laugh startled a fieldmouse. The tiny creature broke cover and scuttled across their path, its paws puffing up small clouds of dust as it fled in terror.

Belina had been loping alongside the group, but now joined her husband and Senna, who was trotting to keep pace.

'I knew I would marry Belina the moment I laid eyes on her,' Ander continued 'I could tell from that first day she was the one!' He smiled lovingly at his wife, and Belina took Ander's hand in hers, laying a quick kiss on his fingers. Years of marriage had not dulled their ardour.

'You might have known, my gentle giant, but I made you

earn my love!' said Belina.

'That you did, my beauty. That you did!' Ander's hearty laugh rang out once more, no doubt spreading panic to all the small creatures in their vicinity.

'I, too, have a sweetheart,' the young attendant said shyly. 'Her name is Meryn. Once I finish my studies, I hope to marry her.' He stared off into the distance as his thoughts turned inward.

Ander and Belina smiled knowingly at each other, both remembering the blush of their budding romance some ten years past.

Belina had been an apprentice ranger when they had first met. Her skills with the bow were already exceptional, and she possessed an innate ability for forestcraft. She could read a trail in an instant, immediately identifying the creature that left it, knowing from tiny signs how long ago it had passed by and in which direction. By analysing the depth of the prints, she could tell the height and weight of her prey, and if it bore any load. Not unusual skills for many outdoorsmen. But rare for a girl of just fifteen.

Belina's natural talents were soon noticed by the local hunters and trappers, and her skills became a highly sought-after commodity. Her agility and flexibility meant she could move through dense woodlands easily, twisting and flexing her limbs acrobatically over and under branches and fallen tree trunks. Her smooth gait and soft footfalls made her almost silent, and she practiced at stealth by creeping up on forest animals to see how close she could get before the creature sensed her and fled. It was a particular point of pride if she managed to smack the rump of an animal and set it bolting away in shock.

One bright summer day, the sun warming her back while she crouched in a thicket, slowing her breathing to make it almost imperceptible, the girl watched the furtive movements of a splendid red fox. The animal paused as it entered the clearing, its full plume of a tail stretched out behind it. The fox seemed to sense something out of place, but did not bolt for the safety of the underbrush, instead standing still, ears swivelling to catch any errant sound.

Belina waited in silence until the fox turned away, then eased out of her hiding place, angling her body around a jutting branch before carefully placing a foot on the bed of pine needles strewn thickly on the ground. Just as she was about to move within touching distance of the fox, an explosion erupted across the clearing, a sudden shock of noise bursting from the bushes opposite. The fox disappeared in an instant, the white tip of its bushy tail flashing as the creature fled.

Belina jumped to her feet in fury. Marching across the grassy dell, she reached both hands into the leafy undergrowth. Using her full strength, she dragged a young man bodily out of a bush and threw him on the ground. 'You idiot! I was so close!'

The boy was a year or two her senior. His hair was tangled and dotted with wattle blossom, but shone the colour of the now absent fox. He stood up and brushed a few pieces of moss from his dirty tunic. 'Sorry,' the boy mumbled, fishing a crumpled kerchief from his pocket. He proceeded to blow his twitching nose. The sound was that of a particularly loud honking goose.

The girl before him rolled her eyes so hard, Ander thought they would fall back inside her head. Despite her obvious annoyance, he couldn't help but stare.

'That was it for me,' said Ander. 'A greater beauty I'd never seen.'

'He needed work,' said Belina, leaning over to Senna, exaggerating her conspiratorial grin, 'but I saw potential.'

Senna grinned back. 'What a romantic beginning! What happened next, how did you come to marry?'

Thorn broke away from the head of the group and turned back. Before either husband or wife had a chance to answer, the Aes-Sidhe called out, 'As much as I would enjoy hearing your adventures once more, alas, the sun is going down. It is time to make camp.'

Their shadows lengthened and stretched far across the ground as the sun drew low. The temperature would drop, and nights were very cold in this part of the countryside. A fire would be a necessity, for warmth but also to keep away any night creatures. There wouldn't be much to harass them in these parts, but later would be a different story entirely as they journeyed into more dangerous locales. For now, however, they could rest easy.

Thorn called for a halt and headed off to scout for a suitable campsite. He strode into the woods, soon naught but a shadow. The others dropped their packs momentarily to stretch and rub their aching joints. It had been a smooth trek today, but tomorrow would be harder, as they reached the rolling hills of the aptly named Barrow Knolls. Jehn hoped that the tiredness in his body would overcome his racing mind and allow him to make up some of the sleep he'd missed the previous night.

A few moments later, Thorn returned, loping easily as if he hadn't been walking with a heavy pack for nearly twelve hours. 'Up ahead,' he said, gesturing back the way he'd come, 'a perfect spot to spend the evening.'

The group shouldered their packs, Jehn and Senna suppressing tandem groans, and they made their way to the campsite. A short distance later, they discovered a small copse of trees, their branches tangling close overhead to form a thick ceiling of green. The ground beneath was dry and soft with leaves. Thorn was right: this was the perfect place to make camp.

CHAPTER 12

Terentius slowed his pace to match Sara's. His annoyance at the reduction in speed was unmistakable as he slouched along, grumbling to himself. Sara was brimming with questions, but given the unicorn's acerbic demeanour, she was hesitant to speak again. Instead, she walked on in silence, stealing glances at her companion, inwardly marvelling at this incredible turn of events.

With a petulant sigh, the unicorn halted abruptly, his hooves digging the grassy soil into small hillocks. He swung his head and glared at the woman meandering beside him. 'Go on then,' he said, through clenched teeth. 'Ask.'

Sara stopped in her tracks, gulping at the unicorn's grim expression. 'I didn't say anything!'

Terentius rolled his eyes in exasperation. 'Your thoughts were plain upon your face and easily read, even without skills such as mine.'

'Skills… You can read minds?' At once, Sara was conflicted between the excitement of this revelation, and the mortifying realisation that her every thought was being broadcast.

Before the unicorn could respond, a torrent of questions flooded out of her. 'Where am I? What did you mean by "a matter of great importance?" What does that have to do with me?' The words spilled out in a blurting rush, and she let them tumble from her lips before she could second guess herself. 'And why are you so... sullen?!' she finished, defiantly raising her chin as she met the unicorn's intense gaze.

'Sullen! The audacity!' His sharp intake of breath whistled through his nostrils, 'I am not sullen! I just have little patience for stupidity. Are you stupid?'

'I don't think so,' said Sara, 'but I doubt I'd be the best judge of that if I were.'

The unicorn broke into a deep, musical laugh. 'Well then, young Sara the human, perhaps there is hope after all.'

Sara's lips thinned instantly, her eyebrows drawing down in indignation. She'd experienced a lifetime of being dismissed as young or immature, even by people not that much older than herself, and it never failed to get a rise out of her. It definitely wasn't fair to have to endure that here, in this new place where no one even knew her!

She crossed her arms. 'I'm hardly young,' she said. 'I'm nearly forty years old.'

The unicorn whickered with laughter. 'Oh! Forty years old, are you? Do forgive me. So old and wise indeed!'

Sara fidgeted with a hangnail on her left index finger as her cheeks grew warm, the colour creeping up her neck. Her heart raced with the old familiar anxiety. This always happened. *I hate this feeling.* She always wanted to have the courage to stand up to someone who'd made her feel small, but usually just clamped up and said nothing. She blinked several times to dispel the hot sting at the back of her eyes. 'Well, I don't know about wise, nor old, but definitely not young.'

Paying no mind to the woman's obvious discomfort, Terentius drew himself up to his full height, the wisp of feathery beard on his chin waving slightly in the warm air. 'I have lived over a thousand years, *young one*,' he proclaimed with mocking emphasis. 'I have seen the rise and fall of kings and queens, and witnessed more than you can even imagine. Should you exceed a century, you will still be but a child to me.'

Sara stopped pulling at the skin under her nail and looked the unicorn hard in the eye. 'You know what? For someone who's lived so long, you don't seem to have learned much about how to speak to people. You don't have to be mean about it. Instead of picking on me, why don't you educate me? If you are so old and wise, you should take this as an opportunity to teach me something, rather than getting all puffed up and pompous.'

Terentius' nostrils flared. Unicorn and woman stared each other down, neither flinching for what seemed like an interminable length of time.

Finally, the unicorn coughed and flicked his tail against his withers. 'I suppose you are right on this occasion, Sara. Perhaps that was uncalled for. You are new to this world and have been thrown into a situation for which you are ill-equipped. I do not fraternise much with humans these days. I forget your particular sensitivities.'

Sara raised one eyebrow. 'Wow,' she said, dripping sarcasm, 'was that meant to be an apology? If so, you need a little practice. I think there's a word for what you are... hmm, what was it... Oh, that's right: "patronising".'

In the back of her mind, Sara's internal voice was screaming at her to shut up and stop arguing with a unicorn. *A literal unicorn! Isn't this what I've always wanted? Why am I being like this?* At home, she would never have the courage to speak to someone like this. She quickly dropped her gaze back to her hands and clasped them together to hide their shaking.

Terentius twisted his mouth into what could only be described as a sneer. It was a strange expression to see on an equine countenance. He shook his head and stamped a hoof in silent irritation, refusing to acknowledge her comment.

Sara shuffled her feet in turn, desperately wishing the cat would return and spirit her away to anywhere but this increasingly awkward situation.

'I loathe to disappoint you,' said the unicorn, with even more caustic sarcasm than Sara herself had mustered, 'but she will only appear when she wishes, and neither you nor I can predict when that may be. Fickle, she is. Like all cats.'

A wry grin played over Sara's face. 'I thought the same thing when she first started appearing to me.'

The unicorn shifted his weight, watching a green and black butterfly dance in the air before it flitted off into the trees. 'Tell me, Sara,' he said, 'are you always this argumentative?'

Sara's eyes flicked to the unicorn, but he continued gazing into the distance. 'No,' she replied, 'but perhaps if I had been, I'd have gotten further in life.'

Terentius smiled as he turned to face her, his eyes softening from their former coldness. 'Well, my dear, perhaps you are right where you need to be.' With this comment, he began to move off, gesturing for Sara to follow. Confused and unsettled, Sara nevertheless complied.

The pair walked in silence for several minutes. Before long, Sara's curiosity got the better of her. 'Terentius, can you tell me what happened to the unicorns in my world? Where did they go?'

'Ah, now that is an excellent question. What do you know of your world's history? Are you familiar with what is known as the middle ages?'

Sara nodded.

'Then as you would know,' Terentius said, 'that unicorns have been present for much of your world's recorded history, and whilst not common, there were enough of them to be heeded by kings and commoners alike.'

'I've read many stories,' said Sara. 'Some date back centuries, to even before the middle ages, though that seems to be where they featured the most. There are unicorns in heraldry, tapestry, and all sorts of art. My mother taught me about them. I loved them, all my life...' she tapered off, embarrassed to be proclaiming this adoration to the very thing she adored.

'Unicorns were well-loved by many humans, but the middle ages were when things began to sour for us in your world. A king got it into his idiotic head that cutting off our horns and crushing them to dust would yield a cure for his impotence.' Terentius' eyes flashed. 'Perhaps curbing his drinking before attempting to mate with his wife would have been more effective.'

'I've read about this. I thought it was just an allegory.' The thought of unicorns being killed for such a stupid premise was heartbreaking.

'Sadly, no. Regardless the efficacy of such a cure, the idea set your world afire,' said Terentius. 'Unicorns were hunted almost to extinction before they were able to flee back to Palantia through the Stitch.'

'The Stitch?'

'Ah well, how best to put it in a way you would understand,' Terentius began, ignoring Sara's frown. 'The Stitch is a kind of doorway that allows passage between our two worlds. However, rather than moving from one place to the next, each entrance exists at different points in space *and* time.'

'It's a wormhole?'

'That nomenclature is not strictly accurate, but explaining it to one other than a great scientific mind would be impossible, so let us just say that time can pass very differently between entering the Stitch on one side, and exiting at the other.'

'That didn't seem too complicated for my tiny mind to grasp,' said Sara, deadpan. 'So, you have been to my world?'

Terentius nodded. 'Yes, but I was just a colt when we fled through the Stitch.'

Sara attempted a calculation in her head. 'Now, I'm pretty bad at maths, but if you are over a thousand years old, and were just a colt when you left my world, it seems like there's a few centuries amiss somewhere. Is that what you meant about time passing differently?'

'Very good, Sara,' the unicorn replied, sounding just like her high school mathematics teacher, Mr Miller. He was the reason Sara was rubbish at maths. The man was constantly vexed by Sara's inability to grasp what he considered fundamental concepts. *You can remember the lyrics of hundreds of pop songs, but not this simple algebra formula, Sara!* She could still feel the sting of humiliation decades later.

Now that she thought about it, Mr Miller and Terentius had a few other similarities. The moral superiority, the attitude of exasperated relief when she finally got the right answer… the beard. Sara quickly pressed her lips together to prevent a giggle from escaping.

The unicorn looked at her sharply.

'Sorry,' she mumbled, 'go on.'

'As I was about to say,' the unicorn continued, 'that particular passage had a discrepancy of several centuries between my leaving your world and returning to Palantia.'

'Is that how I came here, through this Stitch?' she asked, idly wondering how exactly a unicorn was so well-versed in quantum mechanics or whatever science this was.

'Correct,' said Terentius. 'The Stitch isn't a fixed location; it can move and appear as needed. Magical creatures, like myself, can affect its appearance and use it to our advantage.'

'I gather the cat can also, then. She brought me here?'

'Indeed,' Terentius nodded, 'Hummingcats are emissaries between our worlds. They are the ideal choice. Their close resemblance to the mundane cats of your own world affords them the ability to come and go with little notice. They are often sent to seek out potential Candidates.'

Before Sara could ask what that meant, the hummingcat flickered out of thin air and immediately set to washing her face with a dainty paw.

Distracted by the little cat, Sara's question was forgotten. 'Does she have a name?' Sara clicked her fingers at the cat, encouraging the creature to come. The cat pointedly turned her back and continued her ablutions as if they were the most important duty in the world.

Terentius' lip quirked in amusement. 'Her full name is Leandra Lus-a'-chraois. But she will accept the common tongue version, Honeysuckle the Brave.' He scoffed. 'Cats! Such self-important little things!' The hummingcat hissed at Terentius, her sweet features transformed into an unpleasant expression. 'Also easily offended.'

'Loos-ah-cr-ow,' Sara sounded out the unfamiliar name, the syllables feeling strange on her tongue.

The cat returned to her grooming, no longer deigning to acknowledge the unicorn and his flippant commentary. 'I think cats are wonderful,' said Sara, smiling at the pretty feline. 'They are clever and funny and beautiful. I am ever so pleased to have met you, O Honeysuckle the Brave.' The cat rolled onto her back, tail swishing invitingly. Sara approached and sat down beside her. Terentius rolled his eyes and bent to crop the grass at his feet. Sara offered her hand to the hummingcat, who sniffed delicately at Sara's fingers, before pushing her head into the woman's hand. Sara scratched gently under the cat's chin, evoking a humming purr from the little creature's soft throat.

Sara grinned smugly at the unicorn. 'I've never met a cat I couldn't get along with.'

The unicorn snorted. 'She certainly does seem to have accepted you as her own. Consider yourself honoured.'

'I do,' Sara said, bowing her head at the little cat. She gave Honeysuckle another chin rub and then stood up, brushing the grass from her jeans. 'Terentius? What am I doing here?'

The unicorn's mirthful expression turned serious, 'Well then, we should start at the beginning.'

* * *

Ever since humans formed thought, and processed those thoughts in their subconscious, a Dreamer was instated in the world of Palantia to guide its progress and the evolution of its inhabitants. Palantia was far more ancient than the human world, and its recorded history dated back millennia further. This was possible due to the anomaly that occurred between the two worlds, and because of the very nature of Palantia's existence.

'As you now understand,' said Terentius, 'time is not linear in

Palantia and is not beholden to human concepts of relativity.'

Palantia and all its beings were created by the dreams of special humans. They were chosen from the human world for their imaginations and creativity, evidenced by a vivid and active dreaming life that exceeded that of other humans. The Dreamer slept, and was cared for by a staff of attendants, and certain elements of their dreams manifested across Palantia, in innumerable ways. Entirely new animals and plants could originate from a Dreamer's mind, or even new ideas and ways of thinking that spawned all manner of technological, ideological and intellectual developments.

Humans experienced things that could not be conceived of by Palantians until manifested by a Dreamer. Palantia could be heavily influenced by the level of industrialisation and civilisation a Dreamer was chosen from. Whilst the human world had a linear path of evolution—primitive cave dwellings, inventing tools and agriculture, harnessing electrical energy; up to the current age—for Palantia, there was no such linearity. To an outsider, this would seem impossible, but for Palantians, it was simply life.

The transition between Dreamers—as one Dreamer's time asleep ended and the next began—was known as the Awakening. It was a time of great upheaval and change.

'Each Dreamer is different, as are all individuals,' the unicorn explained, 'and thus each Dreamer's era is distinct too. For those of us who live through the time of an Awakening, it is a strange but wondrous experience, as Palantia is flooded with the artefacts of paradoxically disparate realities. I was present at the changing of the last Dreamer, some 800 years past.'

Sara's head swam with this new and complex information.

It challenged her whole understanding of the linearity of time. It did make a kind of sense though. In her world there was that Buddhist concept of the only time being 'now.' She'd also read something about how time is just a construct designed to stop human minds from collapsing.

Terentius continued, 'Each Dreamer sleeps for hundreds of years in the Palantian timeline, but no Dreamer's Awakening can be determined by time alone. There are signs the attendants watch for, of course—an increase in physical movement, or a rise in the number of sleep phrases uttered—and these are indicators the Dreamer is on the verge of waking. However, the specific time of that Awakening cannot easily be predicted.'

He paused to make sure Sara was still paying attention. Satisfied that she was listening closely, he said, 'According to patterns recorded in the journals, it would usually be a matter of weeks or months. The Elders—previous attendants, who stay on past their youth to study Dreamer history for the rest of their lives—are responsible for setting in motion the process of finding and selecting a new Dreamer. As you would expect, such a task necessitates urgency. However, this current batch of Elders have failed in their duty. Despite agreeing that the Awakening is upon us, they nevertheless continue to debate the matter and fail to make any decisions. I'm not at all surprised he felt compelled to step in...'

Sara was about to ask who, but the question stilled on her lips as she noticed the unicorn's grave expression. 'The current Dreamer is surely Awakening, but I am troubled. Very recently, the Dreamer was observed reacting to something beyond the effects of the Awakening. She appears to be experiencing intense pain, the source of which no one is certain. She was clearly in great distress, and that is of considerable concern.'

'What could happen?' said Sara.

Terentius turned his sombre, midnight eyes to her. 'According to the oldest stories, if a Dreamer does not Awaken at the end of their sleep, reality's very fabric will rend and Palantia will be drawn into the void's singularity.'

'Do you mean... a black hole?'

The unicorn nodded. 'I suppose that is the simplest explanation, yes. Essentially, Palantia's existence will fold in upon itself. The resulting temporal displacement will expand until it reaches your own world's reality.'

'What then?'

The unicorn shook his head. 'We cannot know, but I expect we would rather not find out.'

Sara sat down heavily on the soft grass, hardly registering the hummingcat affectionately rubbing her head against the woman's knee. 'This is awful! Why is this happening? What's causing it?'

'Excellent questions,' said Terentius. 'I may have misjudged you.' He kicked at the ground with his hoof, turning up a sod of soil and eyeing a fat worm that twisted in a panic, desperately trying to flee back into the earth. 'I have my suspicions. I intend to meet with our Council and discuss the matter as soon as possible. In fact,' he said, 'we should be on our way.'

Sara got to her feet again and reached down for the hummingcat. The little creature's fur sparked, and in the next moment, she was in Sara's arms. Terentius chuckled. 'Why walk when you can ride!' Sara swung about immediately in excitement, staring at the unicorn's face, her eyes flicking to his curved smooth back.

Terentius' mirth turned to storm. 'Absolutely not! I am not

some lowly steed to carry you from one place to the next. I am a unicorn!' He huffed in disdain and set off without waiting a moment longer. 'Use your own legs!' he called over his shoulder.

Sara scowled a little as she looked at the hummingcat in her arms, 'All right then, Lady Honeysuckle, I guess I'm your "lowly steed". Time to go.'

The woman trotted to keep at the unicorn's heels, hummingcat purring in her very comfortable seat, like a tiny queen.

CHAPTER 13

The campfire burned brightly within the ring of trees, the flames lighting up the thick branches and giving the illusion the trees were on fire. The party had finished dinner: a delicious thick stew made from potatoes and turnips. The dish was made all the more toothsome with the inclusion of a plump rabbit, struck down in the blink of an eye by Belina's arrow as the beast made the poorly timed decision to scurry out of the brush nearby. Ander picked at his teeth with a small bone before cracking it in half and sucking out the marrow with gusto. 'Ah, that was good!' he said, patting his stomach. Belina smiled and nestled against her husband; he wrapped an arm around her and pulled her close, and they watched the fire together.

Jehn pulled an ale skin from his pack and took a swig. Handing it to the Aes-Sidhe, who drank deeply, he asked, 'When did you last pass this way, Thorn?'

'Some two years ago, if memory serves,' Thorn replied, 'Just another of my wanderings, you know how I get. Staying in one place for any length of time invariably has my feet itching for the open road.'

Jehn nodded. 'I understand well such a feeling. But, for me, I think those days are best kept behind me. For the most part.'

'Do not let your past define you, Jehn,' said Thorn, his gaze soft and kind. 'We all make mistakes.'

'Not like mine,' said Jehn. He quickly broke off when he noticed Ander watching with interest. The big man gave a cheeky grin, unabashed to be caught eavesdropping.

Jehn sucked in a slow breath and counted to three silently. *Let it go.* 'What can we expect for the road ahead, my friend?'

Thorn returned the bladder, the ale inside sloshing audibly. 'With luck, nothing too harrowing. There are dangers, of course, as we both well know. But this is a well-travelled area. And not just by the likes of me! There is good sport and prey—very appealing to hunters.'

Jehn was about to take another draw of ale when the ground beneath him shuddered. Ander's empty plate tipped over, spoon clattering. Senna shot to his feet, eyes wide and staring.

The vibrations lasted a mere handful of seconds, and then the earth fell still once more.

'What was that!' said Senna, hugging his arms to his chest to calm his racing heart.

'A small earthquake, I should think,' said Thorn. 'Not unheard of, and nothing to worry about.'

Jehn wasn't so sure. *The Dreamer...*

Ander got up and patted Senna on the back. 'It's all good, my young friend,' he said, 'We've been through worse! Thank the stars we weren't in an enclosed space like a mine or cavern. Then it really feels like the sky is falling!'

'Ander, you aren't helping,' said Belina. She turned to Senna. 'Never mind my husband's brashness. Earth tremors do happen from time to time. Some even say they are the Dreamer shifting in her sleep. You need not be concerned. We are safe.'

'Okay,' said Senna. 'If you're sure…'

'I am. We are. Come, sit with us. Let Ander regale you with a story.'

'Bring that ale skin!' said Ander, laughing.

Thorn passed the skin to Ander, who grabbed it and took an enormous pull. Belina slapped him on the knee in reprimand. She tugged the container from his fist and took a sip, narrowing her eyes at her husband before passing it back to Senna next to her. Ander just laughed, knowing his wife was just teasing.

Senna grinned, unable to stay anxious for long with this happy pair. 'Would you continue the tale of how you two ended up together?'

'Ah yes,' said Ander, grinning at Belina, 'I'd made a wonderful first impression!'

'Wonderful!' said Belina, eyes twinkling with mirth. 'More like woeful!'

'You still married me.'

'Not without some hesitation!' she said, laughing when she was no longer able to maintain her icy facade.

Thorn smiled. 'I know this tale well,' he said, stretching out by the fire, and poking the embers with a stick. 'But the others do not have the benefit of our history, so let us drink with the telling.' Jehn watched the grey smoke of the campfire spiral upwards, and decided he could afford to put aside his worries for the time being and try to enjoy the moment.

'I'd been hunting small game on the other side of the forest,' Ander began. 'I heard the grunting call of a doe and thought I'd try my luck at landing something more impressive than rabbits and squirrels.'

'A greater prize!' said Senna.

'Exactly!' said Ander. 'I was doing quite well, actually. I wasn't an expert tracker, but I knew my way around the forest. I was keeping close on the trail, but didn't notice the wattle tree.'

'In full flower, it was,' said Belina.

'Do you know the wattle tree, Senna?' asked Ander, taking a final swig from the ale skin. He tipped back his head and shook the last drops into his mouth, then stoppered the skin and returned it to Jehn with a wink. 'Bright yellow balls full of pollen, each branch completely covered. I brushed past—silent, like a good hunter—and the flowers just exploded! The cloud of golden dust would've been a pretty sight if I hadn't chosen that moment to take a big deep breath.'

Belina shook her head, a wry smile dancing on her face.

'Hence the sneeze,' finished Ander.

Belina arched an eyebrow. 'Ha! You call that a sneeze? It was so loud, it could've woken the dead!'

'I tried to explain!' said Ander, 'But Belina was having none of it! She just marched off in disgust, and I didn't see her again for months. We ended up on an overnight hunting party together. She was the party's tracker. I'd signed on to help dress and carry the spoils.'

Things had been a little frosty to begin with, but Belina eventually warmed to the young man as they spoke of their shared love of the land and desire for adventure.

'We spent the evenings swapping stories about the different kinds of animal we'd seen and guessing what strange creatures might exist in other parts of the world,' said Belina. 'He wasn't so annoying as that first impression suggested, and in fact, I quickly came to enjoy his company. Not bad to look at either.' She grinned, and her eyes lit up with love for her burly husband.

'She laughed at my jokes,' said Ander, 'truly laughed. She was so genuine, such a kindred spirit. By the end of that first trip, we'd made plans to journey together. To explore the world and find out for ourselves what mysteries it contained.'

After that, the pair were inseparable, and became quite well-known about the environs of the Western Reaches. They accepted jobs that took them further and further into areas they'd never been before, and their wanderlust grew. Belina practised her archery daily, and her proficiency at forestcraft became such as to be almost unmatched. Ander was naturally athletic and well-built, but desired to become stronger. He determined he could best help their ventures in a more physical way, and so he worked hard to build bulk and muscle. Ander trained daily, using whatever materials were at hand to strengthen his body.

'You ate like a horse,' said Belina, 'still do!'

Ander released his embrace and flexed his arm immodestly. 'I need a lot of fuel! You don't want me to waste away, do you?'

Belina laughed. 'I very much doubt you are in danger of that!'

A branch snapped in the fire, sending a spray of sparks up into the night air. Jehn stood up and began clearing away the remnants of the stew. It was getting late, and they'd need an early start if they wanted to take advantage of the full day.

As Jehn stacked away the plates, he wondered if the hummingcat had returned from the other world and brought the Dreamer Candidate with her. If all had gone to plan, Honeysuckle would have deposited the human right at the unicorn's feet. *Once we reached the edge of the 'Shadowing, I should see about an update.*

Story time clearly over, the party began preparations to retire for the night. Thorn stoked the fire and offered to take the first watch. 'I don't need to sleep as much as you all,' he said, silencing the others' polite protestations. 'Ander, I'll wake you in a few hours, and you can take over.'

The big man agreed, and set to laying out a double sleeping roll. He opened one side for his wife to scoot in before manoeuvring his large frame into the remaining space. Belina cuddled against him and closed her eyes. Jehn and Senna positioned their bedrolls close enough to the fire to benefit from its welcoming warmth, but not so close to run the risk of catching aflame in the night.

Thorn swept a watchful gaze over the group before turning back to the fire. As sleep took the other members of the party, the Aes-Sidhe settled in and listened to the chorus of hidden creatures filling the silence with their nocturnal song.

CHAPTER 14

Sara usually loathed exercise, but the walk through this new and strange countryside was such an interesting experience, she hardly noticed the hours slipping by. The ground beneath her feet was firm, but with a gentle springiness born from soft grasses and thick spongy moss. The combination prevented her legs from getting weary, and made the long hike quite pleasant.

They passed through fields of colourful wildflowers, bright oranges, pinks, and vivid colours unheard of in Sara's world: iridescent and shimmering like patches of oil after a rainstorm. They wandered under stands of tall, statuesque trees where Sara spied oaks, birch, and pines, various eucalypts, wattles, and blackwood. The trees were resplendent in foliage and flower, buzzing with nectar-eating life. To her delight, bees were everywhere, ferrying their baskets of pollen all day long, too busy to bother with the woman and unicorn traveling in their midst.

Animal life was equally prolific. Sara spotted animals from her home country—wallabies that sat up from their browsing to watch her go by, echidnas studiously trundling along in search of a tasty ant nest—as well as ones she'd only seen in books or TV: vibrant red foxes, tiny hedgehogs, even a family of river otters when they stopped by a stream to drink.

Everywhere she looked, nature was thriving, and Sara's heart sang at the sight. *My world was once like this, before we wrecked it.*

The hummingcat had cuddled in her arms for the first twenty minutes or so, and then simply disappeared. Sara hadn't seen her since. The magical creatures shared more than just a physical similarity to the cats of her world; both sorts were contrary and did what suited them.

Terentius suggested a short halt, and as she sat down upon a nearby rock, smoothed from exposure to the weather, Sara felt an ache in her stomach, and it occurred to her that she hadn't eaten all day. Actually, it had probably been longer than that, as she'd been running so late to work, she'd not had time for breakfast. *Work!* she suddenly remembered, *what time would it even be there now?* Everyone probably thought she'd just up and quit after the verbal assault she'd received.

Huh, she considered. *I don't think I care! Maybe I can stay here instead.* She noticed the unicorn watching her intently, and she realised he had probably heard her thoughts. She blushed, turning her face away to hide her embarrassment.

If I could stay here, she couldn't help but continue her thought, *all of my problems could be solved in one foul swoop.*

The unicorn's groan interrupted her musings.

'What?!' said Sara. 'What's wrong?'

'You know the term is actually "one fell swoop", don't you?' he said. 'I had begun to think you perhaps weren't an idiot. It seems I was wrong.'

'What are you talking about?' she said, choosing to ignore the unicorn's mental incursion. 'That doesn't make any sense—"one fell swoop"—I mean, what's a "fell swoop" anyway?'

'It means "all at once"!'

'I know that's what it means, but it's not "fell", it's "foul"!'

'Absolutely incorrect,' Terentius said, tossing his head in irritation, setting the tiny jewels in his mane shimmering and sparkling.

'I'm sorry, but no,' Sara argued, refusing to back down when she knew in this case, she was right. 'It's like, you do it all in one big yucky go. Like a job you hate, but if you just knuckle down and get it done, it's done!' She nodded in satisfaction at her explanation.

'It's "fell swoop",' the unicorn insisted in an exasperated voice. 'Its literal meaning is "a sudden downward movement by an attacking bird".' He rolled his eyes at her.

Sara considered this for a moment, her chin resting between her thumb and forefinger as she gazed off into middle distance. 'I get it now. We were both wrong! It's one "fowl" swoop!' and she flapped her hands to demonstrate.

Terentius stared at her long and hard, trying to decide if she was pulling his leg. 'Oh, for goodness' sake!' he said in a low mutter, turning his back to crop at some clover nearby.

She could hear him muttering and grumbling between chews, and she suddenly wished she had a computer handy so she could find out the answer once and for all.

'He's right,' said a small voice beside her. Looking down, she saw a tiny man dressed in brown and grey furs, with a cap made from a gum-nut casing. 'Never try to argue grammar, history, or science with a unicorn, especially not one as old and knowledgeable as Terry.'

Sara's face lit up with delight. '"Terry"!?'

'Don't ever call me that,' the unicorn said, his face full of thunder. 'My name is Terentius Aodhfin and I refuse to acknowledge any abbreviations or familiarisations.'

Sara suppressed a giggle, her previous embarrassment all but disappeared, and she whispered to the little man, 'Who are you? Where did you spring from?'

The tiny fur-clad man doffed his gum-nut hat and bowed deeply, flinging the arm holding the cap low across his body in a dramatic fashion. Despite his diminutive stature, the gesture was stately and impressive. 'Fetcher Thistledown, at your service.' He replaced his cap and jumped down to the ground in front of her. 'You can call me Fetch.'

Sara inclined her head politely. 'It's a pleasure to meet you, Fetch. I'm Sara.'

The unicorn pointedly ignored the both of them and kept on munching the sweet clover, which was interspersed with its red and white ball-like flowerheads. He snorted at a bee that was trying to land on the patch he was partaking in. The bee darted away, not about to fight over the odd clover flower when there were plenty of other less perilous areas to glean.

'Welcome to Palantia, Sara,' said the little man brightly. 'Would you like something to eat?'

At the merest mention of the potential of a meal, Sara's stomached betrayed her and let out an appallingly loud gurgle. This set Fetch falling about in gales of laughter. Sara gave the unicorn an embarrassed glance, but he deliberately turned his rump towards her, tail flicking in irritation.

Fetch, finally recovering from his fit of chuckling, pointed to a small copse of short shrubs behind them. 'Do you like mushrooms? That's my favourite mushrooming spot,' he offered. 'They grow as big as me!' He hopped up and down in excitement.

'Are you sure you don't mind sharing?' asked Sara uncertainly. 'I don't want to take your precious supplies.'

'Not at all!' said Fetch. 'They grow very fast. Take as many as you like!'

'All right,' said Sara, getting up off the rock and brushing away some pieces of moss that clung to her. 'Just over there, you say?'

'Uh huh, uh huh!' Fetch said, brimming with enthusiasm. 'Off you go!'

Sara set off across the spongy ground to the circle of bushes, her backpack abandoned on the ground. She pushed through a thicket of soft, grey foliage, and sure enough, there in the centre was a ring of dusty brown mushrooms. She then noticed the sudden quiet. The pervasive sounds of birds singing and squabbling had stilled, and she slowly turned her head to look back the way she'd come. She could just make out the brown and grey shape of Fetch pacing back and forth near the rock, and Terentius grazing a little further away.

Sara was just about to step into the ring of mushrooms when a thought struck her. *This is a faery ring!* Sara remembered faery rings could be quite dangerous at the right—or wrong—time, and whilst she'd never had to worry about them in her world, Palantia was magical, and who knew what would happen if she crossed the boundary. She could end up in the faery world—across the Veil—and might be trapped there for centuries.

With a gasp, she fled back through the thicket. Terentius' head flew up at her breathless arrival.

Fetch was gone.

As were most of the contents of her backpack, which lay open on the ground next to an empty water bottle rolling gently back and forth in the slight breeze.

Sara's expression darkened and she grabbed the bottle, flinging it in the pack which she zipped with a sharp pull of the toggle. Tossing the backpack over her shoulder, she marched over to Terentius, who stared at her, puzzled. A clover flower jutted from the side of his mouth, and if the situation were less grave, Sara would have found that hilarious. Instead it just made her all the more furious.

'He stole all my things! My keys, my wallet, even my notebook and pen!' she said, in disdain, wagging a finger above the unicorn's nose. 'And he tried to trap me! Why didn't you warn me?'

'Trap you? Whatever are you talking about?' the unicorn said, his bemused expression made more comical as he curled his lip over the clover flower, quickly munching it with his teeth. 'You aren't in any danger!'

'Of course I am. Was. Of course I was! He tried to lure me into a faery ring with his talk of mushrooms. There was a faery ring over there, and I nearly stepped in it!'

The unicorn swallowed his mouthful. 'A what?'

'A faery ring! You know, it's a circle of mushrooms and if you go inside, you get taken to another world and you could get stuck there for a thousand years!'

'Well,' said Terentius, 'I don't know about mushroom circles, but surely it is a little absurd to worry about that when you came through a portal to another dimension with a shiny cat and didn't seem to bat an eye.'

Sara blinked. 'Oh, geez. I'm such an idiot,' she said, inwardly cringing that she'd given the unicorn another reason to be annoyed at her.

The unicorn smirked. 'Well, at least you're not entirely

lacking in self-awareness,' he said as he began trotting towards the copse of bushes. 'Come along, you may as well eat something before we carry on, and I have a hankering for a juicy mushroom or two myself!'

Sara hitched the now-empty backpack onto her shoulder and set off. She could swear she heard a small, piping laugh drift on the breeze as she plodded after the unicorn. She may die of embarrassment, but at least she'd do so with a full belly.

* * *

They had travelled for the better part of the day. Finally, Terentius suggested they stop for the night, and he led Sara to a clearing next to a small stream. She took the opportunity to fill up her water bottle and washed her face in the cool water.

It was warm enough that they didn't need a fire that night, and besides, the hummingcat had returned just as Sara had settled down to rest and had crawled onto her chest, promptly falling asleep. It wasn't the most comfortable of positions for Sara, but the cat was warm and soft, and made her think of Sam, so she put up with a little discomfort to be close to the creature.

The unicorn didn't really sleep, but rather drifted into a semi-conscious state, standing all through the night, his head bowed so low his lustrous horn touched the mossy ground.

Sara closed her eyes and drifted off in a matter of seconds.

When she woke, the unicorn was nowhere to be seen, and the sun was already high in the sky. It was close to midday, and she must have slept for more than twelve hours. She sat up in a rush, realising the hummingcat was no longer there either. Sara was alone. Rising quickly, she attempted to straighten her rumpled clothes with her hands. When she reached up to touch her hair, she pulled a red, dark-veined leaf from within its knotted mess. Dropping the leaf on the ground, she felt around in the pockets of her jeans until her fingers landed on what she'd been seeking. Pulling out a black hair band, she deftly twisted her hair into a bun. At least now it wouldn't get any more tangled.

Sara cast around the clearing, trying not to panic at being abandoned in a foreign world where she knew no one. With shallow, nervous breaths, she made her way to the stream and splashed some water on her face and the back of her neck, then raised handfuls to her mouth to drink.

'Good, you're up,' said the unicorn, leaning down beside her to drink at the stream. Sara started, choking on the mouthful. She quickly wiped her chin with the back of her hand. The unicorn rolled his eyes. 'I trust you slept well. You snore, by the way.'

'Do I?' Sara's relief was apparent on her face, 'I had no idea.'

Terentius looked her over carefully. 'You seem well-rested. Excellent. I thought I should let you sleep. You looked like you needed it.'

Sara wasn't sure if she should be insulted by the comment, but chose to let it go, 'Thank you, I didn't realise how tired I was. Are we going now?' She picked up the pack in preparation, surprised by the change in its weight. She opened it, and to her delight, saw the inside held a cache of nuts, berries, and apples.

'I thought you might like something besides mushrooms today,' said Terentius. 'A local squirrel was happy to share.'

Sara pulled out an apple and bit into it, delighting in the sweet juice that burst into her mouth as her teeth split the apple's green skin. It was heavenly, and by far the best apple she'd ever eaten. She took a few more bites, and then offered another fruit to the unicorn, this one a glossy deep red. Terentius took the apple from her open hand and devoured it greedily, juice dribbling down into his beard. Sara laughed, and then, after a moment, Terentius did too.

* * *

Sara had been nibbling at the nuts and berries in her bag throughout the afternoon. Her energy levels were high; it was a foreign but pleasant feeling. She was still in awe over meeting Terentius, despite his grumpiness. *A unicorn! A real, beautiful, amazing unicorn!*

'Are there other unicorns in Palantia?' asked Sara. 'Or are you the only one?'

The unicorn tossed his head. 'No, there are others. Quite a few, actually.'

'How wonderful! Do you think I'll have a chance to meet them?'

'Perhaps,' said Terentius, pausing to give her a sour look, 'but I don't know why you'd want to, they are silly creatures.'

'How are they silly? You certainly aren't!'

Terentius snorted. 'They are all children.'

Sara's eyes lit up, her mind conjuring images of unicorn foals and fillies cavorting across a meadow of swaying grasses.

Terentius laughed, 'Oh no, not actual children! Just others much younger than I, and far less wise.'

'Far less humble too, I'm sure,' she said, giving the unicorn a cheeky wink.

Terentius' lips thinned in a scowl, and he was about to

chastise her when it became apparent she was not being serious. 'You do have a sense of humour, then.'

The sun was riding higher in the sky now, and Sara enjoyed the summery breeze playing across her face. The sun's rays didn't have the same bite here as her home world, and she was thrilled to be able to be outside without her skin burning in just a matter of minutes. The sweetness of the air, and the musical chatter of songbirds gladdened her. *I could get used to this exercise thing, in a place like this.*

A sparkle caught her eye, and Sara noticed the gems in the unicorn's mane were moving. She cocked her head and tried to take a closer look. One gem split apart, and tiny transparent wings spread out from beneath the two halves. It was a beetle! They were all beetles! Hundreds of minuscule iridescent insects of all the colours of the rainbow made the unicorn's mane their home.

'I see you've realised the true nature of my decorations. They come to me in spring and stay through the summer. Do you like them?'

'Very much so! They are beautiful.'

The unicorn shook his mane gently, which set the beetles quivering. They settled down again when the moment passed.

Sara was curious to find out more about the world she found herself in, and now was as good a time as any. 'Terentius? Can you please tell me more about Palantia and the people who live here? We haven't really seen anyone or anything besides a few animals.'

'Of course you are curious,' said Terentius. 'Well, we have a little time before we arrive at our next waypoint, so take heed.' The unicorn cleared his throat and continued. 'Many of the creatures that live in Palantia resemble those that appear in myths and legends in your own world. You may be familiar with some of them. Your little thief, Fetch, for example, is a spriggan—relatively harmless but with a tendency towards kleptomania. There are a wide variety of others, too—beings your people once called faeries.

'All manner of fae reside in the world of Palantia, and throughout your human history, many have chosen to wander in your world. The fae have a fondness for the arts, and artists in particular, but they also enjoy making mischief. However, as your society and so-called civilisation grew, changes and attitudes emerged that were disagreeable to the fae visitors.

'The fae love nature and wild places,' said Terentius, 'and you would undoubtedly recognise, those are becoming fewer and further between in your world. Most of the fae withdrew to Palantia, where they could be assured their beloved environment would remain unspoiled; though some do still make the journey to play and sate their curiosity.'

'There is a place down the road from my house,' said Sara. 'It's the sort of spot that I fancy faeries would live in secret, hidden within suburbia.' She dropped her gaze, fearing he would judge her childish. 'I call it a "small, wild place". It's where the hummingcat took me through the Stitch.'

'I see,' said Terentius. 'Well, it could very well be a faery haunt, even if it is close to your human houses. Pixies and sprites favour places where they can frolic in nature, but still be near enough to humans to play their mischievous pranks. They are fond of stealing small items, teasing dogs and cats, moving things around. I hear they particularly like to hide keys. They use a type of illusion to block humans from seeing what's actually right in front of them.'

'A glamour!'

'Very good,' Terentius said. 'Most fae here in Palantia work to a common good, and the wisest and fairest, the Aes-Sidhe, adjudicate any issues in the Court.'

'That word—Aes-Sidhe—is familiar. "Sidhe" is an old word for "faery" in my world.'

'The Aes-Sidhe are high fae. They are long-lived—not as long as I, of course—and quite knowledgeable.'

'I see,' said Sara. 'How does the Dreamer fit in to all this?'

'I was getting to that!' said the unicorn, his beard twitching as he frowned. 'You are most impatient!'

'Sorry. Please go on.' Sara popped a blueberry in her mouth and gestured for the unicorn to continue.

'Ahem. Very well. There is another race who hold an important role, more important even that the Court of the Aes-Sidhe. These fae regularly visit your world, passing through the Stitch to forage for the nourishment needed to sustain the Dreamer in her long sleep. The fae gather their harvest, return to Palantia, and preserve the sustenance in special vessels for safe keeping. At regular intervals, attendants of the Dreamer collect the vessels and dispatch them back to their central repository for the care and upkeep of the Dreamer during her tenure.'

Sara's brow wrinkled. 'I'm confused. What is this sustenance?'

'The Dreamer survives on human dreams,' said Terentius. 'The Sluagh—the race of fae who conduct this role—extract those dreams and distil them into physical form. A kind of magical mist, if you would. The attendants "feed" the Dreamer by mingling the distilled dreams with the Dreamer's breath. A small amount is all that is needed.'

'How do these Sluagh take the dreams from humans? Don't

we need them?' said Sara. 'I thought that dreams were necessary, to process everything that happened to you when you were awake.'

'The Sluagh remove the dreams when humans sleep. They take nightmares or other dreams that generate intense energy. Once the extraction is complete, they move on to the next human. There are so many people in your world, Sara, that a Sluagh need only to visit each human but once in a lifetime.'

Sara fell silent, her mind turning this over. She had an active dreaming life and often experienced intense dreams, many of which stayed with her long after she awoke. She suddenly recalled an unnerving experience. *I'd almost forgotten.* 'Terentius, these Sluagh… I think I've seen one.'

'That's doubtful,' said Terentius. 'Sluagh are masters of stealth. Even here in Palantia, they are incredibly difficult to discern if they wish to remain hidden.'

Sara ignored the unicorn's dismissive remark and continued. 'I'd been having a horrible nightmare. I dreamed that my cat, Sam, was being eviscerated by some unknown force. It was so vivid and so horrible; I woke myself up.' She shuddered as she remembered. 'I was laying on my back with my head propped up, and when I opened my eyes, I saw a dark, hooded figure standing at the bottom of the bed.'

The unicorn stopped walking, and turned to her with interest. 'Go on.'

'I couldn't really see its face, because the hood was pulled down low, but I got the sense it had seen me looking at it, and that somehow I wasn't meant to have seen it!'

'And then what happened?'

'It sort of slid sideways, holding my gaze, as if it didn't want to turn its back on me. And then it melted into the wall and was gone!'

The unicorn's expression was thoughtful. 'Well, that certainly does match the form and abilities of a Sluagh. How interesting.'

'Could a Sluagh be responsible for what happened to the Dreamer? I mean, they can extract dreams and probably have other dream-related powers.' Sara's eyes widened at the possibility. 'What if a Sluagh is giving nightmares instead of taking them away?'

Terentius' gaze was steady and serious. 'This is a solid theory, Sara, and similar to my own. I suspect we are dealing with a dream fae of some sort—but if it were a Sluagh, that would go against its gentle nature. I cannot imagine what would have caused such a dark twist to its usually benign powers. For reasons as yet unclear, whatever this creature is, it wishes to cause harm to the Dreamer. I intend to present this case to the Aes-Sidhe Council forthwith. If a fae has turned Unseelie, the Court will act to mitigate the threat.'

'What will happen to the Dreamer in the meantime? Whatever this thing is, it might attack again.'

'We must leave that to the Elders of the Dreamer's Grove. I understand this is frustrating and it pains me to take no further action, but my priority is to ensure your safe arrival at the Court. I take comfort in knowing that the Dreamer will be well cared for by the attendants and others who dwell at the Grove. There is also someone there that I trust. He is an academic these days, but clever—for a human—and resourceful. He will keep a close eye on things.'

Sara felt a sudden wave of tiredness. *So much information, but still so many questions.* 'I don't understand why we don't do something! Shouldn't we go there, protect the Dreamer somehow? Maybe I can help!'

'I'm sorry, Sara,' said Terentius, 'But you are needed in a different way.'

'What way is that? You still haven't told me.'

'I will explain in due course. And now, let us continue on while we still have daylight.' He trotted off without waiting for her to respond.

Sara sighed, her heart heavy. *There's no changing his mind, it seems.* She pulled an apple from her pack and took a bite, following in the unicorn's wake.

CHAPTER 15

The past couple of days had been almost dull for Jehn and his party as they trekked through the Barrow Knolls. The area took its name from the oddly humped hillocks throughout the landscape. They resembled barrow mounds, but were in fact just an unusual geological formation. Jehn thought they were probably a result of the Dreamer's influence—a not uncommon occurrence.

The group emerged from the hills to a thin swathe of grasslands that lead to a forest. The travel had been tiring, but not unpleasant. Until now.

A severe storm front was burgeoning, the sky black with clouds. The companions dashed across the plain into the woods, seeking shelter as rain sleeted hard in their faces. At last, a disused hunter's lodge emerged from the fog, and they burst inside. The lodge had fallen into disrepair some time ago, now featuring a leaking roof and broken windows, but it was better than braving the weather outside. They boarded up the windows as best they could using pieces of abandoned furniture, but the relentless gale blasted through the gaps, howling and whistling throughout the day and part of the night, chilling them with its icy fingers.

By morning, the storm had blown away and the dawn was

cool but clear. After a quick breakfast of fruit and doughy damper, they set off. The party moved into a loose formation; Thorn at the head this time, Jehn and Senna in the centre, and Ander bringing up the rear. Belina moved alongside them, further out so she would be better placed to bring down any unlucky creature, flushed from hiding by the rest of the group. The forest was sparse, consisting of purple wattles and silver birch. The odd maple and oak stood here and there, but overall the forest was new growth. A great fire had blistered through the area some decades ago, and despite a few larger trees which still bore the scars of that conflagration, every other growing thing was new by forest standards.

Jehn switched between watching the surrounding forest and his own feet below as he trudged along on ground blanketed with leaves and twigs. Each step gave a satisfying crunch. The larger trees were far enough apart that their meandering roots would not present any trip hazards, so Jehn's careful observation of his footing was not for safety's sake. He was deep in thought, pondering his last meeting with the hummingcat, where she had shared news of the potential Dreamer. The hummingcat communicated in song, and if the listener joined in, she could pass on insights in the form of emotions and flashes of vision.

Jehn recalled feelings of feline pleasure and satisfaction, and what appeared to be a human woman with long brownish-blonde hair. The images the hummingcat relayed were hazy at best, as cats saw the world differently to people, and so could not be relied upon for visual accuracy. But the cat had been excited by the woman, and her song had conveyed a sense of hope and confidence. Jehn felt assured that the woman would be a fit choice to replace the current Dreamer despite her youth and initial lack of experience.

From his readings in the journals, Dreamers were usually little more than children, as they had the greatest capacity for imaginative thought. Children believed in all manner of things that adults did not, and that open-mindedness was key to being a successful Candidate. The humans chosen matured emotionally and mentally throughout their time as the Dreamer, but the Sleep kept them youthful for centuries. When they eventually awoke, they were blessed with a wisdom far beyond their apparent physical age. Many chose to live out the remainder of their lifespan in contemplation of the universe's mysteries, rather than returning to a life of normalcy.

The oldest Dreamer Jehn had ever encountered was one from the earliest histories. The young man had been chosen at the age of twenty-three. But such Dreamers were extremely rare. Nevertheless, most everyone was young to Terentius. The unicorn had precious little patience these days. Jehn hoped he wouldn't scare this one off.

The scholar looked up from his feet and watched a small bird dart from within a nearby bush and take to the sky. Its yellow and black plumage suggested a honeyeater of some sort. A whistling call erupted from the bird's throat as it flittered above him. The forest was rich with birdlife, and even the party's passing would not entirely halt the birdsong that rang out all around them.

As they moved further inland, Jehn saw an increase in brushy scrub, which took advantage of the clearings between the larger trees. Many were in bloom; grevilleas with their spiky leaves and flowers like animal claws; the lemon lime foliage of diosma, resplendent with tiny pale pink stars; and

101

stands of lavender that released their distinctive scent on the cool air. There were bees everywhere, and their buzzing formed a constant backdrop to the other forest sounds.

'It's beautiful, isn't it,' Senna mused, interrupting the scholar's thoughts, his eyes wandering from place to place, drinking in nature's splendour.

'It is indeed.' The two men walked side by side, enjoying the pleasant moment.

'Enjoy it while it lasts, my friends,' said Thorn from just ahead. 'Another day will bring us to the border of the 'Shadowing.'

The 'Shadowing was the name given to the dark forest that stretched for miles between the Dreamer's grove and the lands of the Aes-Sidhe. It was mysterious and changeable, at times a place of great beauty and comfort, but often twisted and dark. Such was the nature of Palantia, governed as it was by the whims of a sleeping Dreamer, but the 'Shadowing was different still.

Senna cast a worried look at the dark-haired man. 'Can't we go around?'

Thorn raised his arm and called for Ander and Belina to halt. 'Let's take a brief rest.'

The group settled on the leafy ground, passing around a water skin and wolfing handfuls of trail rations. Belina rose, excusing herself, and headed off with her bow at the ready to hunt. Thorn sat next to the young attendant, searching the other's face for a moment.

'As you know, most of Palantia's settlements are on this, the Western side of the world,' said Thorn. 'The forest forms a wide arc that stretches right across the main continent, and curves around at each far end. At the egress of that arc lies the city of Thalanthas, and within, the Court. It is unfortunate, but the only way to reach the Aes-Sidhe Court from this side of the land, without a journey of several months, is to pass through the 'Shadowing.'

'I've heard about that place. The other attendants whisper stories at night to scare each other,' said Senna. 'I'm not really sure if what they say holds any truth, but I admit the idea has me nervous. What dangers could we meet?'

'Anything you can imagine, and a lot you can't!' said Ander, chuckling. A few pieces of trail mix fell from his lips. He deftly scooped them up and deposited them back into his mouth.

Thorn gave the red-headed giant a stern look, silencing his laughter. 'There are many dangers, indeed, but you are with experienced adventurers and skilled fighters. I have been through the 'Shadowing many times in my lifetime, and am familiar with its pitfalls and hazards. Ander and Belina have explored the forest far and wide as well, and even Jehn has had a foray into its depths once or twice. You could not be with a better group.'

Senna gave a brisk nod, but Jehn knew the attendant remained ill at ease. 'We will be through in no time, Senna,' he said. 'You'll be home to Meryn before she can even miss you!'

'I hope so, Jehn,' the boy said, his gaze doubtful, 'I really do.'

Thorn took the lull in conversation to lay down upon a bed of bracken ferns, stretching out to his full length. 'A short respite,' he said, staring up at the sunlight filtering through the outstretched branches of a mottled birch tree. 'Twenty minutes, and then we'll be off.'

Senna followed suit, closing his eyes. His breathing slowed, and he was asleep almost instantly. Jehn was amazed and envious, struggling as he did to sleep at the best of times.

Ander pulled out a small knife from his belt and began whittling a piece of wood he'd picked up along the way. With dexterous fingers, he stripped off the bark and cut the piece down to a manageable size. Turning it over in his hands, the big man smiled in satisfaction and started carving. Curls of wood shavings flew about him as he worked. Jehn watched with interest, trying to discern what the carving would become.

After a quarter of an hour had passed, Belina reappeared, two fat rabbits hanging by their hind feet from a thong about her neck. She tossed them on the ground in front of Ander. He pocketed his knife and carving, and immediately set about field-dressing each animal. With a deft pull, he removed the hide, gutted and cleaned the carcass, and took off the head. Now ready for cooking, he wrapped each rabbit in a piece of dark cheesecloth and stowed them in his pack for later. Given the weather was not too warm today, the rabbits would keep until they made camp at the end of the day.

Ander swept up the remains of the animals and placed them under a shaded spot so they wouldn't rot in the sun. The forest scavengers would find the hide and offal and make short work of them.

The big man washed his hands clean in a small nearby pool, wiping them on the grass and shaking them to flick away the last drops of water. His work finished, he picked up the pack and grinned. 'She hunts, I clean,' he said. 'It's been that way always.'

Belina grinned back at her husband and said, 'Only because you are a terrible hunter!'

'Tease me not, woman!'

Ander growled and grabbed at his wife, but she nimbly leapt

out of the way, 'You'll only catch me if I want you to!' Belina taunted, spinning away a from the big man's feint to the left.

Jehn and Thorn laughed at the couple's antics, which woke Senna from his nap with a start. Jehn touched the young man on his shoulder. 'Time to go,' he said.

The attendant sat up and ran his fingers through his fine hair, picking out a few pieces of fern frond. 'I'm ready,' he said, and got to his feet.

They set off in an easterly direction, drawing closer each hour to the dark smudge on the horizon. The 'Shadowing would soon reveal itself.

CHAPTER 16

The vigil was lasting longer than the Sluagh expected. The female attendant stood over the Dreamer, her expression resolute. She did not look to be leaving any time soon. The Sluagh's patience ran out.

Closing its eyes, it spoke a guttural word and thrust its finger forward, pointing a sharp talon at the attendant. The unsuspecting maiden let out a strangled cry and raised her hands as if warding off an unseen foe. She backed against the Dreamer's dais, mouth gaping, but little more than a whimper emerged from her throat. She crumpled to her knees, eyes bulging in terror. She made a final attempt to cry for help, then toppled over onto the ground. Her dead eyes stared straight at the Sluagh's hiding place.

Quick as a thought, the creature scuttled forward, making the motions of the spell. It cast the nightmare into the Dreamer's mind. While the Dreamer's sleeping form bucked and stiffened on the dais, the Sluagh leaned in and inhaled deeply. The almost imperceptible filament of energy materialised from the Dreamer's temple and disappeared within the Sluagh's greedy maw. The creature licked its lips and sighed quietly.

Not content with a single taste, the Sluagh cast its spell again and again, pulling out thread after thread of the Dreamer's essence and devouring each with a feverish gasp. The Dreamer's body spasmed violently, only the curved lip of the dais' platform preventing it from falling to the ground.

Finally satiated, the creature pulled a glass receptacle from within the folds of its cloak, and directed the tendrils of energy inside, carefully sealing it with a finely wrought stopper. It secreted the bottle beneath its robe, and without a backward glance, slipped away into the trees.

The Dreamer lay upon the dais, alone and unprotected, her skin ashen, breath coming in ragged gasps. The Sluagh's attack had gone completely unseen. The dead attendant's hair lifted as a gust blew through the Dreamer's grove. Overhead, the canopy of aspen trees shook, and yellow, orange, and red leaves rained down upon the two prone forms, one gone from the world, and the other clinging to life by the barest of threads.

* * *

The city bustled with people going about their day, blissfully unaware to the threat in their midst. The sun flashed upon the cobblestone paving, worn smooth from centuries of use. Grand houses stood in regal attention on either side of the wide street.

One home in particular drew the eye, its twin marble columns flanking an exquisitely-carved rosewood entrance. A muddy shadow passed over the building's white stone walls. Unnoticed, the air flickered, and at once the Sluagh stood within the mansion's darkened cellar.

It drew the stoppered bottle from beneath its cloak and

swirled the contents with a lazy flick of its wrist. The delicate filament folded and moved within. The creature ran a sharp tongue over bone-white teeth. It was still high from its last gorging meal, but despite the promise of pleasure, it restrained itself.

Moving to the far wall of the cellar, the Sluagh paused, eyeing the many bottles decorating the wall. Their contents lacked the bright shimmer of today's prize. This was special. It deserved pride of place. Carefully setting the vessel on the highest shelf, it smiled, sly and slow, admiring its collection. The creature fingered the space to the right of this newest addition. Empty now, but not for much longer. The frightful grin widened.

In days past, before it had honed its skills, the Sluagh had not bothered to collect the essences. It had simply consumed each one greedily, forcefully removing it from its host. The urgency had been born of a hunger unknown until the first taste. The creature smiled, remembering. A rabbit. Not much more than a kit, but full of life and thoughts. That first tentative sending of power, the initial connection, the spark… And then came the pulling, the sucking void, leeching the rabbit of its spirit, rushing in a torrent into the Sluagh's being. It had never felt so full of life.

The ecstasy had been so great, it was many months before it could control its urges. Countless beasts met their end at the crook of the Sluagh's hands. A dog here, a deer there, once, a great black bear. *Nothing of consequence.*

In time, the Sluagh learned to control the experience, to extend it beyond a single, fatal time. If it was careful—and not too greedy—the Sluagh could draw from the victim over and over again. Of course, the weaker the quarry, the less able to sustain a continuous flow of essence.

A creak on the staircase alerted the Sluagh to another's presence. It turned slowly, unconcerned, tilting its head to the side as it watched the other make his way carefully down the steps. The man was tall and lean, with raven-black hair held back in a red leather band. He wore a suede tailored jacket in deep blue, with golden threadwork embroidered meticulously across the shoulders and sleeves. Dark cotton pants tucked into knee-high black leather boots completed the sumptuous outfit. The man's features would be considered exceedingly handsome, had his face not been so hollow and gaunt, the skin so pasty and drawn. He looked as if he hadn't slept in weeks.

The man's wearied eyes lifted, and he met the gaze of the Sluagh unsteadily. 'I was just coming to check...' he began, tripping over the words as his voice shook with hesitation. The creature stopped him with a hiss.

'You will not come down here. No matter what you think or feel; this place is mine. *You* are mine.' The creature twisted its fingers in the air, and the man threw up his hands, grasping at his head in pain. 'Do you understand?'

The man nodded fervently, his fine features contorted against the mental onslaught.

'Good. See that it stays that way. Now, leave.' The creature flicked its long fingers at the tall man in dismissal, releasing the spell. The man fled back the way he'd come.

The Sluagh turned back to its shelf of life essence and stood rapt, watching the bottles swirl.

* * *

The man leaned his head against the cool panel of the cellar door. With shaking hands, he slid the bolt across, fixing the padlock in place. He pulled a kerchief from a pocket inside his jacket to mop his brow as he moved unsteadily into the hall. As he passed a large framed mirror, he caught sight of his reflection. The man looking back was stricken with the ravages of age. His eyes had a hunted look, and his mouth hung open, breath coming in rasps, hitching in his throat in shock at his mirror-self.

Trailing his hand against the wall, he put one faltering foot in front of the other and struggled to his bedchamber. The room was large, furnished with a four-poster bed and settee. A basin and jug sat upon a blackwood dresser. Taking a deep breath to calm himself, the man poured a small amount of water from the jug into the basin and slowly washed his face. Avoiding eye contact with the mirror atop the dresser, he let the washcloth fall to the ground. With a heavy, wretched sigh, he fell back onto the bed amidst a pile of pillows and cushions, and stared up at the ceiling. His eyes stung as he fought back tears.

He lay there for some time. How long? Minutes, hours—it was all the same now. Days blurred together and he realised he was beginning to forget his life before. *Before...*

Through hazy eyes, he marked the passage of a spider as it trundled here and there above him. He envied the creature's purpose. He'd had a purpose once. *Hadn't I?* he thought, pushing against the fear and fog. Had made plans, conceived grand ideas. *Was important... wasn't I?* It was getting harder and harder to remember.

So tired. There is no escape from this. Should not even try. No one cares. I'm not worth caring about. Who was I fooling... before?

No one but myself. Who am I now? No one.

The Sluagh was well-versed in the hopes and fears of all living creatures, having seen them in dreams for lifetimes over. It had grown to become a masterful manipulator. It whispered and schemed and put ideas in your head, until you believed its lies. The creature had this man fully under its sway, and he was helpless to break free of its clutches. How easy it was for the dark fae to twist an otherwise rational mind with but a tiny seed of self-doubt. The creature's influence would slip between the slightest crack in certainty and grow there, infecting the thrall with its noisome blight.

It was a terrible irony that the very insecurity it nurtured in its slaves prevented them from ever having the confidence to shatter what was in fact a very tenuous bond.

As the man lay in his bedchamber, mind twisted with self-doubt and fear, the city of Thalanthas carried on its business, oblivious to the plight of one of its own.

CHAPTER 17

E vening was approaching, and Terentius suggested they make camp. A cool change arrived with the sun's descent. Tomorrow's weather would be quite a difference compared to the glorious sunny day just gone.

They found a clearing ringed by thickly wooded trees. A circle of blackened stones was formed in the centre—clearly the site of numerous campfires in the past. The last person who sheltered here had conveniently left kindling and tinder beneath an oiled cloth. Sara thought back fondly on the many summer camping trips she'd taken with her father when she was a child. He had never felt comfortable in the city, and took every opportunity he could get to escape to the highlands or lake country. He took Sara whenever she wanted to; he never hesitated to spend time with her. Those trips were precious to Sara, not just as wonderful memories of her father, but for the invaluable skills he'd taught her. In her everyday life, she'd had few reasons to use them, and she was by no means an outdoorswoman, but she could build a fire, catch and clean fish, even make a shelter if needs be. Her father had taught her not to fear the outdoors, but to revel in it.

Sara stacked the kindling into a pyramid, stuffing bark and wood shavings beneath. There were a few larger logs in the cache, and she put these to the side to use once the fire was started. Satisfied with her preparations, Sara cast around for something to light the tinder. The unicorn had been watching her with amusement. Without a word, he stepped forward and placed a silver hoof within the ring of stones. Terentius brought his horn downwards and struck it sharply against his hoof. A bright spark leapt as the connection was made, flying into the tinder and instantly catching it alight. The unicorn smoothly pulled his hoof away from the kindling flame and gave Sara a wink.

Sara grinned back. Carefully, she breathed on the tiny flame, spurring it to greater intensity. The flame ate up the wood shavings and licked at the bark, which curled and snapped. Finally, the burgeoning blaze burst upwards, wreathing the kindling in its fiery embrace. Delighted with this success, Sara placed first one log, then the other upon the fire, taking care not to smother the flames.

They'd need more wood to keep the fire going through the night. Sara scouted around in the nearby brush, gathering up an armful of branches and returning to stack them in a neat pile beside the campfire.

She eyed her handiwork with pride. 'That should do it.'

'Very good, Sara,' said the unicorn. 'Now come and sit. I want to talk to you.'

Sara nodded and folded herself onto the dry, spongy ground.

'I imagine this has all been quite astounding for you, but you seem to be taking it quite well. I hope, then, that you will also accept what I am about to explain. As I've said previously, the Dreamer is under attack, but secondary to that, she is reaching the end of her sleep, and will soon awaken. A new Dreamer will need to be instated.' The unicorn paused a moment, his expression serious. 'You have been chosen as a Candidate.'

Sara's brow crinkled in confusion, 'Me? Why would you choose me? I'm nothing special!' Her mind raced from thought to thought. She was completely unsuitable, surely. No useful talents, no specialised knowledge. And she'd be leaving her home forever, the people and places she knew. Her rush of thoughts stilled. With Sam gone, what was holding her back? She had no family anymore; her father had died when she was a teenager—a car accident—and her mother had passed away two years ago from a long illness. She had no partner or children, no brothers or sisters, no real friends, and it was unlikely she'd be missed at work. *What is really left there for me?*

'I see you are beginning to understand,' the unicorn said, a touch of tenderness creeping into his usual crotchety tone, 'You have no real ties to your home. That may make your decision easier. But more importantly, you are a rarity in your world, Sara. You *are* special. Most adults in your world would not notice or care about your "small, wild place". They would pass on by and give not a moment's thought to what once was, to that which is now reduced to the merest of places.' The unicorn raised his head, his gaze becoming wistful and distant. Sara held her breath.

After a moment, Terentius continued. 'Even fewer hold on to their childhood beliefs and knowing of the magic and mystery hidden just beyond the edges of your mundane world. You *believe*. You have powers of imagination that are usually lost once attaining adulthood. But you also have experience and maturity. Such a combination of traits is quite astonishing.'

I should feel glad, she thought, *that his opinion of me has changed, but this is so much!* It went completely against her view of herself. All her life, she'd never been exemplary at anything. It was an endless source of frustration for a woman with such a rich imagination and capacity for creativity. She'd pursued different careers and interests and tried her hand at all manner of things: music, painting, sewing, writing. Nothing ever stuck. Average at best, she had come to believe she was destined for a life of mediocrity, and pushing forty certainly didn't help matters. Middle age was knocking at her door, and no amount of wishing and hoping would change that. Sara had achieved nothing of consequence and so was resigned to that being her lot.

Terentius refrained from commenting on this inner dialogue, recognising that Sara must work through it on her own. He hoped she would realise the irony of this kind of thinking. The woman was on the verge of accomplishing something incredible, if she only had the confidence to try. *The fragility of human emotion*, he thought. He would have to proceed with caution.

He shook his mane gently, and the beetles shimmered. 'You do not have to accept this charge, Sara,' he continued. 'You are not bound by a predetermined destiny. You have your own agency, and if you choose not to continue, I will respect that.' He shifted his weight to another hoof and sidled closer to the fire to warm his flank. 'Let us speak of it further in the morning. It has been a long day.'

Sara drew herself back to the conversation, trying to still the turmoil in her mind. 'No, I'm not ready to sleep just yet. I want to know...' she trailed off. *What do I want to know? Am I really considering this, becoming a Dreamer in this new, amazing place?* A small glimmer sparked inside her, offering a tiny

115

voice of hope and confidence. It was hard to listen at times like these, when she felt overwhelmed by the warring sides of herself. One side craved the possibility of being something, or doing something that would leave a mark on the world. The other reminded her that she shouldn't get her hopes up, shouldn't be too big for her own britches. Greatness was reserved for others, not a nobody like her.

The unicorn watched her closely, Sara's internal conflict clear upon her face. The range of emotions her expression betrayed was quite extraordinary. *Poor child*, he thought. *How terrible to live with such insecurity in one's own conviction.*

'Sara,' said the unicorn, 'This decision weighs heavily on you. I understand your reluctance; what I am asking is no trivial matter. But perhaps your mind is best served by rest.'

'No,' Sara shook her head. 'Tell me what I need to know. I think it's better if I have some more information. It might help me decide what to do.' *I doubt it though*, she thought. She'd been having such a nice time, travelling with Terentius. She'd forgotten that she was here for a reason.

'Very well,' Terentius said. 'I do hope you will come to a decision before we reach the Great City and meet with the Council. I will advise them of our suspicions regarding the attacks that have occurred at the Dreamer's Grove, but I also plan to present you as the Dreamer's potential successor.'

'Is that important? What would I have to do?'

The unicorn smiled inwardly, pleased with his not-so-subtle steering of the conversation. 'It is vital that a chosen Candidate be presented for approval by the Council. As representatives for all of Palantia, they must decide if you are suitable.'

Sara frowned. 'But how will I show them I'm good enough?

Am I good enough?'

'You will be, I am certain of it,' Terentius said. 'I will give my endorsement.' He raised his chin proudly. 'I am well-respected.'

Sara laughed despite herself. 'I'm sure you are,' she said, her face breaking into a grin, her concerns momentarily on hold.

Terentius snorted, but refrained from chastising her, though he sorely wanted to. 'I should warn you, then, that the Council determines a Dreamer's suitability by way of a test.'

Sara felt a flutter of fear in her chest and her smile fell. *Damn,* she thought. *I hate tests!* She'd never been good at them. The stress was unbearable, she forgot everything she'd studied. Any time she had to do any kind of test, she always had this moment where she wondered if she could just cut and run. Her eyes darted from side to side, as she unconsciously searched for an exit. *Can't run now*, she thought, *I've no idea where I'd go. Gods, I hate this feeling.* To her horror, she felt hot tears pricking at her eyes and she squeezed the lids shut in earnest. *Damn, damn, damn!*

'Do not fear, Sara,' the unicorn said, his voice deep and calm, 'That is why I am here. I said when we met that I would guide and mentor you, and that I shall.'

'I don't know,' she said, 'I don't want to let you down.'

'I trust you will not,' said Terentius. 'And besides, I will be the judge of that, not you.'

Sara had no answer to that, so she nodded curtly and faced the fire, returning to her storm of thought. The unicorn let her be.

* * *

Sara opened her eyes. She hadn't realised she'd drifted off, and her neck was uncomfortably stiff. The fire crackled, the logs from earlier still burning brightly. *I've only dozed a couple of hours.*

The unicorn stood nearby, facing the forest. The shadows of the campfire danced upon his flank, turning his opal coat to tones of ochre. He shifted his weight, but did not turn.

I should do it, Sara thought, *I should try. He said he'd help me. It can't hurt to try, can it? What's the worst that could happen?*

She blinked the crust from her eyelids and watched a silver cloud drift across the slice of moon, sailing high in the sky.

There's plenty of awful stuff that could happen, her second thoughts reminded, *not the least of which being you stuffing everything up and causing all manner of hurt. That's what you're good at.*

Sara sighed. Arguing with herself was another one of her specialities. *If I don't do this, if I don't try, I won't get to stay. They'll send me back and then I'll return to a boring life, with work, dealing with horrible managers and stupid people and a world were magic is forgotten.*

The unicorn's ear flicked backwards, and finally he turned and walked towards her. Sara looked deeply into Terentius' indigo eyes, seeing herself reflected there in miniature. 'I'll do it,' she said. 'I'll take the test and become the next Dreamer. Well, I'll try, at least.'

Terentius' lips parted in an equine grin, and he half-reared, his front hooves dancing in the air for a moment. 'Splendid!' he said. 'We should begin preparations immediately. Go to sleep.'

'What?' Sara said, her mouth agape, 'I can't just go to sleep like that—' she clicked her fingers, '—especially not after you telling me I'm soon going to be meeting a bunch of important people and I'm going to have to take a test in front of them!'

'Well you had best learn, because your ability to sleep is fairly crucial to becoming the next Dreamer,' Terentius said, dripping with sarcasm.

Sara scowled at the unicorn, 'You really are incorrigible, Terentius Aodhfin,' she said, 'has anyone ever told you that?'

The unicorn laughed. 'Oh yes, once or twice,' he said. 'Now, get comfortable—I'm going to teach you about your abilities.'

* * *

'First and foremost, I want you to understand something of vital importance,' the unicorn began. 'You will not have realised this, but your mere presence in Palantia has unlocked your quiescent talents. All potential Dreamers have these latent abilities, and any Candidate that makes their way through the Stitch to this world will soon after experience a stirring of their newfound powers. Yours seem yet to manifest, so we shall give them a little push along.'

Sara's head swam with this new information, but she was determined to have faith in the unicorn's knowledge and wisdom.

'Lay down, and I will guide you into a restful, meditative state which will ready you for dream journey,' Terentius said, in a soft, low voice. Sara stretched out on the ground, her hair spread out like a halo. 'Good, now listen to my voice. Take deep, comfortable breaths. Bring your focus to your legs, and imagine breathing into that area. Imagine your legs becoming heavy as stone.'

Sara inhaled and exhaled rhythmically, concentrating on

following the unicorn's instruction. She moved through each area of her body, releasing the tension in her muscles until she was entirely relaxed.

'When you are ready, visualise your spirit lifting up out of your body. Feel yourself grow and stretch from your earthly form. You are as the air, light and free.'

Sara's breaths became slower, and Terentius sensed she was on the verge of projecting. 'Now stretch away from your body,' he said, 'and ascend higher.'

Sara felt the pull of the sky, and let herself rise level with the trees surrounding their campfire. She saw the forest spreading out, and the wide, open plain beyond. Further still, the blue hills and mountains marched into the distance. Sara drifted on the eddies of the gentle breeze, revelling in the freedom of astral flight.

Turning over, she looked down and saw herself prone besides the sparking campfire, Terentius standing guard alongside.

'Come back now, Sara,' came the unicorn's voice, gentle but insistent. She smiled and floated back to her body, settling into it and finding it a warm comfort. The astral sky had been cool—almost cold.

Having quickly mastered control over her spirit, and the ability to enter meditation, it was but a simple step further for Terentius to teach Sara to give over to true sleep. She followed the same guided meditation, but instead of visualising leaving her body, this time the unicorn had her imagine herself sinking into it and letting go. Sara fell into a deep sleep on the very first try, and the unicorn had to poke her gently in the side with his horn to get her to wake again. They continued the sleeping exercise a number of times before Terentius was satisfied she could manage without his guidance.

'You have done so well, Sara,' he said, with a tinge of pride. 'However, this next step will not be so simple. Take heed: you must dream now. Release your thoughts at the moment of sleep. When you feel yourself giving over to sleep, unleash your imagination and let it run free. Only then can you sleep and dream a true Dreamer's dream.'

Sara frowned. 'I don't understand. Won't that keep me awake? If my mind is running a million miles an hour? That's a recipe for insomnia, in my experience!'

'Trust, Sara,' said the unicorn. 'You must trust me in this. You must trust yourself.'

Unconvinced, Sara began the exercise. Every time the unicorn woke her, Sara became more frustrated.

'I can't do this!' she said, clenching her fists. Tears welled in her eyes as her cheeks flushed pink. 'I don't know what I'm doing, I don't know why anyone would pick me for this! It's too much! Just when I thought I was getting somewhere... I can't. I'm useless. You need to find someone else. Just send me back. It's okay. I'm not good enough. I'm never good enough...'

'Oh, my dear Sara,' the unicorn said, sadly. 'Whatever happened to you to make you feel you are not good enough? Why do you hurt yourself this way? You are special; but even if you were not, you deserve to be happy. Why are you so hard on yourself?'

Sara let out a heavy sigh. 'I... I don't really know. I guess I've never been good at anything. School was hard, especially after Dad died... But I don't think that's the reason. I don't want to use it as an excuse. Other kids had it hard too. Other adults as well. Everyone has a story, don't they? Everyone has something in their life that is sad. Loss changes you, I get that, but I was always mediocre. Having a dead dad didn't make me more interesting. People don't really care about that. Not really. It makes them feel uncomfortable, mostly.'

The unicorn watched her closely, careful not to interrupt this outpouring of emotion.

'As I got older, I noticed people are pretty self-absorbed. I guess that's normal. But it seems like I cared—care—more about their feelings and what they think, than they do for me. I've had friends that I thought were amazing, that I connected with and wanted to spend heaps of time with. But then they walked all over me if it meant getting ahead in their life. Ditched me in a heartbeat.' Sara stared at her hands, tracing the lines with her eyes. 'That's not to say I haven't met nice people; I have. But they drift away, and find a purpose somewhere else, and then it's back to being on my own again. I got used to it. I'm okay with it. I mean, I think I'm okay with it... I don't know. I'm not good at this either—talking about myself.'

'Why do you think that is?' the unicorn said gently.

'Well... who cares? Who wants to hear my inner thoughts and dreams? Everyone has those, and most people don't have room for mine as well. And why should they? The odd times I do share what I'm thinking, or ideas I want to contribute... it always backfires. I end up feeling stupid that I even said something. This guy at work—' she spread her hands and shrugged. 'It doesn't matter.'

'We are all shaped by our past relationships, Sara, good or bad,' said the unicorn, 'Each one taught you something—about yourself, about the world, about people—they made you who you are and contributed to the values and ideals you hold dear.

And in turn, you have done the same for countless others. No person is an island. Connections bring meaning to life. This is true of any being, whether their lifespans are fleeting like humans, or lengthy like magical creatures such as I.'

The hummingcat took this moment to blink into existence. She sidled over to Sara and lay down at her side, purring.

'I know you're right,' said Sara, rubbing the cat's chin absently. 'I just find it hard to reconcile what my rational brain says with what my twisted up anxious brain says. It makes me feel crazy.'

'Be kind to yourself,' said Terentius softly. 'I believe in you. The only block to unleashing your power is your own uncertainty. You need not doubt.'

'I'll try.'

Sara sank to the very edge of sleep, and she kept returning to the unicorn's steadfast belief in her. Each time she felt the familiar creep of self-doubt, she concentrated on breathing and nothing else. *Inhale, two, three, four. Exhale, two, three, four. I need not doubt.*

Finally, it worked. The unicorn's words broke through the Sara's unconscious block. The mental wall tumbled as the last of her misgivings were dispelled.

She reached inside herself and opened the floodgates. A universe exploded in her mind's eye, and she gasped in surprise and wonder. Sara hurtled through a field of stars, the spiralled arms of galaxies reaching for her as she spun by. She tried to look around, but her body would not respond, and she flew like an arrow through the void. A tiny bright speck appeared before her, nothing but a pinprick against the black, and then she was falling, falling towards a blue-green sphere.

In a moment, Sara's headlong descent slowed, and she

somersaulted in the air, feet slowly reaching down to alight upon lush, thick grass. The land about her was an endless, featureless meadow that stretched far into the distance. She turned around—able to move now—and noticed before her a small hill. Upon the hill, thrust from the earth, was a singular, remarkable tree. Its white, papery trunk was thin and straight, and crowned with leaves of flame—yellow, orange, then finally brightest red at the very top. The stark contrast between trunk and foliage against the intense blue sky was utterly breathtaking.

Sara blinked once, and in that instant found herself beneath the branches on the far side of the hill. She noticed something unusual about this other side. Halfway up the trunk, a second tree emerged from a healed graft. This other tree was almost black, and branched out in a fan. The blackness of its bark had spread down the length of the trunk of the main tree, fusing to become a single entity. There were no leaves, but this second tree was heavy with bright pink blossoms, which gave off a heady scent.

Sara awoke immediately, spinning up out of her subconscious in a rush. She gulped in air as she tried to catch her breath. Terentius was at her side, calming her with soothing words. 'What did you see?' he asked, when finally her chest stopped heaving.

Sara recounted the dream, finishing with a description of the strange conjoined tree.

'Do you understand its meaning?' the unicorn said, intensity in his eyes.

Sara had always felt an affinity for dreams, and over the years enjoyed pondering the meaning of hers and the dreams of others. *Maybe this ability has been in me all along, and I just didn't realise.*

She paused to consider the snippets of meaning, and finally she offered, 'I think it symbolises our two worlds. The aspen is Palantia, and the cherry is my world. I think it means that Palantia came first and my world was joined to it much later—like the graft on the first tree.'

'Do you know the lore of trees?' Terentius asked. 'The meaning and symbolism?'

'Not really,' said Sara. 'I remember reading once that sometimes aspen aren't just a single tree, but a kind of colony, and some aspen forests can spread out a really long way. The whole colony can live on for thousands of years, apparently.'

'In ancient lore,' said Terentius, 'the aspen was known as the whispering tree due to its trembling leaves. It was believed the tree could communicate with other worlds and would provide the ability to pass between one world and the next.'

'Wow!' said Sara. 'That's no coincidence!'

'It would seem not,' said the unicorn. 'What do you know about the cherry tree? Do you have any insight in that surprisingly sharp mind of yours?'

Sara rolled her eyes at the unicorn's sarcasm. 'Well, cherry blossom season is celebrated in some countries. People travel far and wide to see the blossom and have picnics and enjoy the scenery.'

'It is symbolic of new beginnings and revival,' said Terentius. 'The short and somewhat unpredictable timing of the blossom is a metaphor for the transience of life.'

Sara considered this. 'I guess it makes sense, then, that the cherry blossom is the symbol for my world. Human life is brief and intense in comparison to the rest of the universe.'

'Indeed. It is a clear parallel,' Terentius said. 'As with all dreams, there is more than what first appears, but that is for you to discover in time. Let us end the lesson now. You should try to get some proper sleep. We will talk more in the morning.' He shifted his weight to the other leg and settled in for the night. 'You have done well, Sara.'

Sara smiled as she lay upon the soft ground, staring at the unfamiliar stars, and remembering how it felt to journey among them.

CHAPTER 18

J ehn woke feeling well-rested, and realised no one had roused him for his turn at watch. The others were finishing the scraps of last night's dinner. Senna called out to him, 'We saved you a plate, Jehn!'

The scholar nodded and rose from his bedroll, wrapping it up and fastening it to his pack. As he joined the fire, Senna handed him the plate. Jehn wolfed down the leftovers. Belina passed him a hunk of bread, and the scholar used it to mop up the gravy juices. He wiped the bread over the plate, not leaving a single trace.

Ander chuckled and pointed at Jehn's chin. 'You missed a spot.'

Jehn touched the indicated spot and felt a dab of gravy. Wiping it off with his fingertip, he licked the last morsel up and sat back, satisfied.

'Did you sleep well, Jehn?' said Senna. 'You seemed so tired, we decided to let you be.'

'I did, thank you,' said Jehn. 'My first solid sleep in some time.'

'That's good,' said Senna, smiling. 'Ander says we are on the border of the 'Shadowing now. We've been training.' The boy hefted a branch. 'Ander helped carve it last night. He said that a whack on the head with this will sort out any enemies we encounter!'

I doubt that very much, thought Jehn, a shiver of concern plucking at him. *Anything that makes him feel safer though, I suppose.* 'You will cast fear into even the wildest of beasts, I'm sure.'

Senna grinned, giving the makeshift club a few tentative swings.

'Keep your guard up,' said Ander, striding over and poking Senna in the stomach. 'Gotta keep that soft belly of yours well protected.'

'Yes, sir!' said the boy, pulling the weapon back to centre and replanting his feet.

Jehn watched as Ander ran Senna through a few offensive and defensive moves. The scholar was impressed with the boy's determination, despite his own reservations.

Belina and Thorn were making ready to leave. The dark forest of the 'Shadowing loomed a mere two hours' walk from their camp, and it would do to set off soon. Jehn recalled his promise to check in with the hummingcat. He left the group to their preparations and stole away, walking a few moments until he found a quiet spot. Settling down, he closed his eyes and hummed a lilting tune, summoning the cat in his mind. She didn't appear right away, but that was not unusual. Hummingcats—like every other cat in creation—worked off their own schedule and were answerable to no one but themselves. Jehn waited, humming the same few notes every few moments.

Eventually, he felt the hairs on his arms lift. Static snapped in the air. A questioning hum sounded in his ears, and he opened his eyes to see the hummingcat seated on a fallen tree trunk nearby. The cat was in fine condition as always, her variegated coat soft and thick, her tail's voluminous plumage as resplendent as ever. 'Greetings, *mine Milis*,' said Jehn. 'What news?'

The hummingcat rose from her perch, sauntered over and hopped into Jehn's lap. She curled up, purring contentedly. She always liked it when he called her that. The hummingcat was proud, but like most creatures, she wanted to be loved and to love in return. Jehn's heart was always glad when Honeysuckle was nearby, and he knew she felt the same. He would never take for granted the kindness she had shown him, that time, when she found him at his lowest.

Jehn smiled and stroked the feline's delicate head, gently scratching her velvety ears. Honeysuckle gazed up at the scholar, her purple eyes sparkling like gems. She trilled sweetly and it made Jehn's heart sing. The love of a hummingcat was a rare and special thing indeed.

Jehn bent down and touched her nose with his, and his mind flooded with images.

The unicorn stood over a woman as she appeared to sleep. The vision filled Jehn with smug satisfaction—the cat's emotion—and he surmised the unicorn was guiding the Dreamer Candidate to unlock her potential abilities. The woman spoke, but Jehn could not see her face, nor understand her exact words. The hummingcat's vision showed only a rudimentary idea of what was being discussed—two trees, one orange and the other pink. The hummingcat's interest in the subject matter was minimal, so the vision was unclear.

Nevertheless, the cat conveyed confidence in the woman, and so Jehn was assured. 'Thank you,' said Jehn, 'this puts my mind at ease. It seems our mutual friend is conducting his duty and mentoring this new Dreamer well. Depending on the distance between us, and how quickly we make it through the 'Shadowing, I might even have a chance to meet her before she is instated.' *I'll need to get to the bottom of the current Dreamer's situation first, however, and that will mean navigating perils of a more political nature.* He hoped Thorn's presence would help instead of hinder in that venture.

The others would be wondering where he was by now, so Jehn bade farewell to the hummingcat and returned to camp.

'Are you well, *mo chara?*' said Thorn, as he kicked dirt over the last dying embers of the campfire.

'I am,' said Jehn, 'The new Dreamer seems to be a good fit—at least, according to Honeysuckle. She seems quite confident.'

Thorn grinned. 'That is great to hear, Jehn. Is it putting you at ease?'

'Somewhat, I suppose.'

'You feel responsible.'

'I shouldn't, but yes,' said Jehn, his mouth twitching wryly.

'Not many share such a connection as yours with your feline confidant. With that comes a certain obligation, I expect.'

'Indeed. But never mind. We should get a start on the day.'

Thorn smiled and nodded. 'All right, everyone,' he said, 'It's time to go. Let's move out.'

The day began cool with a brooding, overcast sky. The party walked briskly to keep their blood pumping, fanned out in loose formation with Thorn and Belina on the flanks, alert to any threats. When they entered the forest, they would come together to better protect each other if need be.

They made good time with their swift pace and arrived at the edge of the 'Shadowing in under two hours. Thorn called for the group to stop. The Aes-Sidhe's eyes had not stopped scanning the trees, and Jehn then noticed a tell-tale sign of tension—Thorn rubbed his thumb and fingertips together when he was nervous. A very subtle piece of body language, and one that would go unnoticed by any but his closest friends. *He's worried.*

'Friends,' said Thorn, his usual light-heartedness replaced with gravity, 'Most of you have been within before, and are familiar with some of the dangers, but I must remind you that the 'Shadowing is ever-changing, more so than any other place in Palantia. New hazards are likely to have been born since even the most recent past visit, such is the evolving nature of this forest. It will be even more changeable with a new Dreamer present in Palantia. We cannot predict what may happen. Be alert, and Senna,' he locked his eyes on the young attendant, 'stay in the middle of the group. It's there we can best keep you safe.'

The young man gave a quick nod. 'Yes, sir, you have my word.' The attendant's gaze flicked briefly to Jehn, who attempted a thin smile of assurance.

Thorn loosened his silver sword. 'Keep your weapons at the ready, and remain vigilant!'

Casting a final glance over the group, the Aes-Sidhe strode into the gloom. The others followed, Jehn just a few paces behind Thorn with Senna at his heels. Ander and Belina brought up the rear. Belina's bow was now secured to her back; it would only be a hindrance in the thick and tangled forest. Instead, she unclasped her sword sheath and rested her hand lightly on the weapon's pommel. The forest closed about them, and they left the safety of the lowlands behind.

* * *

Jehn breathed in the cool air, revelling in the verdure around him. Everywhere he looked, he was met with a lush richness, in every shade of green imaginable. Here, the glossy foliage of a holly tree, its spiky leaves the darkest emerald. And there a tree with a bulbous green fruit—citrus, he guessed. Here also was a plant Jehn didn't recognise. Its soft silvery leaves were like brushed velvet, and it bore the tiniest, most delicate star-shaped flowers. The blooms were such a pale green they were almost white. The forest was beautiful, and it was thriving.

Jehn drank in the sight, despite the prickling at the back of his neck warning it was not safe here. He marvelled at the variety of shapes and colours of the plant life. 'This place is a botanist's dream,' he said, to no one in particular.

'That it is!' said Ander. 'We brought one to the edge of the 'Shadowing some years back. Weird little fellow, but very interesting. He was like a pig in a wallow. Had a wonderful time.'

'We had to pull him away before night fell,' said Belina, coming in from her position at the group's right flank, 'He'd been simply amazed by the range of plants there. He would've stayed for days if we'd let him.'

'Collecting bits and pieces,' said Ander. 'He had a huge bag full of little jars and he ran from bush to tree and back, filling up all the jars with... what did he call it?'

'"Specimens",' said Belina, 'He was a scientist researching the properties of various plants for medicinal purposes. He was very insistent, and it took both of us to convince him that it wasn't safe to stay after dark.'

'Gods, he was furious,' said Ander, laughing at the memory, 'his face went so red!'

'He wanted to catalogue samples from night blooming

plants, you see,' said Belina, 'but we finally convinced him the danger was too great. We had to promise to procure some for him on our next visit to the area. He wasn't happy about it, but he accepted the compromise.'

'We'll be here at night though,' said Senna, breaking into the conversation with a look of concern.

'It's not the same, young Senna,' said Ander. 'That part of the 'Shadowing was a known haunt for a particular nocturnal beastie. Belina and me, we could've handled it on our own, but not if we were looking out for the doc too. He wasn't a fighter. Opposite of what you'd call fit. Not like you, my boy, and not like Jehn or Thorn here. Built for a lab, not combat.'

'Don't fear, Senna,' said Belina, 'As we've all said, we will protect you—and each other.'

'What happened with the botanist?' said Jehn, hoping to shift the conversation away from the very real dangers they could face.

'His research lead to cures for a number of skin diseases,' said Belina, 'as well as medicine to boost a weakened immune system. The 'Shadowing is quite a wondrous place, despite its changeable nature.'

As they continued deeper into the forest, a low buzzing filled the air. It emanated from head height and shifted from side to side, sounding first nearer, then further away. Jehn pulled Senna closer to him, and the group closed ranks, weapons drawn and ready. 'Stay close,' Jehn whispered. Senna's grip tightened on his branch club.

Thorn carefully pushed aside a tangle of flowering vines, the blossoms sharp and alien with spiky purple centres. The group held their breath, hearts racing with anticipation. Jehn's pulse thudded in his ears and he tried to calm himself. The buzzing was so loud, Jehn felt the reverberation in his chest. He closed his eyes and slowly let out his breath. *Be calm. Be ready.*

The raven-haired Aes-Sidhe turned back, a grin lighting up his features. He beckoned the party forward. Jehn slipped past the vines and emerged beside a small, clear pond encircled with bull-rushes and other reedy plants. A sudden movement caught his eye, accompanied by the strange buzzing sound, and he looked up in awe. Senna pushed through behind him then, and the boy's gaze caught the same remarkable sight.

There above them, zipping back and forth, was an enormous dragonfly. Its crystalline wings spanned nearly the height of a man, and its spearlike body was encrusted with iridescent plates that refracted the light, sending rainbows every which way. The creature's giant many-faceted eyes swivelled as it dipped down to the surface of the pond for the briefest of seconds, before zooming back into the air to continue its enigmatic dance.

The travellers watched in rapt wonder a few moments more, then with a gesture from Thorn, the small group of adventurers left the dragonfly to its pond and continued on.

* * *

They saw other strange creatures throughout that first day, but most fled at their approach. One however, a kind of small feline with the features of a honey badger, stood its ground as they passed, its muzzle rippling in a low growl. Senna stopped to stare at the creature before Jehn hurried him along. Jehn suspected the animal would be far more dangerous to a solo traveller, but in this case, it refrained from attacking a large group. But there could be more nearby; it may not have been a solitary hunter. It would not do to find oneself surrounded by a pack of such tenacious beasts.

The earth quaked again in the early part of the day. The tremors were weak, but lasted for several minutes this time. *There's more to this than just the earth shifting*, thought Jehn.

Thorn lead the group steadily west, taking as straight a path as possible. The mid-afternoon sun broke through the overcast sky and stretched its golden fingers to the earth. The cool of the thick forest gave way to tall stands of eucalypt, dry brush, and dense scrub. The ground beneath their feet crackled with desiccated leaves.

'Mind the cutting grass,' said Thorn, indicating clumps of waist-high grass. The edges of the blades glinted in the dappled sunlight. 'It can slice a man's flesh quick to the bone. Best to keep your skin intact!'

Avoiding the grass made for slow and difficult passage. As the group eased forward, bare hands held high to avoid the razor-like sedge, Ander took the lead, hacking with his axe to clear a path. 'We should start thinking about making camp soon,' he said, axe swinging left and right with abandon, 'Don't want to get caught in the dark without shelter. Or a fire. Big one. This looks like prime hunting grounds for night beasties.'

Ander lifted his arm to strike at a particularly wicked-looking stand of the cutting grass when suddenly the ground swelled beneath him. '*Ifrinn!*' he swore. He stomped his rear foot down, trying to recover his balance. Something struck his thigh like a lancet. He looked down in surprise; the forest floor was scattered with eucalyptus leaves and bark, but the whole area was undulating.

'Ander!' Belina bolted, leaping onto the dead trunk of

135

a fallen blackwood. Ignoring the grass slicing her bare forearms, she grabbed her husband about the waist and heaved backwards. The pair fell to the ground, Ander's face a rictus of shock and pain.

'What's happening?' said Senna, surging forward to help.

Belina ignored the boy and reached for her husband's chest. She plucked a hunting knife from Ander's brace, and plunged downward. The blade sliced through the dull brown stick impaled within the flesh of Ander's leg. Jehn's eyes widened in alarm. The stick was attached to a flat, diamond-shaped creature about three feet in diameter. Glassy hooded eyes stared from either side of its mounded head. Its brown skin was flecked with a bark texture, and a long whip of a tail flicked upwards as the animal bucked in pain from its cleft stinger. Blue ichor dribbled from the wound. Shivering its wing-like fins, the animal swiftly buried itself beneath the forest floor and was gone. Jehn shuddered as he saw the entire area ahead was rippling with an unimaginable number of the creatures.

He heard Thorn's gasp of breath beside him, and met the Aes-Sidhe's gaze. His brow was wrinkled in confusion. 'They shouldn't be here...' said Thorn, 'it's not the right season. They—'

'Help him!' Senna was in tears. 'Stop talking and help him!'

Thorn shook himself from the moment and pushed Jehn and the distraught Senna aside to kneel next to his friend. Ander lay upon the ground, his face red and twisted with pain. Belina cut away his leather pants to get at the wound, discarding the pieces on the ground beside her. The skin was badly inflamed, tendrils of purple snaking out from the centre of the injury. 'Let me see,' said Thorn.

Belina stepped back, her face frozen in a mask of fear,

strands of her chocolate hair unbound and stuck to her forehead with sweat.

The creature's stinger was embedded deep in the muscle. Thorn gently pressed his finger to Ander's leg, his expression darkening as he noted the colour of the surrounding flesh. 'We must act quickly,' the Aes-Sidhe said. 'The groundray's barb is highly venomous. I have to remove it first, before I can treat the poison. Jehn, Senna… I need you to hold him down.'

Jehn took up a place at the big man's head, and Senna at his feet. The two leaned their body weight on Ander, holding him down as best they could. Ander's eyes rolled wildly.

'Belina, in my pack,' Thorn gestured with his free hand, 'there is a flask of clear liquid, and a blue metal tin… bring them both.' Belina returned in a rush, passing Thorn the items. He unstoppered the flask with his teeth, spitting the cap upon the ground. 'Hold him fast.'

'Wait!'

'No, Jehn! There is no time to waste!' said Thorn.

Jehn ripped off his belt and folded the leather strap in half. He clasped Ander's arm and looked him square in the eye. Ander nodded, and took the strap between his teeth. He exhaled hard, his voice muffled by the strap. 'Do it.'

Thorn poured the liquid directly onto the wound. Ander bellowed in pain, and struggled to rise, nearly pulling Jehn from his feet. The scholar pushed his entire body weight onto the other man's shoulders, forcing him back to the ground. Ander's breath came fast and ragged, as he strove to maintain composure against waves of searing pain.

'Onto his side,' said Thorn. The three rolled Ander over so that his wounded leg was on top. 'All of you, hold him down.

Now!'

Thorn grasped the groundray's barb and pushed with all his might. Ander screamed. Thorn forced the barb through the big man's leg, pulling it out the other side as it emerged. Blood spurted from both wounds, soaking the ground. Ander's chest heaved as he gasped for air. 'Quickly, lie him flat,' Thorn said, pushing scraps of Ander's pants beneath the man's leg. Thorn reached for the flask again, and this time poured it directly through the wound. Ander's roar of pain echoed through the forest, sending a small flock of black and white birds to flight, squawking raucously as they launched into the air. Belina let out a strangled sob.

Bending Ander's knee and bracing the leg with his own, Thorn felt around on the ground beside him for the small metal tin. Deftly twisting it open, he plucked out a fingerful of shrivelled grey herbs. Dropping them into his open palm, he spat on the herbs and crushed them together in his fist. He stuffed half the mixture—which had expanded with the moisture from his saliva—it into each wound, packing it deep with his fingers. Ander's pain tolerance gave out and he fell unconscious.

Thorn sighed heavily and wiped his palm on his pants. Jehn and Senna released their hold on the big man and rocked back on their heels. Belina reached into her top to pull out a silk bandana. She handed the turquoise cloth to Thorn. 'Bind his leg with this,' she said, her voice quavering with emotion. Thorn took the cloth wordlessly and set to dressing the wound.

'Is it over?' said Senna. His eyes darted to Ander and back to Thorn. 'Is he going to be okay?'

Jehn moved aside so that Belina could sit beside her husband.

She leaned over to look at Ander's face, which was bathed in sweat, but otherwise calm. 'I hope so,' said Thorn. 'I think I expelled the venom, but we will have to wait and see. We must watch him closely. He is strong and healthy, but will need to rest. We must try to find somewhere safe we can shelter for the night. Perhaps tomorrow also. Let's make a litter, this giant won't be moving himself, at least not right at this moment.'

Belina traced her finger along Ander's jawline and bowed her head so she could kiss him softly on his mouth. 'My big bear,' she whispered, 'don't let me lose you.'

* * *

They worked swiftly, conscious they had but a few daylight hours left. If it came to a fight, they would be sorely disadvantaged without Ander. Thorn left to scout the area for a safe place to rest.

Binding together long branches and a thick net Senna triumphantly discovered inside Ander's pack—'He likes to be prepared', Belina explained—they fashioned a crude stretcher.

Now came the difficult job of placing their friend upon it. Unconscious, Ander was a dead weight, and it took all their strength to lift the man.

Thorn returned as they were catching their breath. He wordlessly gestured a path to follow. He and Belina took the front of the stretcher while Jehn and Senna took the rear. Together, they carried the stricken Ander through the scrub and down a dry riverbed. Even with the aid of Thorn, Ander was a heavy burden.

Sweating and huffing, they rounded a bend to find a small

cliff rising above them. When it rained heavily, this would make a spectacular waterfall, but now a small cavity was revealed, just above the watermark.

'There is not much room within, but it is dry and cool, and will serve us for the night's shelter,' said Thorn. 'I've checked thoroughly. There are no secret entrances from the other side, so our backs will be protected.'

Jehn eyed the cave as they crossed the empty pool and set the stretcher upon the dry ground, considering how best to get Ander up into the space.

'It won't be easy, *mo chara*,' said Thorn, at Jehn's hesitation, 'but we will manage. Senna, the rope in my pack, if you please.'

Thorn and Belina clambered into the cave with the ends of the rope tied to the stretcher. With considerable strain, the four hoisted and pulled the stretcher to swing Ander inside, setting him down against the cavern wall.

Belina gingerly pulled aside the turquoise scarf to inspect the wound. The purpling flesh had begun to calm, and was returning to its natural colour. 'It seems to be healing,' she said. 'the wound has even started to close.'

'An old Aes-Sidhe remedy,' said Thorn. 'I always bring some on my travels.'

Belina rose from her husband's side and stepped across the dusty cave floor to grasp Thorn's hand in hers. 'Thank you,' she said, 'thank you so much.'

'Of course, Belina, he is a great friend. I, too, do not wish to lose him,' Thorn rubbed his finger and thumb together absently. 'He is not out of the woods just yet, however. We must watch and wait.' Belina's features were drawn with worry. 'Why don't you sit with him? Your face should be the first thing he sees when he wakes.'

140

Belina smiled thinly and sat down next to her husband, crossing her legs and resting her elbows on her knees. Holding her head with her hands, she settled in for a long vigil.

'I'm going to find some wood for a fire,' said Jehn. 'Thorn, will you join me?'

Senna sat at the cave's entrance, watching them as they went. The two scoured the banks of the dried-up riverbed for fallen sticks and bark.

'It is most fortunate you came prepared,' said Jehn. 'But you are worried.'

Thorn shook his head and sighed. 'They weren't there last time.'

'What?'

'The 'rays. They've migrated. I should've been more careful. This is just the kind of country they like to inhabit, but I've never seen them this far south.'

The Aes-Sidhe stared at the tree line.

'Don't blame yourself,' said Jehn, 'we both know this place can change in the blink of an eye.'

'I know that,' said Thorn, 'but I should have guessed.'

'Perhaps the recent quakes—'

'It's possible... but even so, I need to be more vigilant.'

'Ander will be fine,' said Jehn, 'You got to him in time.'

'We don't know that, Jehn. It was close. Too close! I was complacent.'

'He is strong, like you said. By tomorrow morning he'll be back to cracking jokes, you'll see.'

'That may be, *mo chara*, but he will not be ready to travel.'

Jehn shifted his bundle of kindling onto his hip. 'How long are we delayed?'

Thorn turned to meet Jehn's gaze. 'Longer than I'd like.

Even if Ander heals overnight, which does seem likely—he's a bear of a man, that one—even then, he will struggle to regain his full strength for a long while. The venom is debilitating. The smallest amount will have a lasting effect. At the very least, we will need to take a slower pace. A different route, as well. We can't risk another encounter with those 'rays. They aren't aggressive, but as poor Ander has witnessed firsthand, they will defend themselves if they are provoked. Or stood upon.'

Quite the setback, thought Jehn. *Will we make it through in time?* Anything could happen to the Dreamer while they tarried.

'I would estimate at least a few more days on top of our initial journey, and that is only provided we don't run into any more trouble,' said Thorn. 'But this is essentially unknown territory for me. We'll have to track through a part of the 'Shadowing I've not gone through in years. Decades. Who knows what we may encounter, especially with what is happening with the Dreamer.'

'We'll make do,' said Jehn. He kept his fears to himself, and quickly donned a mask of confidence. 'I have the utmost faith in you, Thorn, my old friend. And Belina's forestcraft skills will no doubt help us to avoid anything we can't handle. And failing that, Senna has his club.'

Thorn laughed, though the tremor in his voice betrayed him. 'You're right, of course, Jehn. We'll be fine. It's just going to take a little longer than originally planned.'

The sun dipped below the horizon and Jehn was suddenly chilled. Shaking off the ominous feeling, Jehn hefted his bundle and the two headed back to the cave to settle in for the night.

CHAPTER 19

Sara woke feeling more restful than she ever had. The hummingcat was curled at her side, the creature's small fuzzy body warm and content. Sara snuggled against the cat, stroking the soft fur and watching it shimmer with each movement. The hummingcat let out a purring sigh and twisted onto her back, exposing a soft underbelly of mottled cream and marmalade.

Sara hesitated. Some cats—her own Sam a prime example—offered swift retribution to any unsolicited touch. But the hummingcat's soft belly fur lured her, and she decided to risk being swatted.

It was like tickling a cloud. The hummingcat's purring intensified and she stretched her forearms, pummelling the sky with her paws. Sara rubbed the cat's underside and delighted in the happiness emanating from the creature.

As she stroked the little cat, an image formed in her head of a group of unfamiliar people, dressed for travelling. Sara could only vaguely make out the shapes of most of them, but one man stood out quite clearly. Chin-length russet wavy hair framed his angular face. He had a sharp nose and a strong jaw, and the clearest, most piercing blue eyes she'd ever seen. He seemed wise and kind, but neither young nor old. She felt a great sense of comfort at that face as if it belonged to someone who could take care of her if she ever needed.

Terentius cleared his throat, and Sara opened her eyes, not having even realised they were shut until that moment. The hummingcat broke off her song and blinked up at Sara, eyes wide with innocence.

'Little mischief-maker!' At Terentius' stern voice, the cat turned and disappeared with a flip of her fluffy tail.

Sara tilted her head, 'What's the matter?'

'Oh, cats and their catty ways. Never mind,' said Terentius, with a slight smile. 'Now then, when you have breakfasted and readied yourself for the day, I would like to talk to you more about your upcoming test.'

Sara sucked in air through her teeth and grimaced. Terentius had assured her he would prepare her for the trials, so she tried to hold back her nerves. She scoffed some fruit and washed it down with a swig of water, wiping her mouth on her sleeve. The unicorn rolled his eyes. 'Delightful.'

Sara mumbled an apology and stood. 'Do we walk and talk?'

'An excellent idea,' the unicorn said.

They set off, moving out of the forest and into a field scattered with daisies and buttercups. Bees and butterflies danced among the flowers as a cool breeze ruffled Sara's hair.

'As I've said previously, the Council will determine your suitability to become the new Dreamer. The Trial of the Dreamer,' said Terentius, 'will be rather comprehensive and involve several tests and questions.'

'Several! I thought there would just be one test!'

'Calm yourself, Sara! For goodness' sake, you are an exasperating human. I cannot imagine past mentors having such a troublesome student as you. It's fortunate I have unlimited patience.'

Sara's mouth dropped open at this blatant lack of self-awareness.

Terentius snorted. 'Shall I go on, or would you like to continue your inner criticism?'

Sara flushed and nodded.

'The Council will wish to test and analyse different aspects of your personality. This is to ensure you are of sound mind, and that you possess the acuity and aptitude necessary to become a Dreamer. This is a demanding post; one you may hold for hundreds of years. The Council will not instate you if there is any doubt as to your suitability.'

Sara's heart fluttered at the enormity of the task ahead of her, and at the sheer weight of years that may soon be upon her shoulders. *I could live a thousand years!*

'Indeed. It is a task of great importance, but one I do believe you are fit for,' said the unicorn. 'In the past, Dreamers have been tested on factors such as creativity and imagination, patience and wisdom, moral balance and integrity, and the extent of their compassion. We cannot know for certain what the Council will see fit to test you on, but it would be prudent to train and prepare for these same factors.'

'This sounds like a job interview,' said Sara.

'I suppose it is, in a way,' said the unicorn. 'It would do for you to consider possible scenarios you may be asked about as well. Such as your vision for Palantia.'

'My vision?'

'Yes, what kind of world do you wish to make?'

Sara stopped walking and took a long, deep breath. 'That's a big question, Terentius.' She tugged on her lip while she considered. Finally, she answered, 'I want it to be better than my world. I want it to be full of kindness and respect for all the inhabitants, people, animals, plants. I want the citizens to strive to be the best they can be. To be brave and kind... and nice to each other!'

'Hold onto that passion, Sara,' said Terentius, 'this is exactly the response the Council will be looking for. While we travel to the Great City, keep that feeling in your heart and let it grow. By the time we arrive, you should have much to say when asked the question.'

Sara began walking again and Terentius kept pace with her. They continued in silent contemplation.

'Terentius?'

'Yes, Sara?'

'How will the Council test me on the other things you mentioned? Creativity, kindness, all that? What will I be expected to do?'

'I can only offer you examples from Dreamer Trials past. Creativity tests involve being posed a problem whereby you must use your imagination to find a solution. Now, wait, Sara,' Terentius said as she opened her mouth to interrupt, 'You may think this could be solved by lateral thinking, but this is not a test of logic. Your creativity and your imagination are key. You may solve the problem in any number of ways. It is up to you to determine the most effective method, and that which you choose will tell the Council much about you. Later I will teach you how to manifest and control that which you imagine. This is one of the fundamental skills of a Dreamer.'

'What do you mean by "manifest and control"?'

'Exactly what it sounds like. You must be able to create something from your mind and direct its action.'

'Do you mean willing something into existence?' said Sara.

'I can't do that!'

'You can. I will teach you.'

Sara chewed her lip as she rolled the idea around in her head. Creating something from her mind was definitely magic, and she was absolutely not magical.

'I'll be the judge of that,' said Terentius.

She frowned and shook her finger at him. 'Get out of my head, Terry!'

'I have told you not to call me that!'

'Well, stop snooping in my private mind thoughts! It's very rude!'

The unicorn shrugged, not at all contrite.

Sara stared at him, but soon lost her nerve to his steely gaze. *I don't know why I keep thinking I'm going to win a staring competition with a thousand-year-old unicorn.* Terentius suppressed a smirk.

'What are some of the other potential tests? How would I be tested on something like compassion? I mean, I get how you could see that over time, if you observed someone and their actions. But how do you test for that in an interview situation? Would it be a scenario kind of question? Such as, "You see a box of abandoned puppies in a rubbish bin, what do you do?"'

Terentius closed his eyes and sighed heavily. 'Sara, please be serious. A test of compassion is incredibly important. It determines if you will be a benevolent Dreamer. If you fail such a test, it is not safe to instate you as Dreamer. A Dreamer without compassion would bring tragedy and indifference to Palantia whether they meant to or not. A compassionate Dreamer will ensure the coming age will be a peaceful one.'

'I am being serious, Terentius,' said Sara. 'I want to make

sure I am prepared. And anyway, didn't my "vision of Palantia" answer kind of cover this?'

The unicorn smiled. 'All right, Sara, yes. Your vision answer does infer that; however, you may not be asked that question.'

Sara frowned.

'I acknowledge this is confusing,' said the unicorn, 'And in all honesty, my assistance can only go so far.' He flicked his tail. 'To answer your question, a test of compassion would likely be something other than a scenario such as your example. It is highly probable this part of your trial will require evidentiary testimony.'

Sara's heart skipped a beat. 'Testimony…? This really is a trial.'

'Never fear, Sara, you are a compassionate human and that is easily proven. The hummingcat has shown me.'

'What do you mean? How has she shown you? She hardly knows me.'

'Cats are very good judges of character. A cat will not befriend one with cruelty in their heart, and a hummingcat is particularly perceptive to the values and morals of a person. This one has observed you for some time. She told me all about you: about your own cat, and your garden, and your respect for all the creatures that live in your neighbourhood. She said you are patient and kind, and she would not have brought you to Palantia if she did not think you worthy.'

Honeysuckle trilled proudly and flipped onto her side, swishing her tail in the grass and winking an amethyst eye.

'Huh,' said Sara, stroking Honeysuckle's fur and scratching her ear. 'I didn't realise you were such a spy!'

The hummingcat let out a burst of notes that sounded very much like laughter, and then blinked out of existence.

Terentius rolled his eyes, 'Hummingcats have such a flair for the dramatic.'

'I guess if you can teleport all over the universe, you may as well have fun doing it!'

'I suppose so,' said the unicorn, grinning.

CHAPTER 20

With the dawn came a stirring from the stretcher, and much to the relief of all, the patient woke.

'What happened?' said Ander. He attempted to raise himself to a sitting position, but Belina pushed him back down onto the litter.

'You're fine, everything is fine.' She laid a hand on his forehead and found it to be cool and dry. Any chance of fever had passed.

'A small setback, my friend,' said Thorn, stepping around the packs strewn on the cave floor. 'And you call me the Thorn in your side!'

Ander's usual hearty laugh was curtailed by a wince of pain. Belina pulled back the blanket covering the big man to take a better look at his leg. The poultice was dry now and crumbled at a touch. Thorn brushed the last of it away and gently prodded around the wound site.

'Ouch! Watch it!'

'You are healing well, *mo chara*,' the Aes-Sidhe said, 'but you should continue to rest. We can stay a while longer.'

'Rest! And delay our journey? Let me up!' Ander ignored his wife's protests and pushed himself up with his hands. The veins in his neck strained taut as the big man struggled to lift his bulk from the stretcher. Grunting, he lost his strength and his arms gave out. He fell heavily, gasping for breath.

'What's wrong with me?' he said between ragged intakes of air.

'You were stung by a groundray. We were able to treat you before the venom killed you,' said Thorn, reaching to clasp his friend's arm, 'but it is extremely potent. Anyone with a lesser constitution would not have survived. You will be in a weakened state for some time. Please—'

'Weak! No, I'm fine,' Ander's pleading eyes caught Belina's. 'You said everything was fine.'

'It is, my bear,' she said, smoothing Ander's hair from his forehead, 'You just need to rest a little more. Get your strength back. We can afford another day,' she glanced at Thorn, who nodded, 'Just you wait, you'll be back on your feet in no time.'

'We can't wait! The Dreamer—'

Jehn peeled himself away from the cave wall, where he had been silently watching the discussion. 'It is out of our hands now, Ander,' he said, shrugging. *We really should go, but we can't carry him. It would take just as long as staying put another day.*

Ander clenched his fists. 'You should leave me here. Go on without me. I'm no use to anyone like this.'

Maybe we should, thought Jehn, but guilt had him immediately chiding himself. *He's a friend. He needs to rest. But losing another day...*

'I'm not leaving you, love,' said Belina, 'Not in a million years.'

'Another day, Ander,' said Thorn. 'We will wait another day.'

Jehn suppressed a sigh and walked to the edge of the cavern. Senna was below, sitting on a boulder, composing a letter to his sweetheart. The boy turned and waved, mouthing something that Jehn could not hear. Jehn shook his head and gestured at his ear. 'I can't hear you!'

Senna got up from his seat and trotted to the base of the cliff. 'Is Ander awake?'

Jehn nodded, and gave the boy a hand up as he scrambled up to the entrance.

'Ander! You're awake! I'm so glad! How do you feel?' the boy's words trailed off as he noticed the sombre mood.

Ander turned his head away, quickly wiping away the threat of tears.

* * *

Jehn stood at the cave's entrance, shuffling from side to side. The mood inside remained uncomfortable and he didn't want to be a part of it. He stamped his feet against the cold. The day had turned bitter soon after morning, with a sharp wind that iced into the bones, bringing with it the threat of a long freeze.

The change in weather had come without warning. Jehn supposed the delay had a silver lining. Being caught out in this would have been unpleasant and likely dangerous. He watched the eucalypts thrash in the gale, branches snapping back and forth. Lengths of bark, small sticks, and clusters of gum nuts flew through the air, scattering the empty riverbed.

Jehn was finding it very hard to shake the uneasy feeling that had plagued him since they entered the 'Shadowing. If Thorn hadn't been so prepared, hadn't acted quickly, it would have been disastrous. He hoped there would be no further setbacks, but such a thought was practically an open invitation for the fates to meddle.

Waiting chafed Jehn's patience. Every hour that passed was one where the Dreamer remained at risk. There was nothing to do in the current circumstances, but nevertheless, Jehn was irritated. He picked up a leaf and absentmindedly tore it into tiny pieces, stripping it to the veins. Frowning, he threw the pieces into the wind, watching them scatter and eddy before disappearing amongst the debris.

If he's not ready to travel tomorrow, I'm leaving without him.

* * *

Jehn was in a dark mood. The night had been interminable. A day of pacing the small cave in such close proximity with the others had him irritated and ill-tempered. By mid-afternoon, even Senna had stopped trying to engage with him and had left Jehn alone with his doleful thoughts. The lack of exercise brought with it a return of Jehn's chronic insomnia, and so he'd spent the evening in wakeful annoyance.

'Senna, would you mind helping prepare some breakfast?' said Thorn, breaking the uncomfortable silence. 'Something warm to fill our bellies.'

'Of course,' said Senna. He began sorting ingredients while Thorn set up the cooking pot.

A short while later, the pot was bubbling with a thick fragrant porridge. Senna handed Belina a bowl and a spoon for Ander. 'I've added some dried fruit and spices. It's quite good.'

Belina took the bowl gratefully, and coaxed Ander into a seated position, piling their packs behind him. The big man's eyes were downcast, but the sweet smell was just too enticing, and he began shovelling the warm oats into his mouth, swallowing in great gulps. Senna passed him a second helping, amazed by the big man's gusto. After three servings, Ander's hunger was finally sated.

Jehn helped himself to a bowl while he sat on his haunches in front of the fire, wordlessly watching Ander's display.

'It is good to see your appetite remains intact,' said Thorn. 'This is surely a sign that you are well on the road to recovery!'

Ander grinned weakly.

'Would you like to try to stand?'

Ander nodded. Tentatively, he swung his legs off the litter. With significant assistance from Belina and the Aes-Sidhe, the big man struggled to his feet, favouring his good leg considerably.

Jehn took this as motivation enough. 'We should get packing now that the weather has cleared. The sooner we leave, the sooner we can arrive at the Great City.'

The group exchanged hurried glances. 'Jehn,' said Thorn, 'We should not be too hasty. Whilst Ander appears in remarkably good stead after his ordeal, he will be suffering the aftereffects of the venom for some time. I thought I had made that clear.'

Jehn pressed his lips together, silencing his desired retort. *Gods be damned!*

'I agree with the scholar,' said Ander. 'I don't want to lie around anymore. I need to be up and moving. That's gotta be good for me, right? A man can lose his fitness in just a matter of days, you know. Need to get back into condition. Stop fussing, woman!' He scowled at Belina, who was attempting in vain to comb Ander's hair into some semblance of order. She pulled her hands away, smiling.

He looked around at the group. 'Well? What's the plan? Are we moving out?'

Thorn shook his head. 'I don't think that's a good idea.'

Ander looked to Jehn, seeking an ally. 'If he thinks he's ready, who are we to hold him back?' said Jehn, shrugging. He kept his expression carefully neutral, but Thorn narrowed his eyes in suspicion.

'I do not advise it,' the Aes-Sidhe said. Ander frowned, and turned his back to fossick through his pack.

Thorn quietly gestured for Belina to join him. 'I've said my piece. I cannot stop him if he wants to go. Perhaps you would have more luck.'

Belina shook her head. 'Ah, my lord, he is his own man. I think it best we support him in this and be at the ready if he needs us. Besides—' she glanced at Jehn, 'I don't think we could wait another day without splitting the party anyway.'

Jehn averted his gaze. *Who knew I was so transparent?*

Thorn sighed. 'He'll need to rest more than usual, but he'll protest. We'll have to insist.'

Belina nodded and re-joined her husband to help with the gear.

'As soon as we're packed up, we can go,' said Thorn, his usual cavalier attitude tempered. He poured sand on the remains of the fire and gathered his belongings.

A few minutes later, they carefully lowered themselves to the riverbed's dusty floor.

'We'll need to climb here,' Thorn said, indicating the cliff-side above them. It was about thirty feet in height, with plenty of hand and footholds, but with Ander's condition, this would not be an easy climb. 'I'll head up first and throw down a rope.'

'Don't do me any favours, Thorn!' said Ander.

'Thank you, my lord,' said Senna. He turned to Ander, 'I'm not much of a climber. This will make it easier for me. So, it's not just to help you. Why struggle when we don't need to?' He glanced at Belina and she nodded her silent thanks.

If Ander noticed the look, he did not acknowledge it. 'Very well, my friend. And have no fear, I will catch you if you fall!'

Thorn looped a length of hemp rope over his head, beneath his left arm, then commenced his ascent. The Aes-Sidhe made swift work of the climb, deftly finding places to grab among the rocky outcrops that protruded from the defunct waterfall. Had the waterfall been flowing, it would have been near impossible to climb unassisted. The cliff wall was stained with lime and dried algae, and the rocks that made great handholds now would be slick and perilous. *Small mercies*, thought Jehn.

Thorn disappeared at the lip of the cliff wall. Moments later, the rope snaked down, smacking against the rocks. Jehn reached for it and gave it a tug. The hold was secure. Thorn reappeared above them, leaning over precariously. 'It's clear,' he said, 'you can come up.'

One by one, they ascended the dry waterfall, hefting the packs on their shoulders. Ander was determined to make the climb without help. His bare arms glistened with sweat, even in the cool morning air. Hand over hand, he pulled himself slowly up the cliff. Halfway up, he stopped, gripping the rope and panting heavily, his breath coming in puffing clouds.

The rest of the party reached the top. Thorn and Jehn heaved on the rope. Ander was too out of breath to protest. They helped him over the edge and lay on the ground together, exhausted.

Jehn sucked in deep breaths. Perhaps this wasn't such a

good idea, after all.

'Don't say it,' said Ander, between huffs.

Thorn chuckled. 'All right, my big friend. I won't say I told you so.' The Aes-Sidhe got to his feet. He offered a hand to Ander, who accepted it gratefully.

Together, the party stood above the dry riverbed and gazed across the spectacular vista spread out below.

A swathe of blue-green gum trees marched into the distance. Snow-white parrots festooned every branch like enormous blossoms. On the nearest tree, one bird arched its neck, a comb of bright orange feathers rising like a crown. The parrot stretched its impressive wings, flashing the same orange on the underside of its pinions. With a ratcheting cry, it launched into the air.

As if this were a signal, the entire flock took to the wing. In a long, rolling wave, they eased into the air, filling it with their raucous song. Senna clapped his hands to his ears to block the sound. The others watched in wonder as the white cloud, hundreds strong, lifted and soared away towards the horizon.

CHAPTER 21

'You know,' said Sara, 'I have been thinking about my Dream and what else it could mean.'

'Oh?' The unicorn was grazing while Sara sat by a stream, dipping her toes in the cool water and rolling the smooth pebbles around.

'Yes, you said there was more, but I had to figure it out myself.'

'Well then,' said Terentius, swallowing a mouthful of grass and chickweed. 'Do explain.'

'So, I said before that the aspen tree represents Palantia. It's older, stronger, and further along the timeline—I got that from the autumn foliage.'

The unicorn nodded to indicate her to continue.

'The cherry tree is my world and needs the other tree to survive. It's become part of the aspen tree and can't survive without it. And even though the aspen tree is strong on its own, it would be terribly damaged if the cherry tree was removed from it now. The two trees—the two worlds—are now linked and can't be separated. To do so, would be bad for both of us. What do you think?'

Terentius pondered while chewing a fresh mouthful, 'I believe you have the symbolism correct, Sara,' he said. 'And what else?'

'What else?' Sara's brow wrinkled as she considered, 'Isn't that it?'

'Maybe so,' said the unicorn, 'but often even average dreams can have multiple interpretations. The same is assuredly the case for a true dreaming, a Dreamer's dream. What was your role in the Dream?'

'Well, I was an observer; I didn't really do anything.'

'This was your first proper Dream. You should try again and see what it tells you.'

'I can do that?'

'When it pertains to sleep and dreaming, you can do anything, Sara.'

Sara pulled her feet from the stream, drying them on the nearby ground. She left her shoes and socks off for now. Clothing on damp skin gave her the creeps. 'Should I try now, or do you want to keep moving?'

'There is no time like the present. Shall I guide you?'

'Thank you, but no,' she said, 'I want to practise by myself.'

'Very well. Just visualise the trees in your mind as you reach the edge of sleep.'

Sara lay down on the soft, lush grass. The tiniest of breezes wafted over, ruffling her hair. Sara stilled her mind, concentrating on the buzzing of insects around her, and dropped down into the Dream.

The tree rose before her atop the grassy hill. Sara searched for any small details missed the first time. All appeared as before. The meadow stretched out in every direction, grass rippling like wind across a pond against a clear and cloudless sky. The tree dominated the vision, and as Sara stepped closer, it seemed to grow taller and wider, filling up her field of view.

She walked the perimeter of the tree, trailing her hand along its smooth white bark, warm to her touch. She paused and rested her cheek against the tree, slowing her breathing. A low pulse, right at the threshold of her hearing—the tree's heartbeat. The rhythm filled her with calm and a sense of belonging. Pulling herself away regretfully, she continued her circumnavigation of the tree until she came to the graft where the cherry emerged. It was high above her reach, and still abundant in delicate pink blossom, the petals raining down upon her whenever a small gust chanced this way.

The graft had changed. No longer was it smoothly sealed. Now the graft was open and torn, and deep red sap oozed freely from the jointure to the base of the trunk. Sara put her finger to the fluid and found it hot and thick, not sticky as tree sap should be. A metallic, coppery odour assaulted her nostrils. *Is this... blood?*

Sara cast about for a way to inspect the tree's wound. Before her eyes, a wooden ladder materialised, and without hesitating she picked it up and leaned it against the trunk. She was up the steps in a moment, now face to face with the graft. *I need to do something.*

She brought her two hands up, placing one on either side of the wound below the cherry tree's smaller trunk. Concentrating hard, she pushed the split bark together, holding it in place while she imagined the tree healing itself.

Suddenly she was back in the field with the unicorn, sitting bolt upright, hands stretched in front of her. He was watching her with interest, but didn't say a word.

'I think it's me,' said Sara, in sudden understanding. 'I need to prevent the rift between our two worlds.'

The unicorn peeked into Sara's mind and saw the Dream

in her thoughts. He smiled. 'You are ready, Sara,' he said. 'I knew you were the right choice!'

Sara stared at him, then shook her head, chuckling. 'I thought you said I was an idiot!'

'I said nothing of the sort!' said the unicorn, stifling a grin, 'though I may have implied something along those lines, I suppose.'

Sara pointed an accusatory finger at the unicorn. 'Hah!'

'Don't point,' Terentius said, laughing, 'it's rude.'

* * *

They set off again once Sara grounded herself with some food, a little water, and a few deep breaths.

It was another pleasant day, and Sara was beginning to wonder if it was always this perfect in Palantia, or if she'd just been lucky.

She was about to ask Terentius when she felt a rumbling beneath her feet. It rolled up her body, vibrating deep in her chest. She gasped and looked to the unicorn. He stood stock-still, nostrils flaring. 'What's happening?' Sara cried.

The unicorn remained silent, his eyes squeezed shut.

After a few tense minutes, the tremor stopped, and the unicorn let out a long breath. He glanced at Sara, his lips thinned over his teeth. *He's embarrassed!*

'Are you okay? What was that?'

Terentius averted his gaze. 'Just a small earthquake. Nothing to concern yourself about.'

'You were concerned.'

'No, no,' the unicorn said, 'I'm fine. Just best to stand still when the earth shakes, wouldn't you agree?'

'Yes, but—'

'Time to move, child! We'll never get to the Great City if you insist on dilly-dallying!' The unicorn trotted away, leaving Sara gaping in his wake. She frowned as she jogged to catch him up.

He eventually slowed his pace. 'Mercy, Sara,' said Terentius, 'your puffing and blowing is a travesty. I've never met someone so unfit!'

Sara prickled. 'Geez, Terentius, give me a break! You don't have to take it out on me because you were scared and embarrassed about it.'

The unicorn tossed his head and scowled at her. 'Scared! Of what? A little shaking of the ground? Nonsense!'

'Fine. If you aren't going to be honest, that's your problem.' Sara crossed her arms, stiffly. It made walking at this pace even more difficult, but Sara was stubborn and didn't feel like being the mature one right at this moment. *Great, I thought we were getting somewhere, but no, he's back to being a jerkface.* Sara heard Terentius' snort, and knew he'd sensed her thought. *Too bad!* She stalked ahead, her previously light-hearted mood now dark. She kicked a stone in her path, sending it skittering into the grass.

To make matters worse, grey storm clouds were quickly scudding across the azure sky, washing out the brightness of the day and turning the landscape ashen. The temperature dropped with the disappearance of the sun, and Sara suppressed a shiver. *It better not rain.*

It did.

The first drop hit Sara's bare hand and she stared in shock. The rain was uncomfortably warm. Another drop fell, and another, each one getting warmer still. Sara yelped in pain.

Red dots speckled her skin and she looked to Terentius in horror. The unicorn's flank quivered against the rain, but he seemed not to notice the heat.

'It's burning!' said Sara, 'Terentius, the rain... there's something wrong with it.'

A drop fell on the unicorn's unprotected nose and he winced. 'What...?' His ears pulled back as he took in a breath. 'It smells like sulphur! Quick, Sara, to the trees!' The pair ran full tilt to the shelter of a stand of pines, the rain pricking at their exposed skin.

Pushing beneath the branches, they found a mercifully dry space. The thick canopy prevented any of the burning rain to penetrate, and Sara and Terentius were able to catch their breath.

As quickly as it had begun, the rainstorm relented. Exchanging a glance, the woman and unicorn emerged gingerly from their sanctuary to a bright blue sky once more.

'Is that normal?' said Sara, rubbing her hands where the rain had burned her. Some of the red spots were starting to blister.

'Not at all,' said Terentius, 'something more is afoot. Perhaps the Dreamer... or you.'

'Me?! What have I done now?'

'Do you remember me saying that your arrival in Palantia would unlock your latent abilities?'

Sara nodded.

'It may relate to that. The emotions and sensations of a Dreamer are inextricably woven together. You are coming into your powers. Your emotions may be the cause of this burning rain.'

'Well, great. Another thing to worry about!'

The unicorn smiled. 'It may be something else entirely, Sara,' he said, kindly, 'our current situation is quite unusual—a Dreamer perhaps on the verge of Awakening, but experiencing an assault on her mind as well. You, a Dreamer Candidate, here at the same time. Palantia may be adjusting to accommodate the presence of you both. We must continue to hone your skills and prepare you as best we can. And just in case, you must aim to keep your emotions in check.'

Sara's face reddened. 'But—'

The unicorn caught her gaze, 'I will be sure to mind my own as well.'

Sara let out her breath and nodded, 'Okay. Thank you. This is a lot to deal with. I'm not great with stress!' *Pretty bad with it, actually.*

'I think you fail to give yourself credit, Sara,' said the unicorn, 'You are doing remarkably well for someone whose entire life has been turned upside down. I am impressed.'

Sara raised an eyebrow, 'Are you, now.'

The unicorn rolled his eyes, 'Don't go getting too proud of yourself, Sara, your head may swell.' Terentius laughed. 'In your case, that may be quite literal!'

* * *

'I wanted to come back to your Dream, Sara,' the unicorn said. Sara had been lost in thought, not paying attention to how much time had passed. She glanced at the sky. The sun had dipped noticeably, so it had to have been at least an hour that she'd been turning over in her mind the possibility her mood could control the weather. *I'm not sure that's such a great power.*

'Yes, what about it?' she said, combing a few stray strands

of hair from her face and resetting her messy bun.

'You recall the part where you imagined the ladder?' said the unicorn, 'You should keep that in mind when it comes to your Trial. Your ability to manifest an item you needed in the Dream and to control its use—This is a skill you may be tested on. I said I would teach you, but I believe you already have the inherent capacity for it. We should practice, however. I'd like to see if you can use this skill outside the Dream.'

'That really does sound like magic, Terentius. It's one thing to be able to control what's happening in a dream—we have books that teach you that in my world—but it's something else entirely to make stuff happen when you're awake. I'm pretty sure I don't have magic powers. If I did, I reckon I'd know by now.'

'You are quite mistaken, Sara,' said the unicorn, inwardly shaking his head. *When will she believe in herself?* 'Perhaps not in your home world, but here you will find yourself to be quite a force to be reckoned with, once you gain control over your abilities. Now, sit down and find your focus. Concentrate on the pause between your breaths.'

Sara settled into the meditation. *This won't work.*

'No negative self-talk, please,' came the unicorn's stern voice.

Sara's cheeks reddened slightly, and she cleared her mind as best she could.

'That's better. Now, we will start small. Put your hands in front of you. Imagine an apple. Consider its shape, its colour. The weight of it in your hands. What would it feel like to bite into? Imagine every aspect of the apple. Pour all your concentration into it.'

Sara let her imagination take over. She could see the fruit

clearly in her mind. Blush and shiny, with stalk and leaf still attached—the epitome of the perfect apple.

'Now, breathe in deeply. Breathe in the image of the apple.'

Sara inhaled, holding the breath.

'Exhale and open your eyes.'

Sara let out the breath and opened one eye, just a crack. Both eyes snapped open as she felt the object in her outstretched palms. A mirror image of her mental picture, the apple manifested.

Sara laughed. 'Oh come on, you just put that there! You nearly had me!'

The unicorn shook his head. 'No, Sara,' he said, seriously, 'you put it there.'

Sara rolled her eyes in disbelief. 'No way.'

'Yes way,' said Terentius. 'This is your doing.'

'"Yes way"! Oh Terentius, who knew you were such a comedian.'

The unicorn was not amused. 'This is no joke, Sara,' he said. 'Your powers are developing quickly.'

'You're serious?'

'Indeed. Let us try something else. To convince you, why don't you decide on the item this time.'

'Okay.' Sara closed her eyes and concentrated. She brought the object into her mind, shaping it with her imagination, building up the layers of its creation. On her final exhale, she opened her eyes. In her hands was a bar of chocolate. She laughed with glee. 'This is incredible!' She ripped open the wrapper and took a bite. 'It's good!'

'Let me try, please,' said Terentius, as he eyed the chocolate with curious interest. Sara broke off a piece and let the unicorn take it from her open palm. Terentius' eyes widened as the sweetness broke over his tongue. He swallowed, sighing with pleasure.

Sara laughed. 'You like it?'

Terentius nodded, grinning, 'What a delightful flavour. I've never had anything like it!'

'Well, if Palantia is without chocolate, I guess my old world isn't all that bad after all!'

The unicorn licked his lips. 'Well done, Sara. You truly are quite skilled. I wonder what else you can achieve.'

They spent the afternoon putting Sara's newfound abilities to the test, the unicorn giving her suggestions and having her manifest them. He observed every nuance of the creations before increasing the complexity of each attempt.

Finally, Terentius asked Sara to conceive a living creature. 'This will be your most difficult challenge yet, Sara. The creation of an entirely new life form will require every ounce of your creativity, imagination, and concentration. Are you ready?'

Sara nodded, her eyes wide with excitement. 'Let's do this!'

The unicorn watched intently, noticing the small furrow to Sara's brow as she brought her powers to bear. It was almost effortless, and the unicorn couldn't help but be in awe of this human and all she had accomplished in but a few days. *She is something special.*

Sara's powers of imagination were robust, and once she opened her eyes, she uncupped her hands to reveal a round fluffy brown ball cradled therein. The fluffball rolled over and its fur parted, displaying a wholly enormous eye. The creature blinked once. Sara giggled. 'I'm going to call it the gigantimous eye beast.'

'Completely impractical!' said Terentius, laughing in return.

167

The unicorn was delighted. Never before had he seen nor heard of a Dreamer with the breadth of Sara's powers. The future of Palantia looked bright indeed.

Sara practiced until the sun dropped low in the sky, and then the two settled back to watch the small menagerie of odd creatures frolic nearby. After a while, each wondrous new creature roamed away, until finally the last had disappeared from view.

CHAPTER 22

' I think we need to stop,' came a hesitant voice, breaking Jehn's concentration. Senna trotted alongside the scholar. Jehn had set a steep pace despite his inner misgivings. His anxiety to reach the Court grew with each passing hour. *I have a bad feeling. Something is off.*

'What?' A frown marred his brow, deepening the lines etched there.

'He's dead on his feet,' said Senna, lowering his voice so as not to draw attention. He tipped his head in the direction behind him.

Jehn stole a glance.

Ander plodded along at the back of the group, head nearly on his chest, feet dragging and stumbling over roots and stones. The big man's labouring breath was so apparent, Jehn was shocked he hadn't noticed until now. *What's wrong with me?*

Belina caught Jehn's eye and her expression was a mix of concern and disappointment. Jehn's heart twinged with guilt. Thorn was nowhere to be seen. Jehn recalled the Aes-Sidhe passing by and saying something, but he hadn't listened—hadn't really wanted to.

Jehn's gaze flicked to the sky overhead. The rainforest's

thick canopy prevented a clear view, but he guessed it was mid-afternoon. They'd been walking for hours non-stop. The guilty twinge became an undeniable pang.

'Let's take a break,' he said, pulling his pack from his shoulder.

Ander crumpled to his knees and Belina helped remove his gear. The man was soaked with sweat. Jehn passed him a water skin, which Belina intercepted silently. She unstoppered the skin and helped Ander drink. He nodded gratefully, too exhausted to speak.

'Where's Orinthorn?' said Senna. 'He won't know we've stopped.'

'I'm sure he's not far away,' said Jehn, hesitantly, but to himself, he thought, *I have no idea.*

'He said he would scout ahead,' said Belina, her tone flat as she rearranged items from Ander's pack to lighten the load. 'He told you two hours ago.'

Gods, thought Jehn, *I need to keep it together. They are relying on me.*

'Ah yes,' he said, averting his face to hide his confusion, 'that's right. Don't be concerned, Senna. Thorn will be keeping the trail ahead clear for us. We remain safe.'

The boy nodded, still uneasy in this place. *And rightly so.*

'My boots are saturated,' Ander said, his voice shaky as he battled to remove the lacings, 'my feet are rotting in their socks! If I even make it to the Great City, I'll have no toes left!' His laughter lacked his usual booming timbre and failed to reach his tired eyes. Belina helped Ander pull off the boots; they made a sucking sound when they finally came free.

Jehn reached into his pack, suddenly aware of a gnawing in his belly. He scrabbled around, his fingers searching for trail rations. Only two left. The hunger subsided in an instant, replaced with a sinking in his gut. They were running out of food.

'We'll need more food soon,' said Jehn, keeping his tone light.

'Not much game around during the daylight hours,' said Belina. 'I can hunt tonight.'

Jehn nodded. He set a mental reminder to forage the next day to supplement their dwindling supplies.

Twenty minutes passed, and Thorn did not return. Ander leaned against a tree, his eyes closed, chest lifting and falling rhythmically. Senna sketched circles in the mud with a stick, while Belina rested on her heels, standing at ease surveying the forest.

Jehn closed his eyes. *Just for a moment. I'm so tired, not sure what's come over me...* The scholar's head bowed, and he let go the strap of his pack, causing it to fall onto the damp ground.

A faint rustling came from the trees, just off the trail. Jehn opened his eyes, idly noticing the thick gumminess to the lids. His head felt dull and heavy. His gaze lifted to a spot to Senna's left.

An enormous triangular head crowned with feathery antennae loomed from the trees. Two spiny jade arms snapped out with serrated claws and clasped the boy about his torso, pinning his limbs. Senna's eyes widened in shock, but he was unable to even struggle.

Belina's bow was nocked, and a split second later, an arrow let fly, only to clatter off the hard carapace of Senna's captor. The boy screamed, the sound piercing the otherwise still forest. Ander's eyes snapped open, and he fumbled with his axe, adrenaline rushing him to his bare feet.

Senna's scream grew high and strangled, cutting off with a sudden, awful silence. Jehn's stomach rose, bile burning his throat as the reality struck home.

The boy's lifeless, decapitated body listed sideways as the mantid released its hold, giving a final clacking of its saw-like jaws to swallow its prize. The monstrous insect disappeared into the forest without a sound.

Jehn retched and vomited on the ground, his stomach contents mingling with mud and the crimson ribbons trailing from Senna's mangled corpse.

Tears streamed down Belina's stricken face, and Ander stood, shaking and staring, barely able to comprehend this terrible thing. 'Wh-why did I take my boots off?'

Across the clearing, a twig snapped. Belina's arrow was away before she took another breath. Emerging from the trees, Thorn feinted to the side. As the arrow flew at his chest, the Aes-Sidhe took the glancing hit across the shoulder. He met Belina's eyes in surprise before his gaze slid to the terrible shape lying on the wet ground.

'No...'

Jehn began to sob, his body heaving as he gasped for breath. Belina's hand went to her mouth, aghast at what she had nearly done. Thorn came to her, his eyes glistening as he gently lowered the bow. The Aes-Sidhe looked to Jehn, searching his friend's face for an explanation, a reason for this tragedy.

Jehn slumped to his knees and buried his head in his hands. *My fault! We should've waited! I pushed... If we'd waited another day—just one more day! Oh gods... Senna. Not again.*

* * *

A young Jehn, bright-eyed with excitement and youthful confidence, pushed through the branches of the thicket. 'Hurry up, Cale. You're so slow!'

The other, some years younger, with but the promise of a man's beard, hefted his pack and scurried after Jehn. 'I'm coming!'

'You told me you wanted to come,' said Jehn. He flashed a grin over his shoulder at his brother.

'I did. I do!' Cale's breath puffed in the cool autumn air. The boy was not comfortable in the outdoors and preferred his books and stories. Jehn found it utterly and incomprehensibly boring. There was adventure everywhere in the world if you just went out to find it.

'Well, why don't you act like it?' he said. 'Or do you want to go back home and stick your nose in a book?' Jehn took great pleasure in teasing his brother. He was so quick to bait.

'No... let's keep going,' said Cale, his eyes darting about uneasily.

Jehn had been trying to convince Cale to take a trip with him for ages. He wasn't quite sure what had made his brother change his mind, but Jehn was not about to let the opportunity pass by.

A bird called from high up in a tree, and Cale nearly tripped over himself in surprise.

'It's just a crow,' said Jehn, 'not even a big one. Not like the ones we used to see in the fields at the farm.'

'Those were ravens,' said Cale absently, 'Same family, but a different species.' He paused, his expression thoughtful, 'Did you know—'

Jehn sighed. 'Are you going to wax lyrical about birds now? What do your books say a raven will do if you do this?' He pulled a slingshot from his pocket and aimed it at the bird.

'Don't!'

'Why? It's just a stupid bird.' He let the stone loose and it whooshed through the air, whacking into the leaves above the bird's perch. The raven feinted away, leaving a single midnight pinion in its wake.

Cale's fists clenched, but instead of retaliating, he sped forward, overtaking Jehn and disappearing into the trees.

'Cale, wait!' Jehn gave chase, his long legs eating up the distance, and he soon caught up to his slower brother. 'I was only playing,' he began. Cale stood with his back to Jehn. 'What are you looking at?'

Cale moved aside and turned to Jehn, 'That.'

The split was a silver gash in the air. Jehn's eyes widened in boyish excitement. *Adventure*!

He circled around, but there was nothing behind the odd phenomenon; in fact, as he moved around, it seemed to disappear. It was like one of those optical illusions you could only see from just the right perspective. Cale peered at the split, his face scrunched up and perplexed. He kept his hands firmly clasped behind his back. *No touching what you don't understand.*

Jehn laughed. 'Oh, Cale, are you scared?'

'No!' said Cale.

'I think you are,' said Jehn, 'I think you're chicken!' He pushed his brother playfully, causing Cale to stumble over a stray root. The boy thrust out his hands to break his fall. Instead, his fingers brushed the split, and Cale was pulled through like a vacuum.

Jehn blinked in surprise and confusion. 'What... Cale!'

There was no reply. The split sparked and halved in size.

Jehn hesitated, unsure what to do. The clearing was perfectly still; not even the whine of late season cicadas broke the silence.

Jehn took a deep breath and launched himself at the silver gash.

His body stretched and contracted, and he was sure his eyes would pop from their sockets. Bile filled his mouth. Then the stars in his head turned outside and Jehn found himself laying on a surface of black velvet.

After a moment to still his spinning head, he gingerly got to his feet. His stomach heaved as his mind tried to comprehend the void he stood within.

Carefully, Jehn cast around, trying to find a landmark or sign to find his way. 'Cale? Where are you?'

A lightening of the pitch black drew him forward—or perhaps it was just his eyes adjusting. *No... there's something there.* 'Cale? Why won't you answer me!'

The light in the distance sparked.

Another split! A way out!

Jehn ran toward the light. However, instead of an exit, it was a window—yet not one of glass and iron. Rather, it was a thinning of the void. The light Jehn had seen was coming from the other side. He pressed his face against the pseudo-pane and found the material to be warm and almost viscous. It clung to his cheek, but he did not draw away. He was enthralled by what he saw on the other side. Perfectly square buildings rose to the sky, covered in mirrors that blinded if looked at directly. Automated carriages sped up and down black, slick streets. It seemed a kind of city, but not like any Jehn had seen or heard of before; not even Thalanthas, the Great City of the Aes-Sidhe. The city spread far into the distance, much further than Jehn's human eyes could discern.

Oddly, there were no people anywhere, just carriages—of all different shapes and sizes—moving in a crazy, frenetic pace. Despite this, the city had a soothing, smooth sense of order. Everything seemed as it should be. The carriages did not slow, but nor did they come in contact with each other. It was an intricate dance for which Jehn did not understand the steps.

He stood transfixed, soaking in the vision, trying to comprehend the reality of this strange truth.

'Jehn!'

The voice annoyed him.

'Jehn?'

Trying to take him away from the city. *Shut up! Leave me be!*

A hand grabbed his arm, but Jehn shook it away, kept staring at the wondrous vista. He could watch it forever. Would never look away. *Why would I want to?*

Two hands grasped him, spun him around. Took him from the sight, took him away! Jehn lashed out, fists flailing against the soft flesh of his oppressor, this awful thing that stole his liberty. How dare they!

He hit his foe hard against the side of its head and it went down. Crumpled on the floor, it was just a pathetic thing now. He kicked it and it didn't move. His breath slowed and returned to a more natural rhythm as the red mist slowly cleared from his eyes.

Jehn stared. It was just a boy. Just...

'Cale?'

Time passed.

Or did it? In truth, time held no meaning. Jehn lost all sense of place and self, and simply lay prone, his mind fractured, torn between his terrible grief and the siren call of the strange city. His body ached. He hid his face, the heat of his tears drying upon his cheeks.

A querulous note murmured from the void, and the hairs on Jehn's bare forearms lifted. He ignored the sensation and let himself withdraw deeper into his torpor.

The note sounded again, closer. Still, Jehn did not respond.

A few moments more, and then came a trilling staccato. Firm, questioning. Urgent.

Jehn raised his head and blinked against the sizzling, sparking scintillation before him.

The hummingcat tilted her head and let out a short burst of melody, the final note rising up like a question.

Jehn frowned. He was just on the edge of knowing, like a word caught on the tip of one's tongue.

The cat pressed against him, joined her mind to his, and Jehn burst into tears, his emotions flooding out in a dark rainbow. The cat rubbed her soft head on Jehn's face, and in a shock of realisation, he understood her.

* * *

They buried Senna's body—what was left of it—beneath a stone cairn. The ground was too thick and muddy to dig a decent grave, and so a pile of moss-covered rocks was the boy's final resting place. Jehn's heart was heavy. He resolved to break the news to Senna's beloved Meryn once he was finished at the Court. *My fault, so it's my responsibility.* He couldn't get the image of Senna's death out of his head. It kept repeating over and over, clear and vividly awful. The strap of Jehn's pack was stained with the boy's blood, and no matter how hard he tried, Jehn could not seem to clean it off. *It will serve as a constant reminder of my failure to protect him.*

The earth quaked again during the interment. With each tremor, the cairn rattled and shifted, but not a single stone fell. Thorn attributed it as testament to the boy's strength and stability. Jehn was not so sure. Two quakes in a matter of days... It was unusual, yes, but Jehn felt there was also something more at play.

The party made camp that night beneath the dense weeping boughs of a thick-trunked willow, choosing to skip the fire due to the cloying damp. Any wood they might find not completely saturated would only smoulder and fill their shelter with choking smoke. They instead dined on trail mix—*with one less mouth to feed, there's more to go around,* thought Jehn darkly—and a few slices of hardening yellow cheese. They spent the night downcast and silent, lost to their own thoughts.

The following day was much brighter, but the cool temperate climate of the rainforest prevailed. Ander's toes had survived the night, and come morning, Belina produced from her pack a pair of fresh, dry socks. Ander took them sadly.

As the group trudged ever onward, Jehn withdrew in a haze of grief and guilt. He heard the voices of his companions, but was so burdened by his emotions, he ignored any attempts to engage in conversation. It was just too hard. Too painful. *My fault.*

Soon, they began to pass trees laden with myriad fruits of all shapes and colours. Jehn barely noticed. 'We should harvest what we can,' said Thorn. 'Fill your packs, but don't encumber yourselves.' The inferred warning remained unspoken.

Belina and Ander took themselves away in silence. The man seemed much recovered physically, but had said barely a word since the day before. Jehn supposed that was understandable. *He probably blames himself too. But that's my fault as well. It all is.*

Jehn's mind grew foggy and thick, but he nevertheless went through the motions of harvesting from some of the nearest trees, careful, at least, to stay within earshot of the rest of the group. He chose a tree that bore pale, greenish-yellow fruits with waxy skin. The individual fruits were a hand-span in length and ridged in such a way that, when cut, the slices would form stars. Jehn plucked a fruit from the tree, rolling it over in his hand. The action was in slow motion, as if through water, and his hand seemed to resist moving any faster. *Strange...*

A shadow moved at the corner of the scholar's eye. Glancing to his left, there was Senna; the boy's pack swung around so that it was suspended at his front, the flap open. The attendant was methodically working his way around his tree, plucking round dusky orange fruits from the branches.

What?

The boy turned his head—*His head!*—and stared at Jehn, his mouth opening to speak.

Jehn's hands fell limp to his sides, and he crumpled to his knees upon the spongy earth. His vision spun, narrowing to a black tunnel and closing in fast. With a heavy jolt, Jehn's eyes snapped open and he gasped.

'Jehn!' *Senna?* 'Jehn! You're awake! Are you okay?' *Senna!*

The fog began to clear, and Jehn could make out the worried faces of his companions gathered around, peering down at him. The cacophony of their anxious questions rang in his ears, and he raised his hands to block the sound.

Thorn motioned for silence. He reached out and gently

removed Jehn's hands. 'Jehn. Are you hale?' he asked, his voice a whisper. 'You've been unconscious for nearly a day. We didn't know what was wrong with you!'

Senna's face appeared next to Thorn's. 'I knew,' said the boy, 'or at least, I had a strong suspicion. I think whatever's been hurting the Dreamer has followed us. Well, followed you, specifically.'

'What?' Jehn's mouth tripped over the word. His tongue was a thick, dry lump and his jaw worked furiously to build up saliva. 'How are you here? You're dead... Am I... am I dead too?'

Senna and Thorn exchanged a confused look. 'I'm fine,' said Senna, 'Definitely not dead. Neither are you!'

Jehn let out his breath in a rush, and deep mournful sobs wrenched from his chest. Senna's eyes widened in surprise at the scholar's reaction. Jehn was always so calm and collected. To see the scholar in this state was quite a shock to the young attendant.

Thorn pulled Jehn to a sitting position and flung his arms around his friend. He held Jehn tightly, and the others rallied around him, soothing the scholar's grief and terror, whispering words of support and concern.

Once the outpouring of emotion had finally ceded, Jehn was able to get his breath. He wiped his face with his sleeve, glancing at his friends with reddened eyes. 'It was a dream, then,' he said, finally. 'A nightmare.' He raked his fingers through his hair, feeling the sweat at the roots. 'By the gods, it was so real!' He seized Senna's hands in earnest. 'You say you think I was attacked? Like the Dreamer?'

'It's just a theory,' said Senna, 'But it makes some kind of sense. You were reacting in a similar way. It appeared at first you were having a seizure, but we couldn't wake or calm you. Then you went so very still, it seemed to be over. But you'd suddenly cry out… We had to hold you down to stop you hurting yourself.'

'But why me?' said Jehn, his brows knitted as he tumbled the idea over in his mind, 'Why would it come after me?'

'You are a threat, *mo chara*,' said Thorn, handing Jehn a waterskin and encouraging him to sip. 'Perhaps this thing—whatever it is—saw you back at the Grove, heard what you planned to do, and was somehow able to track you.'

Jehn's heart fell, as the pieces began to fall into place. 'Honeysuckle.'

'Your cat?' said Senna.

'Not just any cat,' said Jehn, sighing, 'a hummingcat.' Well that secret is out. *"Cat out of the bag", and all that. Hah!*

'You have a hummingcat for a pet?!' Ander jostled Senna aside and pointed in triumph. 'I *knew* you were more than you seemed!'

'Honeysuckle is not a pet, Ander,' said Jehn. 'She is a creature of her own agency. But she is also my friend. And probably in danger now.'

'I don't believe so,' said Senna. 'Perhaps this attacker simply used her as a way to follow you. To keep tabs on you.'

'That would imply it can sense where she materialises,' said Jehn, rubbing his chin. 'Or it can move through the Stitch!'

'It's fae,' said Thorn, his expression mournful. 'This thing attacking the Dreamer is an Unseelie fae.'

* * *

Jehn pulled a plump red fruit from the heavy bough. The tree was so laden with pomegranates, the branches hung almost to the ground. The fruits were large, and each would make a meal itself. *A fae, Thorn said. Unseelie. Not a good situation at all.* Jehn had studied Palantia's fae during his many years at the Dreamer's Grove. The library had literally volumes on the subject, so diverse were their species and so long their history. *What kind could it be, though? And why is it doing this?*

A split second's warning was all Jehn got. Senna's cry rang out and the boy raced towards the scholar, his pack discarded on the ground, contents spilling out and rolling down the ferny slope. The young attendant's makeshift club was raised above his head, fear marked across his face. 'Above you!'

In an instant, the companions flew into action, weapons drawn, faces masks of determination. Jehn's stomach dropped as he looked up.

An enormous reptilian head was suspended above his own, armoured scale plates almost an exact match for the foliage around it. As the sunlight shifted, the creature's colouring deepened instantaneously, changing to imitate the darker tones of the forest. Jehn leapt back, tripping over his pack and tangling his feet in the straps. He flailed, scrabbling at the ground beneath, desperately trying to pull himself away from the reptile, but his legs refused to extricate themselves.

Senna's scream was incomprehensible as he brought the club down on the creature's snout with all his might. The giant lizard drew back, blinking in surprise. It let out a low, sharp hiss and spun to face the attendant, blue tongue twisting in its mouth. The creature's breath reeked of carrion; scraps of decaying flesh mottled its razor-sharp teeth.

An arrow flew through the air and struck the beast in one eye, shaft sinking right down to the fletching. The beast recoiled, shrieking, and disappeared into the trees.

Ander and Thorn reached Jehn and Senna, the big man quickly hoisting the scholar up. Jehn kicked the pack away from his feet and pulled Senna towards the group. They formed a circle, backs to one another. The forest was eerily silent. They cast around, heads whipping left and right as they sought their foe. The lizard was nowhere to be seen.

'Is it gone?' whispered Senna.

'No,' said Thorn, his voice low, 'It's still out there.'

Belina broke from the group to prowl the perimeter of the clearing, a new arrow nocked to her bow. She kept her distance from the trees, and circled round, searching for her target. A chittering sounded from their western side. As one, they turned to face it.

The branches swayed and parted, and the creature emerged from the canopy, mottled green scales rippling in anger. Its jaws parted and it hissed as it lunged forward.

Thorn was into the fray in an instant, silver sword flashing as he pirouetted around the beast, hacking and thrusting at every opportunity. He was a marvel to watch, violent poetry in motion as he avoided the monster's vicious attacks. Thorn landed blow after blow, and soon the beast began to waver. Blueish blood dripped from innumerable wounds, yet it refused to give up, snapping and slashing at the Aes-Sidhe as he danced this way and that, sword a blur.

Finally, Thorn appeared to falter, going down on one knee. The lizard charged, jaws gaping. The prince tucked his body in and rolled forward towards the creature, raising his sword skyward. The beast realised its mistake too late, and, failing to forestall its forward motion, skewered itself on the Aes-Sidhe's upright thrust. Pulling the blade out at the last second,

Thorn spun sideways, and the lizard fell forward, its heavy form thudding onto the ground in deathly stillness. Grinning, the Aes-Sidhe bowed, flourishing his sword.

Jehn shook his head and gave a slow clap. Ander and Senna laughed and joined in. 'All right, my old friend,' said Jehn, 'I concede that was impressive. Worth a little pomp and circumstance.'

Belina smiled and stepped forward to inspect the reptile's corpse. Nudging it with her foot, she remarked, 'What a master of disguise, this one. I could barely make out its outline when I shot it.' She looked down to admire her handiwork. The arrow was not there.

She frowned, confused, 'But—' Before Belina could finish her thought, something struck her face. She screamed in agony, clawing at her eyes.

A second monster launched from the trees at its blinded prey. The beast clamped its jaws around Belina's torso. She screamed anew as its fangs sunk into her flesh. Ander reacted on instinct, flinging two of his throwing daggers before his companions even blinked. Both blades embedded deep in the creature's remaining good eye; the shock caused beast to release its hold on Belina.

Jehn and Senna lunged forward, each grabbing one of Belina's arms and dragging her out of the creature's reach. Thorn leapt ahead to this new threat, but Ander had his axe in both hands and was roaring like a beast himself, hacking into the lizard without mercy. The creature may have been swift and stealthy, and monstrous in size, but it was no match for the uncontrollable frenzy of violence dealt it by Ander. The axe rose and fell, rose and fell, and with each strike, blue blood splattered the clearing. The beast went down, unmoving, but still the red-headed giant struck, his eyes wild with frenzy.

'Ander, stop!' said Senna, 'It's dead!'

The young man made to reach for his big friend, but Jehn held him back, 'Don't,' said the scholar, 'He's not Ander right now. He won't see you. He is in the fury.' Jehn looked to the woman moaning in pain nearby, 'Quickly now, we must see to Belina.'

Senna nodded and backed away from Ander, who was now slick with the blood of his mangled victim. Thorn watched for a moment, his expression a mix of concern and awe, then turned away, moving to Belina's side. The woman's clothing was torn in several places, and stained red with blood. But it was her face that was of greatest concern.

Belina remained conscious, whimpering, with her hands locked over her eyes. Thorn tried to carefully remove them, but she protested weakly, 'No, no, please.'

'I need to look, Belina,' he told her, softly, 'Let me see.'

She nodded, sobbing faintly.

The Aes-Sidhe gently pulled the woman's hands from her face. Her skin was red and sticky, and already beginning to blister.

'Bring me water,' he called, and Jehn hastened over with one of the packs, pulling out a flask and handing it to the dark-haired man. Thorn carefully trickled the water over Belina's face, gently washing off the remnants of the creature's venom. He looked up at Jehn, his expression grave.

The clearing fell silent. Ander's berserker rage finally ebbed, and he stood amongst the gore and carnage of what remained of the lizard monster. Jehn caught Senna's eye and gestured for him to go to the other man. Senna slowly walked over to Ander, avoiding looking at the butchery around him, and lightly laid his hand on the other's arm. Ander looked down at the young attendant, no recognition in his eyes. Then his senses returned to him in a flood, and he spun around, running to his wife.

Thorn rinsed Belina's eyelids as delicately as he could, profoundly conscious of the pain the slightest touch would cause. 'Jehn,' he said, 'Would you please shade her face?' Jehn moved over so his shadow fell across Belina.

Thorn leaned close and carefully lifted the woman's eyelids. His expression betrayed nothing. 'I won't hurt you,' he said, 'I just want to rinse your eyes now.' The Aes-Sidhe poured water into first one eye, then the other. 'You're doing so well, Belina. We're nearly done here.' Rummaging around in the pack, Thorn drew out some gauze and a length of cotton bandage, placing them on the woman's chest. 'Whose pack is this?' he said, 'Jehn, is it yours?'

The scholar nodded.

'Do you have your medicine? The one for your allergies?'

'I do,' said Jehn, bringing out a blue vial. The liquid had an oily motion to it and clung to the sides of the tiny bottle.

'What's happening?' said Ander, desperation colouring his voice.

'Jehn's medicine will help reduce inflammation. Now, please stand back, Ander. I'm doing the best I can.' The Aes-Sidhe unstoppered the vial and dropped two drops of the liquid into each of Belina's eyes. He soaked the gauze in water, and smoothly wrung it out, separated it into two pieces, and laid each over the woman's eyes. Jehn gently lifted Belina's head so Thorn could wrap the cotton bandage around it, covering her eyes. He secured it with a knot at one side.

Satisfied with his treatment, Thorn then set about looking

over Belina's wounds. He peeled away the torn jerkin, gently teasing the cloth from where it was stuck to her bloodied skin, and exposed her torso for inspection. She groaned, and Ander moved forward to kneel beside her, clasping her hand in his two giant ones. *She looks so frail*, thought Jehn.

Senna waited alongside with water and extra bandages, ready to assist with his basic first aid training. *He is far more equipped for this that I ever gave him credit.*

Thorn's fingers cautiously probed the holes in Belina's flesh. They were not as deep as first feared. Miraculously and mercifully, the attack had failed to hit any vital organs. The damage was mostly in the top layer of muscle, and would heal itself over time with proper cleaning and treatment.

Thorn gestured to Senna for the flask. The Aes-Sidhe flushed the wounds, then administered a portion of the same liquid he'd used to clean Ander's leg earlier. Belina stiffened but did not cry out. Jehn looked over at Ander. The big man's eyes were glistening with unshed tears, and his mouth was a thin line as he watched first his wife's face, and then the Aes-Sidhe at work.

'The bite was not venomous,' said Thorn, 'but the beast was a carrion eater, so the wounds could become infected. I'll stitch her up and apply the poultice I used for you, Ander,' he gestured at the big man's leg. 'We must keep a close eye on each of the wounds to make sure they don't fester.'

Ander nodded.

'Senna,' Thorn said, 'in my pack...'

'I'll get it,' said Jehn. Moving various supplies aside—a bundle of candles, a box of flint and tinder, a small leather journal—he finally found what he was looking for, a small sewing kit. He brought the box and its contents over to the patient.

Thorn nodded gratefully, and, after sterilising the needle with a few drops from his antiseptic flask, began threading it carefully through Belina's skin. She grimaced at each pass of the needle.

After what seemed an age, Thorn's handiwork was complete. He laid a small amount of the moistened herb over each wound and directed Senna to cover and secure them. The attendant set about doing so, and Thorn stood up from his kneeling position, stretching and shaking out his legs.

'I don't think the creature was planning on killing her, otherwise it could have done so easily. The bite wounds are too shallow. In that, she was lucky.'

Ander's face flushed with anger. 'Lucky!'

Thorn fixed Ander with a serious look, 'She's alive, Ander.' The Aes-Sidhe rubbed his thumb against his forefinger. 'Alive, and her wounds will heal.'

Jehn's eyes narrowed at the tell. 'Her wounds, you say.'

Thorn's gaze broke from Ander and he faced the scholar. 'Yes, her wounds are serious, but she will recover from them.' He sighed and rubbed his face. 'I understand what you allude to, Jehn. Indeed, her other injuries are far more grave. The creature's venom has damaged Belina's eyes. I hope to have offset any further harm with the drops I administered. For now, all we can do is wait. In this, I suppose, time is both enemy and friend.'

'Do you think she has lost her sight?' said Senna, in a whisper, his face drawn.

Thorn ran his fingers through his silver-shot hair. 'I can't be certain. Perhaps. As I said, only time will tell if this is temporary or permanent. But Ander, you must be prepared.'

Before he could respond, Belina broke her silence, voice cracking, 'I fear it is as you say, Whitethorn. It is not just the pain. It is something more. I feel different.'

'Hush, my beauty,' said Ander, touching her face and leaning close, 'don't speak now, you should rest.'

'I agree,' said Thorn, 'We'll stay here a while. We are in no immediate danger for now.' The Aes-Sidhe wiped his sword on the grass, but did not return the blade to its sheath. 'Make her comfortable. I will return.' Without a further word, he strode off into the depths of the forest.

Jehn hunkered down upon the grass and looked up at the sky, his mind in turmoil. *This whole journey has been a calamitous disaster.*

Senna sat next to him. The attendant plucked a blade of grass and twirled it between his fingers. 'I wish I was back in the Dreamer's Grove, Jehn,' he said, after a long moment of silence. 'I thought this would be an exciting adventure, not peril at every turn.'

The scholar shrugged, 'It is what it is, I suppose. We couldn't have predicted—'

The two gasped as one, realisation dawning as they remembered the last words the Dreamer had spoken. *'You have to be sure,'* the Dreamer had whispered, *'be careful of your eyes.'*

'She warned us,' said Senna, 'She warned us, and we didn't understand!'

Jehn's gaze flew to Belina, her eyes shrouded in bandages. Ander lay at his wife's side, whispering words of reassurance in her ear. Jehn felt a chill. *Portent and prophesy.*

'We need help,' said Jehn. 'I don't think we can make it on our own. We've delayed so long now! Who knows what else lay ahead? I need to contact Honeysuckle.'

'Are you sure that's wise?' said Senna, 'What if that thing tracks her and comes after you again? We're sorely disadvantaged as it is.'

'I know, Senna! But what other choice is there? We need to get word to the Court, and I'm afraid of the consequences of leaving the Dreamer unprotected any longer. If this thing is fae, like Thorn suspects, it could be free to move where it likes.'

'It's too big a risk! We can't afford to lose you! Please, Jehn! There must be another way!'

'There isn't. I have to try, I have to—'

A cracking boom assaulted their ears. Jehn and Senna leapt to their feet, staggering as the ground rippled in undulating waves. They watched in shock as a fissure splintered the earth, jagging across the clearing, whipping the grass into a turmoil. The trees bent and moaned in protest, roots thrusting upward as the ground swelled in fury.

Ander hunched over Belina, shielding her body from the branches raining down. 'Not again!'

Jehn and Senna clung to each other, working desperately to keep their footing. The clearing filled with the acrid scent of sulphur, and they realised in horror a shimmering heat was erupting from the fissure. Small licks of flame danced within the cracked earth, and a low rumble sounded, full of menacing promise.

Jehn sucked in a hot breath over clenched teeth, eyes wildly seeking shelter and finding none. Senna stared in terror, his young face white as bone.

Jehn's desperate voice rang out over the quake's clamour, 'Leandra Lus-a'-chraois, please hear me! I need you!' Overcome with the energy needed to force the connection, Jehn collapsed to his knees as the earth's violent upheaval finally stilled.

CHAPTER 23

The hummingcat zapped into sight as Sara and Terentius passed from a small forest into a lowland area. Sara saw a building far off in the distance—*a farm*, she thought, though she couldn't be certain—as the horizon faded into haze.

The cat's ears were pulled back against her skull, her amethyst eyes wild with alarm. A ridge of fur rose along the hummingcat's spine, and her tail was so puffed out, it looked akin to a feather duster.

'Oh my god!' said Sara, 'Honeysuckle, what's wrong?'

Terentius came to an abrupt halt, bowing his head to the distressed cat. He closed his eyes and Honeysuckle pressed her face to his.

'What's going on?' said Sara, worry biting at her.

'Wait,' said Terentius.

Tense moments passed as unicorn and hummingcat communed. Sara grew ever more anxious, but kept her mouth firmly closed. Finally, the unicorn raised his head and met her questioning gaze. His midnight eyes were clouded with concern.

'Our friends are in trouble,' Terentius said, a tremble to his deep voice.

'What friends?'

Terentius sighed. 'Oh Jehn, you silly boy, you couldn't leave well enough alone.'

'Who's Jehn?' said Sara. 'Leave what alone?'

'Hist, child! Enough of your mewling! Let me speak.'

Chastened, Sara looked away. The hummingcat's fur had smoothed down, but her eyes were still showing white around the edges. Sara coaxed the feline into her arms, stroking Honeysuckle's ears and cheeks. The cat pushed her head against Sara's chest, nuzzling close. Sara held the little creature tightly, cooing softly to calm her. She could just make out the smallest purr, more a feeling than a sound.

'You recall my saying the Dreamer would be protected?' said Terentius.

'Yes,' said Sara, 'the guardian person. I remember.'

The unicorn continued. 'Alas, it seems that protector—Jehn—has taken it upon himself to seek counsel from the Court and lead a travelling party through the 'Shadowing. It's a dangerous forest that separates the lands near the Dreamer's grove and the city of Thalanthas,' he explained, noticing Sara about to interrupt again. 'The hummingcat says that Jehn is more frightened than she has ever felt. During the connection, I saw fire, smelled brimstone. At least one of Jehn's group has been terribly injured. The cat thinks they are in great danger. We must make haste.'

'Make haste! How? Aren't they miles away? We won't get there for days!'

The unicorn bowed his head again to the hummingcat, and the small creature flashed, disappearing from Sara's arms, re-materialising upon Terentius' wide back. The cat caught Sara's eye and slowly—deliberately—winked.

'Get on,' Terentius said, tossing his head and stamping a foot into the earth.

'What!' Sara's eyes swept from the unicorn's face to the cat and back again.

'Before I change my mind!'

Sara didn't need to be told twice. Securing her pack upon her shoulder, she approached the unicorn's glossy white side. He was so tall, his shoulder well above her head, and she wasn't quite sure how to mount him. Terentius let out a long-suffering sigh and knelt his forelegs to the ground, allowing her access to the broad plain of his back.

With a last look in his indigo eyes, she leapt onto his back.

'Hold on to my mane,' the unicorn said.

Sara wound her hands into the luxurious double mane, sending up a spray of jewelled beetles. She clasped her knees tight to his flanks.

'And, Sara?' said the unicorn, with the merest hint of mirth, 'Don't forget to breathe.'

The trees and grasslands flew by as they galloped across the ground, faster than should have been possible. The air buffeted Sara, and she nearly lost her seat. She leaned low against the unicorn's neck, her body shielding the humming-cat, who appeared to be having no trouble whatsoever staying on board. Seconds passed, and already the countryside was a blur, just smears of green and brown with blue sky streaking past at breakneck speed. Sara felt a tightening in her chest and realised she was holding her breath. She let it out in a huff, and sucked in a lungful of fresh air, trying to stabilise her breathing.

Sara looked ahead, trying to see where they were, but it was unfamiliar—they were on a new path. There was a shimmer in the distance, and then they were upon a wide river, cluttered with jagged rocks, the water churning over and around in a mad dash towards the distant sea. She tried to yell a warning, but Terentius plunged ahead, reaching the bank in an instant. Sara felt his hindquarters bunch, muscles rippling beneath her, and the unicorn soared through the air, effortlessly, impossibly, clearing the river as if it were but a tiny stream.

Sara laughed with unrestrained joy. Old life and future fate were forgotten as she revelled in the fantastical wonder of riding a unicorn at the speed of light. She twisted around to look behind her, and saw that every kick of the unicorn's hooves threw dazzling sparks and stars into the air. A trail of wildflowers arced away behind them, spreading out in a wide swathe. She yelled in exultation, and Terentius threw back his head and trumpeted musically along with her, delighting in the thrill of running free.

After an impossibly short amount of time, the unicorn slowed. Sara saw a dark line of trees ahead.

'The 'Shadowing,' Terentius said.

Sara's stomach flipped unpleasantly at the sight of the forest, and she felt a hitch in her throat. 'They're in there? I don't like it.'

'Nor do I,' the unicorn said, 'But we must.'

They reached the edge of the sinister place, and Terentius pulled to a halt. Sara looked down at the hummingcat. She was asleep. Sara shook her head in astonishment. *I shouldn't really be surprised. Cats can sleep anywhere.*

'Wake up, Honeysuckle,' she said in a low voice. 'We're here.'

The small group faced the thick, tangled forest together, Sara still seated upon the unicorn's back, her hand upon his withers, not yet ready to break the connection from their incredible ride. 'I will let no harm come to you, Sara,' said Terentius.

Sara nodded once and let her arm drop, then made to dismount.

'Stay upon my back,' the unicorn said, 'it will be far safer that way.'

Terentius trotted into the darkening trees, and Sara watched in wary silence as a hazy mist settled about them. The hummingcat was alert, ears swivelling constantly as she picked up tiny sounds out of Sara's earshot. The forest quickly revealed itself as a murky swamp. Each step the unicorn took caused a sucking noise that set Sara's teeth on edge. The trees were gnarled and draped in strings of grey moss, their trunks glistening with dampness.

Their passage did not go unnoticed, and was punctuated often by inhuman shrieks and moans. Terentius picked up his pace and moved through the gloom. Sara was not sure how he managed to keep his footing, but he did not hesitate even a moment as he plunged ahead.

The ground grew muddier as they moved further into the swampy forest, and now large pools of dingy water stood stagnant everywhere Sara looked. A pervasive, dank smell of decay and rot assailed their nostrils, sending the hummingcat into a fit of delicate sneezing.

Sara hushed the little creature, stroking her throat and rubbing the sides of her whiskered face with her fingers. They entered an area of thick, black trees with vicious branches, and something winged and scaly burst from one side, nearly colliding with Sara as it rushed by. It let out an ear-splitting screech and disappeared into the mist.

Their path took them alongside a body of water large enough to be considered a small lake, and Sara felt even more uneasy. 'Terentius,' she said, 'This feels like a bad place. Like something old and dangerous lurks here. I am not at all keen in meeting it.'

'Indeed, Sara,' the unicorn said, his voice barely above a whisper. 'There is no doubt such a beast may lay in wait beneath this black surface. But it is the way we must go.'

The unicorn stepped upon the stinking beach, and sure enough, a ripple broke the glassy lake. Rather than wait to see what might choose to drag itself from its brackish lair, Terentius instead bolted like a fiend.

The unicorn flew across the boggy lake shore, leaping over tangled roots and fallen branches. Vines snaked across the ground to snare him, but he did not falter. Sara turned back to see if anything had indeed emerged from the watery depths, and watched in horror as a monstrous black pincer thrust skyward, festooned with weeds. Terentius sensed her fear and broke into a full gallop, daring to spur on his super-speed even in this dangerous terrain. The giant crustacean clacked its claw at them, but did not attempt to pursue, and instead sank beneath the water, returning to the depths.

Terentius kept up his headlong flight for a few moments more before finally slowing to a trot. Sara smoothed the hummingcat's raised hackles and whispered soothing sounds, feeling her own heartbeat beginning to slow from its accelerated pulse. They eased through the quagmire, the thick, viscous mud impeding Terentius' stride. Sara and the hummingcat kept a wary eye on the surrounding murk, hoping to have no more close encounters. The shrieks and moans from unseen denizens echoed out from the mist, but whatever the creatures were, they stayed hidden.

Eventually the ground began to harden, the trees losing their ghoulish demeanour, straightening and turning a more natural shade of green. The air became less foul, and the unsettling sounds of the swamp creatures gave way to pleasant bird song. The danger seemed to have passed, and now it was well past time for Sara to give Terentius a piece of her mind.

'You've had this ability all this time, and kept it from me!' she said. 'We could've been at the City in no time! Why did you make me walk all that way!'

The unicorn slowed his pace to an easy canter, 'And where would be the lesson in that?' he said, twisting his head back to glare at her, 'You needed to learn a thing or two before you were thrown right into the Trial, don't you agree?'

'Well, uh,' said Sara, blushing, 'Yes. Of course. You're right again. I'm sorry, Terry.'

The unicorn groaned and shook his mane in annoyance. 'For all that is sacred, Sara, I've told you over and over not to call me that!'

Sara smiled silently, and the hummingcat trilled a few notes.

'Oh, never mind,' said the exasperated unicorn, 'what's the point!'

Sara grinned, trying not to think triumphant thoughts.

'Bah! Children!'

CHAPTER 24

Thorn stepped into the clearing, worn and dishevelled, the left sleeve of his tunic torn. Jehn weakly lifted a hand in greeting. The scholar was more exhausted than he could remember, but worse than that was his sense of shame. *I shouldn't have reacted like that! I needed to keep a level head, and I panicked. Idiot.* He could only imagine the hummingcat's reaction if his desperate call had reached her. *Though, to be perfectly honest, we are in dire need of help.*

Senna leapt to his feet, his young face a storm of emotion, 'Where have you been?' he said, jutting his chin in defiance. 'You left us!' The attendant's hands were bunched into fists, barely restraining his anger as he stood his ground in front of the Aes-Sidhe.

Thorn placed his hands upon the boy's shoulders, 'I am sorry, my young friend. I had meant but to scout the perimeter. The quake caught me off guard, and I found myself trapped between a rockfall and my quarry. No humour intended,' he said, catching Senna's dark look, 'Whilst there are no other beasts the likes of which we fought this day, other dangers lurk—lurked—nearby.'

Senna glanced at the other's torn clothing. Thorn inspected the tear, pulling the cloth away to show a bloodied gash across his bicep. 'A scratch,' he said. 'The creature that inflicted it will not do so again.' He picked up a piece of abandoned fruit from the grass, and brushing it off, took a bite. 'What have I missed? Jehn, what ails you?'

Jehn opened his eyes with some effort. 'Ah, well,' he said, blushing, 'an overreaction, perhaps.'

The scholar filled Thorn in on the discussion before the quake, and what came after. 'It seems you reacted as you saw fit in the moment, *mo chara*,' said the Aes-Sidhe. 'And in all honesty, perhaps it was not a bad thing.' Jehn smiled to hear his own thoughts echoed by his friend.

Thorn stepped around the crack in the earth—which was no longer venting steam—to where Belina lay upon the ground, propped up on the pile of packs. 'How do you feel?'

The woman touched her face and sighed. 'Before, when I'd close my eyes, I could still *see*—light and shadow, movement through my eyelids. Now there is nothing.'

'Then it is as I feared,' said Thorn, 'My skills are satisfactory for most field injuries, but it seems yours were beyond my experience.'

'What do we do now?' said Ander, tears shining in his eyes, 'We're in real trouble this time. Hardly a hale or whole one among us. How are we gonna get to Thalanthas in this state? We need a gods-be-damned miracle!'

A trumpeting call rang from the forest depths. Ander and Senna leapt to their feet, quickly loosing their weapons to take an offensive stance. Jehn's heart leapt. He pushed himself upright, and, curling his thumb and index finger into his mouth, let out a loud, sharp whistle.

'What are you doing, you fool,' said Ander, his knuckles white as he clutched his axe. 'We've lost the element of surprise!'

'Wait and see,' said Jehn.

The forest swayed, trees bending forwards and leaves rustling with such ferocity that it seemed an awful storm wind was assailing them. The thick green wildwood parted with a crack.

A magnificent white beast burst from the trees, pulling up with a half-rear, hooves pawing at the ground, flicking up sods of earth.

'Terentius Aodhfin, as I live and breathe!' said Thorn, clapping his hands together. 'You're timing is, as ever, impeccable!'

The shift in mood was immediate. Belina let out a sob of relief.

The unicorn bowed his head nobly at the Aes-Sidhe. 'Greetings, Anwyl Orinthorn, it has been too long.'

'An age!' said Thorn, 'And we have you to thank, little one!' The hummingcat leapt from Terentius' back and rushed to Jehn, who lovingly gathered the small animal into his arms.

'Lus-a'-chraois, the little brave,' he sang,

'has won the quest she doth was gave;

a hero's path be marked and paved,

and thus, our souls are saved!

'Oh, Honeysuckle, *mine Milis,* my little sweet! I am so sorry to have worried you! I overreacted. I'm fine, really.' The hummingcat purred and rubbed her face against Jehn's chin.

* * *

He's her friend. And he sang to her! Sara glanced furtively at the rest of the group. Besides the tall, dark-haired man who had greeted them, and Honeysuckle's friend, she spotted three others clustered together: a teenage boy, a huge red-headed man dressed somewhat like a barbarian, and a woman who was lying on the ground.

Terentius knelt so that Sara could dismount, and she slipped off the unicorn's back to stand awkwardly beside him.

'The cat was very insistent,' said the unicorn, 'I doubt I could have denied her. She would never let me hear the end of it if something had happened to you. But it seems you are hale, friend Jehn?'

Jehn shrugged, his long fingers gently tweaking Honeysuckle's tufted ears. 'I am now, though you can see we aren't in the best of shape for travelling.'

'Yes, I see. Incidentally, this is Sara,' said the unicorn. 'She is to be our new Dreamer. Well, I should say, she is a Candidate. But a strong one. She will take the Trial when we reach the Great City.'

"Incidentally!" Gee, thanks a lot, Terry, Sara thought, narrowing her eyes at the unicorn. He tossed his head and ignored her.

The tall, dark-haired man stepped forward to take Sara's hand. 'Welcome to Palantia, lady Sara,' he said, bowing elegantly. His black hair had silver strands, but she could not guess his age. 'Your arrival is most fortuitous.'

'Uh,' Sara returned the bow with an awkward curtsy, 'Hi.'

He laughed, 'What a delight you are, lady Sara!' He kissed her hand, and Sara blushed furiously, unsure where to look. 'It is sweet indeed to be anonymous for once!'

'Orinthorn is rather well-known in Palantia, Sara,' said Terentius.

The dark-haired man caught her eye and winked. 'Call me

Thorn. Over there is Senna,' he pointed to a teenage boy, 'with him, Ander and Belina. And that's Jehn.'

'You're to be the new Dreamer?' said Jehn, inspecting her with curiosity. 'I was expecting someone younger. You're—'

'Too old?' said Sara, cutting the scholar off.

Jehn's cheeks flared bright red and he ducked his head. 'No, er, ah...' he trailed off without finishing.

'Sara!' said Terentius, 'I never!' He stamped his hoof and shook his mane. 'Whatever has possessed you to be so impolite?'

Sara blushed and looked away. *Mouth shut, Sara. You don't know these people!*

The red-headed man impatiently nudged Thorn out of the way to face the unicorn. 'Nice to meet you, Sara. And good to see you, Terry, but please, can you help my wife?'

The unicorn closed his eyes for just a moment, but did not reprimand the big man for this transgression. 'Ander Findomar,' he said. 'To the point, as is your wont. Let me see her then, and I will do what I can. Belina, my dear, I am here.'

Belina's chestnut hair clung to a face drawn and pale. She nodded weakly, unable to offer more. Senna sat down alongside her and held her hand, remaining silent to the introductions.

Sara gasped, unable to contain her concern. 'What happened to you?'

'We were attacked by monsters. Giant lizard creatures,' said Thorn. 'Belina bore the worst of it.'

The unicorn nosed Belina's body, then gently laid his pearlescent horn against each of the wounds left by the attack. Belina sighed in appreciation at the respite from the pain.

As the others gathered around, they watched the bandages

fall away and the flesh reseal before their eyes, leaving nothing behind but smooth skin. Ander grasped Senna's arm in hope. The boy winced at the big man's grip, but did not protest.

Senna carefully pulled back the gauze covering Belina's eyes so that the unicorn could better survey the damage. 'The skin around her eye sockets is less inflamed than before,' said Senna. 'Your treatment has done some good, Thorn.'

Belina took a shaky breath, and with effort, opened her crusted lids, however, her eyes were entirely white and covered in a milky film.

'Your eyes!' said Sara, 'Did the monster do that? It looks really bad, does it hurt?' She noticed Terentius glaring at her. 'Uh… I'm sorry… I really hope it can be fixed.' Sara trailed off, embarrassed for saying something wrong, yet again.

'You are kind, lady Sara,' said Thorn, with a small smile. 'I can see already why you are a good Candidate. Empathy is a vital characteristic for a Dreamer.'

Sara nodded, unsure how to respond to the dark-haired man's remark. In the end, she chose silence. *And staying out of everyone's way.*

Terentius' expression was grave as he lay his horn against Belina's face. He closed his eyes in concentration, and luminescence flared from within the spiralled horn. The blisters receded, and the reddened skin returned to its natural hue. Sara found she was holding her breath, wishing hard for the woman's sight to return.

The unicorn's power cleared the hazy fluid from the woman's eyes, but his healing ended there. Belina's eyes remained clouded. Her sight had not returned.

'I am so very sorry, Belina,' Terentius said, his deep voice coloured with sadness. 'I can take away your pain, and heal your wounds, but it seems anything greater is beyond my abilities.'

Belina's breath hitched in her throat, and her lips pressed together tightly, muffling the sob that threatened to escape. 'I understand, my lord, and you have my gratitude for all you have done. I thank you.' Her expression was blank, but the stiffening of the tendons in her neck told another story. Sara knew Belina was forcibly restraining her emotion, and her heart fell. *So unfair.*

'That's it?!' Ander shook off Senna's hand as the attendant tried to still the big man. 'There's nothing else you can do? She'll never see again? Never hunt? Never track?' He stared at the unicorn in disbelief. Terentius bowed his head in regret.

Belina rose unsteadily to her feet, 'There are more things to life than hunting and tracking, my love. I will adjust. I must. You must.' Ander rushed to support her with one hand at her back, the other taking hers in a tight grip. 'Accept this, Ander,' she said, turning her sightless eyes towards him. 'This is the way it is now.'

The big man made to argue, but something in his wife's expression stopped the objections in his throat, and he squeezed her hand in acquiescence.

'I regret I can help no further, my friends,' the unicorn said, 'but I will guide you to safety. And then I must take Sara to the City. The Trial of the Dreamer awaits. We also have the matter of our current Dreamer's affliction to deal with.'

'We have some ideas about that,' said Thorn.

'As do I, Orinthorn,' said the unicorn. 'Perhaps it is prudent for us to discuss the matter before our departure.'

Senna joined Jehn, who remained seated, the hummingcat purring sleepily in his lap. Jehn was still mentally and physically drained from his own ordeals, but he realised he also felt abashed from his misstep with Sara. He was inwardly surprised at that feeling. Jehn was not usually one to care too much about what others thought of him. He'd certainly had plenty of time to get used to making his fellow scholars discomfited. But Sara was different. She intrigued him. *And this has not been a great introduction.*

Senna scratched the hummingcat's ear and her purring increased. 'We think it's a fae,' he said. 'It attacked Jehn too.'

The unicorn looked at the scholar sharply. 'Is that so?'

'It does seem to be the case, from all the evidence,' said the scholar, wearily. 'Senna thinks it tracked me. I was trapped in a nightmare for the better part of a day. I'm unsure why, though my connection with Honeysuckle is likely part of it. Perhaps to delay us, or to find out what we know.'

'Or to find me,' said Sara, who had been listening to this exchange with interest. It all seemed greater than mere coincidence. Attacks, earthquakes, Dreamers and Dreamers-to-be. More was at play that just casual happenstance. *We've been brought together for a reason.*

'To find you?' said Jehn, 'That does seem possible.' He rubbed his chin and flicked a stray lock of russet hair from his face. *There's something so familiar about him*, thought Sara, *He's quite nice to look at...*

The hummingcat woke and stretched, delicately extricating herself from Jehn's lap to flash over to Sara's feet. The little cat buzzed musically, and quite suddenly Sara made the connection. Her eyes flew to Terentius, who was watching her with amusement. *Mischief-maker, indeed!*

She thrust her hands in her pockets, avoiding further eye contact, and said, 'I think it's a Sluagh.'

Thorn, who was putting the first aid supplies back into his pack, froze and said, 'What leads you to that conclusion, lady Sara?'

'Well… Terentius has been teaching me about Palantia and the Dreamer, and how Sluagh come to my world to extract dreams. It doesn't seem like too much of a stretch to think that a fae who can manipulate dreams could maybe do something bad with them.' Sara shrugged, 'It's just a theory.'

'An unnerving one, if true,' said Thorn. 'Any fae turning Unseelie is cause for alarm, but a Sluagh…'

'If Sara's theory is correct,' said Terentius, 'which seems to be the case—given what happened to Jehn—we should proceed without further hesitation. As I said, I will lead you out of the 'Shadowing, but from there, I must take Sara and fly to the Court. The situation is clearly more urgent than I had originally deemed.'

'We must continue to Thalanthas, too,' said Thorn, firmly. 'Although your wisdom is well-considered throughout Palantia, the Council has become more… insular since last you visited. You may find resistance where such did not exist in the past. My presence may lend weight to your voice.'

Terentius frowned. 'Does Uinnseann Elised no longer stand as High Counsellor?'

Thorn paused, then ran his hand over his chin. 'No, he still holds the position, but of late, he has been indecisive. Distant. Even with me.' Thorn's eyes grew sad. 'My brother is not the man you once knew, *mo chara*.'

His brother… thought, Sara. *This Thorn fellow must be someone important, then.*

Jehn lifted the hummingcat from his lap, setting her gently on the ground. Honeysuckle turned in a circle twice and then curled into a tight ball, promptly going back to sleep. The scholar rose to stand with his friend. 'You have not spoken of this before, Thorn,' he said, placing a hand on the other's arm. 'Why did you keep this to yourself?'

'Ah, Jehn,' said the Aes-Sidhe, 'You have more than enough worry in your heart as it is. I did not wish to burden you with my own troubles.' He smiled sadly.

Terentius sighed. 'In that case, let us away before we lose more daylight. Our path will be somewhat circuitous, but I will nevertheless lead you to a point that will provide the most direct route to the Great City. Ander, please assist Belina. She can ride with me.'

A flash of jealousy sparked, but Sara pushed it down, finding it immediately replaced by guilt. *I shouldn't be so selfish when this other person is in such dire need.* She glanced at Jehn to find him watching her intently. She quickly turned away, cringing at the thought he'd seen her jealousy towards Belina. A covert glance back found the scholar flushed of cheek, his eyes tracing the horizon, looking anywhere but at her. Sara found this awkwardness endearing. *Maybe he's as socially inept as me.*

Ander helped his wife to get comfortable and placed her hands within the unicorn's thick mane. The woman was resolute and straight-backed, as Ander adjusted her pack and bow. He patted her leg and she nodded in response.

With Belina in position, and the rest of the group ready to leave, Terentius lead them into the forest.

CHAPTER 25

The Court of the High Council was in session. The chamber—palatial and opulent—was adorned with ornate figures of plants and animals carved meticulously into every wooden post, panel, or piece of furniture.

The Aes-Sidhe's love of nature was reflected everywhere. The flowing style of the architecture called to mind bending, twisting tree limbs. Curtains and carpets were dyed in subdued shades of brown and green with decorative leaf patterns throughout. The trickling splash of a fountain murmured in the background. The folk of Thalanthas adored the mercurial nature of water in all its forms, and so it was a frequent presence in landscaping and design.

A large crescent table dominated the centre of the room. The space within the inner curve held a speaker's platform—a place for petitioners to address the Council. For now, the platform stood empty. Carved wooden seats lined the outer curve of the table, and were presently filled with twelve nobles dressed in their Court finery.

The tension was palpable. Even a sweeping glance would quickly uncover the suppressed emotion around the table. A clenched fist here, a tight frown there; the Court was maintaining composure, but barely.

All eyes were trained on the figure in the head of the table's arc. The man stared down at the polished wood, his fingers idly tracing the grain. His clothes lacked the pressed crispness of his colleagues', and his eyes were distant, as if his thoughts had taken him far away from this moment.

A tall, statuesque woman, clad in shades of green from head to toe, surged from her seat. The wooden legs screeched a protest on the timber floor. The woman slammed her hands upon the table. The man in the centre did not even flinch.

'We must act immediately, High Counsellor!' the woman said, leaning forward in earnest. 'This situation cannot be left unattended a moment longer!'

Murmurs of assent echoed around the room, the other members nodding in agreement. Buoyed by her colleagues' support, the woman's eyes sparked with ire. 'The Dreamer has been attacked, and messages arrived just this day that indicate an attendant has been killed! This is no physical malady, your Honour. Something of malevolent purpose is causing this!' She banged her palms against the polished surface once more to emphasise her point.

The High Counsellor strained against the arms of his chair and slowly, painstakingly rose to his feet. His raven hair, loose from its leather band, clung to his face and neck. His ashen skin glistened with a sheen of perspiration.

Despite her passionate condemnation, the green-clad woman's expression was a mixture of concern and pity. The High Counsellor was a shadow of his former self, but past offers of help and words of concern from her and other Council members had fallen on deaf ears, and in some cases had been met with open hostility. Regardless of her own feeling and deference towards the man, his lack of action could no longer go unchallenged.

Uinnseann Elised drew himself up to his full impressive height with a visible struggle. 'I have heard your concerns, Silvana Verdantine,' he said, voice gravelly as he regarded the woman, 'a thousand times, it seems. My response remains the same. We will not act until further information is gathered. To do so beforehand would be folly.'

'Folly!' said Silvana. 'What folly? To fail to act is folly!' Her fellow Council members punctuated her impassioned speech with cries of 'hear hear'. 'We must do something. I beg you, High Counsellor! At the very least we should send a contingent of guards to the Dreamer's Grove, perhaps even a diviner or spellbinder. The Dreamer is unprotected, and we all know what could happen if—all the heavens forbid—she were to die before a new Dreamer is inducted. Please, High Counsellor!'

'I said no!' The High Counsellor's eyes were ablaze. 'My word is law!'

Silvana bristled. 'This is a democratic council, Your Honour. We do not put this forth as a light request. This is dire situation and requires a serious response! You are bound to consider the consensus of your fellow counsellors.'

Fury flashed in Uinnseann's eyes, and he smashed both fists down upon the table with such force that nearby cups were overturned, their contents spilling like quicksilver across the surface. 'I am also your King, you insufferable wench!'

Silvana's mouth dropped open. Her seat mate, a younger Aes-Sidhe dressed in neutral browns and greys, hastily took her arm and pulled her back into her seat.

'This meeting is adjourned,' said the King and High Counsellor, and he slammed an ornate wooden gavel downward, striking the sounding block so forcefully it threatened to split in twain. He pushed away from the table, and in a whirl of dark velvet cloth, strode from the chamber, leaving his other council members staring at each other in shock.

* * *

Uinnseann stood in the hallway of his stately home, fingering the key in his pocket as he stared at the cellar door. His indecision was crippling, but with a shaking hand, he thrust the key into the lock and slid back the bolt. Picking his way down the creaking stairs, his pulse raced; he felt a conflict in his very being. He feared the Sluagh's presence, but also worried what it might mean if the creature wasn't there. *Nothing good, nothing good at all...*

The King cleared his throat before reaching the landing, belatedly realising the triviality of the gesture. He need not have bothered; the cellar was empty. Unsure what to do now, Uinnseann stood in the middle of the room, wringing his hands together and darting glances back and forth. If he left now, the Sluagh would know he'd been there, and it would be angry. *Best to stay and wait.* He could explain his presence before the creature took its rage out on him.

His eyes wandered around the room, finally settling on the shelf furthest at the back. Something was glittering there, and Uinnseann's curiosity twinged. He took a hesitant step forward, and then shook his head, mumbling to himself. *Mustn't move, mustn't touch.* Yet, his eyes were drawn again to the shelf and its mysterious contents. He shuffled forward another step.

He reached out, his slender fingers just grazing the bottle at the very top of the shelf, before an agonising spike of pain shot through his temple. He shrieked, crumpling to the ground, clasping his head in his hands. The pain did not relent, and he rolled into a ball, moaning and sobbing, rocking back and forth.

The hem of a black robe swished past him, and Uinnseann dared to look up, wincing through the searing, stabbing pain. The Sluagh loomed above him, widening and expanding—filling up the entire space with its malevolence. Uinnseann shrank back, trying to make himself smaller, whimpering like a trapped animal.

The Sluagh finally ceased its mental attack and shot out a scaly hand to grasp the King's throat. Uinnseann struggled to his feet, his knees like water.

The creature's voice was a hissing sibilance. 'I told you last time, King,'—the honorific delivered with sneering disdain—'You are not to be in here. Do I need to teach you this lesson in a way you can understand?'

Uinnseann cringed and cowered, recoiling from the shadowy figure, 'No, no, please!'

The Sluagh tightened its hold on the King's throat. 'And why should I spare you such a teaching, one that is so clearly necessary?'

'They know,' Uinnseann managed to choke out, 'they know!'

The Sluagh's emerald eyes narrowed. 'What could they know? They know nothing.'

The King plucked at his robe, barely daring to meet the creature's gaze. 'They suspect! They suspect you are the reason the Dreamer is ill.'

The Sluagh laughed, a cracking, horrible sound, like breaking bones. 'You are paranoid, King.' It thrust a taloned finger at his chest. 'Did the voices in your head tell you that?'

Uinnseann struggled to speak, his confusion evident upon his stricken face. 'They want to in... inves... investigate.' His hands dropped to their sides, fingers twitching unconsciously.

The creature blinked its eyes languorously at the King, encouraging his honesty with a cooing tone. 'And how did you respond? Did you maintain our position?'

'Yes, yes! I told them it was not yet time.'

'Good.' The Sluagh released its hold on the man's throat. Uinnseann fell in a heap on the cellar floor, wheezing and heaving to catch his breath. 'You will continue to resist the demands of these fools. They will not act without your authorisation.'

Uinnseann sobbed. 'They want to send guards. Magic-users, too! They will find out!'

'Get up!' The King quickly scrambled to his feet, head bowed. The Sluagh's voice dripped with scorn. 'They may send whomever they want. It is too late. Already far too late. I have another prize in mind. The game is already in motion.'

The King nodded feebly, his mind struggling to gather its scattered thoughts. His mouth gaped, but no words would come.

The Sluagh smiled slyly, its head swaying as it stroked a finger along the shelf holding its bottles of dream energy. 'Soon, there will be a new flavour to add to my collection.' It took down a small bottle, swishing the contents. 'Even the most delicate flavours, the strongest energies—tastings I've taken from far and wide across this world—these will pale in comparison to what I have discovered.' The creature sighed with twisted joy, its eyes reflecting Uinnseann's terrified visage in the dim light. 'I could not have planned it better! My extraction from the Dreamer sent one of those detestable mortals to seek out a Candidate! The fool thought the Dreamer was Awakening!' The creature scoffed. 'Did you know, little King, that an uninducted Candidate is a greater force than even the Dreamer herself?'

The King's eyes darted left and right, his broken mind working on instinct, trying to find a place to hide, to escape from the Sluagh's building mania.

The Sluagh hissed at the meek display, its snout wrinkling with contempt. It pushed the King towards the stairs. 'Get out of my sight, you disgusting wretch.' It turned its back on him, uncorking the small bottle, and with a mocking laugh, inhaled the pale green essence.

Uinnseann Elised, King of the Aes-Sidhe and High Counsellor of the Court of Palantia, scuttled up the stairs and fled through the open doorway, slamming it shut as he passed the threshold.

CHAPTER 26

The unicorn led the companions through the darkening forest. Trees loomed overhead, their upper branches mingling to form an impenetrable canopy blocking the sun's passage, shrouding the path in a strange grey half-light. Creepers hung from the trees, swaying and writhing despite the non-existent breeze. The air was heavy and still, pushing down like a weight, making it difficult to breathe. Sara walked briskly in the middle of the group, her heart thudding in her chest with an unsettling beat. *Terentius knows what he's doing, I have to believe that.* She chanced a look at Jehn. His eyes flicked to her and he gave a tight smile.

Mist rose off the ground in pale tendrils, coiling and twisting about their feet as if it were alive. A nervous tension shivered through the party; all were on edge, constantly scanning the surrounds for any unexplained movement. The only sounds were their own shuffling feet and the occasional unsuppressed cough. The forest was otherwise deathly silent.

Sara watched the unicorn push through a thicket. The thorny branches scraped across his hide and left lines in his coat. Belina remained ramrod upright upon the unicorn's back, swaying her head side to side.

'I read that if you lose a sense, the others improve to

compensate the loss,' whispered Senna, sidling alongside Sara. The boy passed her a piece of fruit from his pack.

'I hope that's true,' said Sara, 'Losing your sight... what an awful shock.'

'She is strong,' said Senna. 'Have you noticed? She's already learning to adapt.' He gestured, and Sara then realised Belina's head movements were in fact deliberate. The woman was listening intently. *She refuses to let her newfound blindness beat her. I wish I had that kind of determination.*

The companions trudged onward in silence, the oppressiveness of the forest defeating any desire for further conversation. *I hope we're out of this horrible place soon. Even the swamp didn't feel this wicked.* It was as if a deep and ancient anger was brimming just below the surface.

Belina's head whipped around and she cocked her ear, straining to hear something the others did not. Terentius' own ears twitched, and the flesh across his rump quivered as if he was shaking away an irritation, but he said nothing and continued pacing ahead.

Something flickered at the corner of Sara's eye, but when she turned to look, she saw nothing but the same thick tangle of vegetation that had persisted throughout the day. She noticed Jehn watching her then, his expression questioning, and she shook her head not to worry. He came towards her anyway, matching her stride and walking so close next to her that they were nearly touching. She felt a flutter in her stomach and gave him a quick smile. He smiled back, and opened his mouth to speak, but stopped suddenly, grabbing her arm.

He frowned and looked at the trees, scanning their dark depths. Ander and Thorn pulled up behind them and stopped as well. 'What is it?' whispered the Aes-Sidhe, his voice low

217

and urgent. The previous day's attacks had left him shaken, and he was not about to be caught unprepared again. He unsheathed his sword. Ander freed his axe from his shoulder strap in response and held it loosely by the haft.

'I thought I saw something,' Jehn murmured.

'Me too,' said Sara, as softly as she could.

Ander called to Senna, 'Sst!' He lifted his arm, signalling to halt. Seeing the group standing some paces back, the attendant called quietly to Terentius to wait.

The unicorn turned about. 'We must continue,' he said, in a low deep voice, 'We are not alone.'

He eyed the trees to either side of the path and Sara felt a rush of fear, her body stiffening. She was not a brave person, and would freely admit that she was happiest when she was safe and comfortable. Being a hero and facing danger for glory and honour was not high on her list of preferred pastimes. *I don't like it here. I want to feel safe again!* She felt a hand clasp hers, the fingers strong and slender. 'I have you,' said the scholar. 'Stay close.'

Sara nodded, only slightly comforted, but it was better than nothing at all. As she squeezed his hand, Sara noticed the mounds of Jehn's palm were thick with the remnants of old callouses. Unexpected of one who spent his days poring over books and scrolls. *More than he seems, perhaps. Terry did say he was an academic* now. *When we get out of here, I'll have to find out more about this mysterious scholar.*

'Hist!' The unicorn's voice rang out in the stillness. 'I said, move!'

Sara felt it then—the sense of something old and wrathful watching—and from the hurried glances between the companions, she knew she was not alone. They began to move, urged by the unicorn's insistence and their own barely restrained fear. *We aren't welcome.*

A low moan wended among the trees to their left, echoed by another at their rear. Out of habit, Belina nocked an arrow from the quiver to her bow and held the string taut. The moans were all around them now, with a pitch starting low and tremulous, rising sharper and higher until it peaked in an ear-splitting shriek.

Wind whipped the leaves from the trees and sent debris swirling viciously about their faces. Sara's hair was torn from its bun and streamed out above her head in flaxen tendrils. Despite the rising bile of terror, Jehn noticed. He'd never seen hair as beautiful as those wind-tangled strands.

'Run!' bellowed the unicorn, interrupting the scholar's distraction and causing Sara to stumble in surprise. 'For the love of all the gods, RUN!'

As a group, they bolted, leaning into the storm and sprinting past the unicorn who swung about to guard their rear.

Ander tried to turn back against the maelstrom, but could make little headway. 'Belina!'

'Go, Ander! Terentius will protect me!' Belina spun her torso around then, and let fly an arrow towards her husband's head, sightless eyes tracking back and forth. The arrow soared over Ander and struck a tree trunk behind him. Sara's wide-eyed gaze followed the arrow's trajectory and saw a shadow writhing beneath the shaft. *What the hell is that?!*

More shadows swirled above the woman and the unicorn, engulfing them in a cloud of darkness. Sara screamed in horror, tearing her hand from Jehn's grasp and running towards the shadowy mass. The wind whipped her hair into her face, and she stumbled over a root and went down. Jehn threw himself to the ground at her side, shielding her against the onslaught of sticks and branches whirling in the air around them.

The wind screamed and shadows streamed in from every direction. Jehn looked up to see the sky above them thick with the creatures, mouths stretched open in wailing shrieks as their long, crooked fingers reached downwards, clawing furiously. Sara let out a strangled cry of terror.

In an instant, the hummingcat flickered into view in front of the prone pair, her back arched sharply, tail whipping. Jehn reached out to grip Sara's shoulder, and the hummingcat leapt at them, her fur crackling with sparks. The air shimmered like a heat haze, and with a sizzling snap, they were gone.

* * *

Senna cried out, but his warning was lost amidst the confusion. Ahead, Belina and Terentius disappeared within the blackness as the second cloud of shadow creatures rushed forward, enraged that their prey had escaped.

The forest was now so dark there was little the others could do to help even if they possessed the means. They staggered against the gale, hands in front of their eyes as they sought to find their friends.

A shrill clarion call blasted through the forest and Terentius' horn thrust through the inky cloud like a divine spear, shredding the shadows with every slashing swing. The darkness parted slightly, and they could make out the unicorn's alabaster form, rearing tall upon his back legs, his white tail a frothing tangle. He lashed out with his argent hooves, sparks flying into the air, his glittering mane flying in the storm like the wings of a vengeful angel. Shadows tore and were flung to pieces as the unicorn fought like a mad thing, his furious screams reverberating through the trees. The shadow creatures' moans and shrieks turned to fear-drenched howls as the unicorn ripped them to pieces.

In but a few moments, all that remained were wisps of shadow, quickly disintegrating into motes and then noth-ingness.

The unicorn returned to the earth, his sides heaving with exertion, foam coating his mouth and nostrils. A coruscating light radiated up and down his spiralled horn, its movement slowing by the second until it faded entirely. Belina still had her seat, bow yet drawn, and quiver nearly empty. The trees surrounding them were littered with her arrows; the shadows they had pinned still squirming.

'I told you to run, you foolish children!' Terentius' eyes rolled in annoyance as he cantered towards them.

Thorn approached, letting out a low whistle. 'Well, it seems our ranger friend is not as hampered by a lack of eyesight as we first thought. You old scoundrel,' he said, pointing a finger at the unicorn, 'you should have told us!'

The unicorn regarded the Aes-Sidhe seriously. 'It was not I who worked this miracle, Anwyl Orinthorn.' He turned his head to look over the group, and in alarm, said, 'Where is Sara?'

Terentius' eyes rolled as he cast around, the whites unnerv-ingly bright beside his midnight irises. Foam formed in the corners of his mouth as he frantically stamped his hooves. 'Sara! Sara, answer me!'

Senna emerged from the trees, shaking his head, his face tight with tension. 'It's no good. I can't find her. Jehn's missing, too,' he said, 'And the cat.'

Ander kicked at the shadowy remains on the ground, 'That cat took them somewhere, I'm sure of it. Spirited them away. They are probably in Thalanthas already!'

Thorn nodded. 'That seems likely. That the cat took them, at least.' He lay a hand on the unicorn's shoulder. 'Fear not, my old friend, I'm sure they are safe. Safer than us perhaps…' The wights were gone—or dead—but the forest closed overhead, ominous and unforgiving. What had taken place this day would not soon be forgotten. 'We should move from here.'

Belina slid from Terentius' back to join Ander. She stepped easily over roots and branches as if she was seeing them clear as day. The whiteness of her eyes seemed to impede her no longer. 'Something comes,' she said. 'It is not yet close, but I agree with Thorn. We need to go.'

'I've lost her,' the unicorn muttered. 'Of all the ridiculous things… I told you to run but would you listen? No, of course not. Stupid, stupid children!'

Thorn moved to hold the unicorn's gaze, 'It's no one's fault,' he said. 'We couldn't have foreseen this. Come, Terentius. We need to go. Sara is safe, you mark my words. Jehn is most likely with her, and the hummingcat knows what she's doing. Between the two of them, our Dreamer Candidate will be safe and well looked after. We will find Sara when the time is right.'

Terentius nodded vaguely, his expression distant. This shock would weigh heavily on the unicorn. Thorn could not remember a time he'd ever seen the unicorn this downhearted. He sighed, unconsciously touching finger to thumb, and leaned his head against Terentius' side, offering what comfort he could. *It will be all right,* mo chara, he projected. *I hope you are right, Orinthorn,* came the reply, *for if not, we are all surely lost.*

The companions gathered to the unicorn and ushered him ahead into the forest. They trudged in silence, speech suppressed by the sense of threat, but for now they encountered nothing. The trees lost their stifling closeness and the forest began to thin. The day's shadows lengthened and stretched around them, but these were just shadows, nothing more.

CHAPTER 27

Sara hit the ground hard, her breath rushing from her chest in a sharp whoosh. She blinked in confusion, noting the blue sky overhead, whips of horse tail clouds high above. Before she could recover her breath or her wits, Jehn appeared in the air above her, flailing his arms and legs in a way that would be comical in the right circumstances. These were not such circumstances, however. Their eyes met and widened in horror, just as the scholar fell to earth, landing heavily right on top of Sara.

Jehn's face reddened instantly, and he scrambled to extricate himself, becoming more and more flustered with each passing second. 'Oh gods, sorry, I'm so sorry!'

Rolling aside, Jehn stared up at the sky for a moment to collect himself. His embarrassment was soon forgotten once he realised the ground beneath them was not earth, but sand, pricked with sharp dry grass in clumps. The crash of wave-break echoed in his ears, and he turned his head towards the sound. 'Where are we?'

'I don't know,' said Sara. 'What happened?'

Jehn got to his feet and offered her a hand up. The warmth of the sun beat down on their heads as they took in their new surroundings. A gentle breeze lifted Sara's hair from her shoulders. 'We're on a beach!' She cringed, a hot rush of awkwardness following such an obvious remark.

Jehn didn't seem to notice. 'Yes, it appears we are.'

A sizzle sounded behind them, and the hummingcat burst from a split in the air, landing on the sand, a tangle of blackness at her feet. She growled and bared her teeth at the shadow, but it was still. The creature was dead. Sniffing at it in disdain, the cat strode towards the pair as if the shadow were of no consequence.

'Honeysuckle!' Sara fell to her knees and coaxed the hummingcat on to her lap. Jehn came and sat beside, reaching over to scratch the little cat's ears. Honeysuckle purred and rubbed her face against Sara's hands.

'I would hazard a guess this was her way of protecting you, Sara,' said Jehn. The hummingcat trilled and nipped at his fingers, 'Us, then. Thank you.'

'We have to go back,' Sara said, 'Terry, the others, they're in danger! Those things—'

'Wights,' said Jehn. He rubbed his chin thoughtfully. 'But I've rarely heard of them swarming in such numbers before, and never with such hostility!'

'I don't care what they are, we have to go back! Take us back, Honeysuckle!' The cat stared at Sara a moment and then began a methodical grooming routine. It was clear she would be doing no such thing.

'I expect they were drawn by our unique confluence of power,' the scholar continued, heedless to Sara's concern. 'Wights are attracted to the living, you see, but usually pose no danger to an individual traveller. How fascinating! It would be unusual for such a group of travellers to converge on their territory at once; I suppose they were both enticed and inordinately threatened by our presence. Wights possess the ability to drain a being's life force; being caught in the midst of such a large group was extremely dangerous.'

'Are you even listening to me? All you are doing is making my point! How do we get back?'

'Back? I don't think we can,' Jehn said. 'I'm not sure where exactly we are, and if Honeysuckle doesn't want to take us back, she won't. I expect the others are all right, however. Yes, I'm sure they are...' he trailed off, and pressed his lips together in a thin smile to hide his uncertainty.

Sara stared at him, shaking her head in disbelief.

'I'm sorry, Sara. I think we will have to find our own way to the Great City, and hope to meet the others there.'

The hummingcat stretched languorously and rolled off Sara's lap onto the sand. She flopped on to her back and proceeded to writhe back and forth, revelling in the feel of the warm grains within her fur. Sara watched, amazed the little animal could be so carefree after being in such danger mere minutes earlier. *Perhaps she's only doing what she's meant to do.* After all, she had brought Sara here to Palantia to be tested as a Dreamer Candidate, and that had not yet occurred. *Cats may be inscrutable at times, but I'm sure they take duty and honour quite seriously.*

'Thank you for saving us, Brave Honeysuckle,' Sara said, tentatively touching the hummingcat on her exposed belly. The cat pummelled the air with her paws and winked one eye at the woman. Sara smiled. 'Well then,' she said, 'that's that.' She got to her feet. 'I suppose we should try to figure out where we are. Any ideas?'

Jehn stood up, brushing sand from his clothing. He squinted up at the sun, 'I... I don't know...'

Sara looked up and down the beach for any sign that could help their plight. The western end was stacked with grey boulders, carpeted with lacy white lichen. The eastern end was shielded by a high sheer cliff.

'Wait,' said Sara, 'I know this place. I've been here before...'

'That can't be—'

'...but something doesn't feel right. It's familiar, but some-how... off. Like a dream you can't quite remember.'

'Say that again,' said Jehn, as he grabbed Sara by both arms, searching her face.

'Like a dream...'

'Honeysuckle!' said Jehn, startling the cat awake, 'Where are we? Where have you taken us?' The cat blinked once and went back to sleep. 'Gah!'

Sara picked up a handful of sand. It was made of small shells and pieces of broken coral. A tiny crustacean peeked out from the hollow of a miniature spiral. *Hermit crab. This... I've done this before.*

The turquoise water lapped at the edge of the shore, barely a ripple upon the mirror surface. The sun was warm and the air heavy with fragrance. *Sweet... like hibiscus, or frangipani.* 'Are we in Fiji?!'

'Where? I've never heard of such a place.'

'I swear, this looks just like a place I went to on holiday once.'

'In your world? No... that can't be possible.'

Sara carefully replaced the handful of shell-sand. The small crab dug itself in and disappeared. 'I'm not a hundred percent sure on how this Dreamer thing works, but Terentius said I have latent powers. He's been teaching me. I can do a lot of things I didn't know I could. Maybe I have teleportation abilities.'

'I don't think that's it,' said Jehn, the machinations of thought chasing over his features and settling into a picture of worry. 'Palantians can't go to your world unless they are fae. I think we are somewhere else. Somewhere we... *I*... shouldn't be.' He scanned the horizon, a barely discernible separation between sea and sky. 'Honeysuckle would take us somewhere to keep us safe, and for her, the safest place is the Stitch.'

'Isn't the Stitch just a passage between places?'

'Yes and no. It is a path between two points, yes. But it is also a place. Technically speaking.'

'That doesn't make a lot of sense,' said Sara, 'though not much about this whole business does.' She looked at the hummingcat, lying on her back with her paws in the air. 'If this is the Stitch, why does it look like somewhere I've been before? And why shouldn't you be here?'

Jehn sighed. He lay down upon the sand and crossed his arms behind his head, gazing up at the sky. A single fluffy cloud scudded across the vast blue void. 'I don't have an answer for your first question,' he said, 'But for the second...' he closed his eyes for a long moment. 'Perhaps it would be a relief to finally tell someone.'

Sara propped herself on one elbow and waited. *All is about to be revealed!* The hummingcat woke from her slumber and hopped on to Sara's side, curling up there, a barely detectable weight. The cat watched Jehn closely, her ears tilted forward.

Jehn smiled. 'She has taken to you. It is rare, you know, for a hummingcat to bond with anyone, let alone two people. Perhaps she knows something we don't.' Sara's heart fluttered at the man's words and she smiled back. 'All right,' Jehn continued, letting out a sharp rush of breath as he worked up the courage to share his story. 'I was hardly grown when I met Honeysuckle. That was the day I killed my brother.'

As Sara's eyes widened in shock, the hummingcat trilled and zapped over to Jehn. The little cat rubbed her face on the man's chin, then turned back to Sara. The cat's gaze locked on the woman's, and Sara's heart beat calmed. Involuntarily, she stretched her hand to touch the cat's fur, which appeared to be lengthening, stretching out in a shimmer. The luminescence caught Sara, linking her to the cat, and through Honeysuckle, to Jehn. A flood of memories poured into Sara's mind, and she closed her eyes against the rush of emotions. She felt the full spectrum of Jehn's experience: the excitement of the adventure, his love for his brother, Cale—even tinged with irritation, as it was—the fear and confusion of falling into the Stitch, then worse. The very worst. Sara's chest heaved and tears streamed down her face as she was there at Jehn's grim realisation; his brother dead, by his own hand. No matter that he was not in his right mind, had not known what was happening, what he'd done. The grief was thick and suffocating, and Sara lost her breath right there with Jehn.

The hummingcat trilled a low note, and Sara broke from the reverie. Aghast, full of sorrow, she reached for Jehn, and he fell into her arms. The scholar sobbed in silence, and Sara held him, stroking his back and whispering sympathies, until his grief stilled. Jehn pulled away slowly, and Sara released her hold, dropping her hands to take his. 'It's okay, Jehn,' she said, 'it was an accident. A horrible one, but an accident, nonetheless. You were just a kid. It's not your fault.'

The scholar gave a small smile, 'I know. I know that, rationally. I've made my peace with it, best I can. But the guilt—the grief—it comes for me at times. Like a crow—no, a raven—pecking at my vulnerabilities. You have seen it all now. Seen more than any other.' His breath hitched in his throat as he saw himself staring back in the reflection of her eyes. The world dropped away, and time stood still. He moved—or was it she?—and then his heart and head were filled with fireworks.

* * *

Sara opened her eyes, the sparks in her head subsiding. Her lips curved in a slow smile. Jehn grinned in return, his eyes gleaming. The pair fell back on to the sand and lay there, hands entwined, as they stared up at the impossible blue sky.

Sara breathed in the warm, salty air. *I feel at peace. This is the first time I've felt so calm since I've been here. It really is like a holiday. Maybe that's why it looks this way, this pocket Stitch universe.*

The waves on the shore kept their rhythmic motion, and the slight breeze continued to caress—just enough to keep the temperature perfect. *Not too cold, not too hot. Goldilocks.*

Sara turned her head to gaze upon the man beside her. Her heart softened at the sight of him: his sharp nose and high cheekbones, sparkling eyes. His lips. *Mmm.* She leaned over and kissed him again, and he responded with enthusiasm.

Seconds, minutes, hours. Time melded, and nothing else mattered but this moment.

* * *

'The sun isn't going down,' said Jehn.

'I hadn't noticed,' said Sara, tracing the scholar's jaw with a finger.

Jehn captured her hand in his and kissed it. 'You're sweet, but see?' He pointed at the sky. 'The sun is still at its zenith. We've been here for what seems like hours, but there is no evidence of the passage of time. It's as if this day has been crafted solely for this moment, a never-ending, timeless now.'

Sara laughed. 'That's very poetic for an academic.'

Jehn grinned. 'Perhaps, but do you agree?'

'You're right. Time isn't moving. Makes sense if we are in the Stitch, though, as you suspected. Terentius explained that time passes differently between worlds.'

'Yes, but don't you think this feels strange? If I start to think about the strangeness of it, I get a small discomfort in the pit of my stomach. As if it's not a good idea to question the matter. My instincts are telling me one thing but my mind another.'

'Well, could that be because you aren't meant to be here? I don't have that feeling. I feel relaxed.' Sara's brow wrinkled. 'Where's Honeysuckle got to?' The hummingcat was nowhere to be seen; a surprising turn of events after successfully orchestrating this romantic interlude. *She's been angling for that, practically since I met her! Not that I'm complaining in the slightest.*

'She'll come back when she thinks she needs to,' said Jehn. 'I can't shake this feeling that if we don't act soon, we'll slip into a dream we can't escape. We should probably work out what we should do next.'

'I can think of a few things,' said Sara with an exaggerated wink.

Jehn laughed. 'You are just too…'

'Old and decrepit?'

231

'Hey, now, that's not it! Why do you do that? You said something like that when we first met. It's not what I was going to say at all.'

'Oh really?' said Sara, 'Well, what were you going to say, then?' *Flirt!*

'I was surprised you weren't a child. Most Dreamers are. The average age of recorded Dreamers through Palantia's history is about sixteen years old. Honeysuckle had shown me a very vague image of you, and I filled in the gaps in my expectation from my reading. You toppled my expectations in a most wonderful way. Though, I admit, now I've gotten to know you, I find myself wishing you weren't so extraordinary.'

'What do you mean?'

'Well, if you pass your Dreamer Trial—which seems likely—you will sleep and Dream for Palantia for centuries. I will be long dead and gone when you wake again, and you will remain young and beautiful. I don't think even Terentius would be there for you when you wake.'

Sara's heart fell. 'I hadn't thought of that. I hadn't thought beyond passing the tests and being accepted. I don't want to miss out on what this—us—could be! I don't want to never see you again. Or Terentius. Honeysuckle. Even the others! I don't want to leave you behind and wake up with no one.'

'You will be able to go back to your world and things won't change there.'

'I don't have anything for me there.' Sara's eyes began to glisten, tears threatening to flood over. She gulped in air. 'It's not fair! I don't want to be the Dreamer if I lose everyone I care about!'

Jehn enfolded her in his arms, holding her as she sobbed, torn between this new blossom of affection and a strange, underlying vacillation of unease. *Who would've thought I'd find someone so perfect, so wonderful, who understands and accepts me, only to lose her to such an important fate.* He stared at the sparkling ocean, his own eyes prickling. *But whoever said life was fair?*

CHAPTER 28

The Sluagh's eyes snapped open as it felt the ripple upon the fabric that melded Palantia and the detestable human world. A drawn thread.

Its snout curled into a sneer of disgust. That Stitch-touched man had found the Candidate. The pulse of their connection thrummed on the air, an invisible current.

The Sluagh's taloned hand swept across the table, knocking trinkets flying and toppling a fat candle pillar. The flame guttered and choked on the onslaught of molten wax, which snaked across the table and dribbled to the floor. The Sluagh closed its eyes to pray for patience.

No matter. He can't protect her. He may have been touched by the magic of the Stitch, but he is just a human. Corruptible, vulnerable to influence. Like all the rest of these pitiable creatures. Even the Aes-Sidhe, who hold themselves so high and mighty. Especially them. Insecurities lie in everyone, everything. Each can be plucked and played like an infernal instrument, if one knows the song of their dreams. And no one knows that song better than I.

The Sluagh hummed a low deep-throated note, the thick minor tone bubbling forth, astringent, unsettling. The sound shivered the pane of glass above the table, where the street outside could be just barely discerned. The Sluagh ceased its baleful music and waited.

Moments passed and still the Sluagh waited in silence.

Finally, a soft sound upon the small window. *Tap, tap. Tap. Tap, tap. Tap.*

The Sluagh smiled and reached to pull a fine chain. The pane of glass angled inwards, and over the threshold crept a dark shape the size of blackbird. Its spindly striped legs seemed far too small to hold its meaty bulk, the creature's thorax fully two inches in girth. It sidled onto the windowsill and twitched the long antennae sprouting above its ink black eyes.

Rather than continue its shambling crawl, the creature spread thick, hairy wings and lazily flapped to the table, dropping a shower of powdery scales. The Sluagh coaxed the giant moth into its hands and held the loathsome creature to its face.

'Systheh namatha fyohk,' the Sluagh whispered. 'Mnenath frehagh thriix.'

The moth quivered, its wings spreading to full span, more than a foot wide. The black undersides pulsed with concentric red circles.

'Not yet, little one,' said the Sluagh, stroking the furry abdomen, 'Save that for your prey.' The Sluagh slunk to the window and threw the moth into the air. The malodorous wings flapped once, and the creature disappeared, leaving nothing but a cloud of shimmery grey dust in its wake.

CHAPTER 29

The sun shone overhead, unmoving, a constant against Sara's churning thoughts. *This sucks.*

Jehn's hand brushed hers and she clasped it tightly. 'We can't stay here,' he said. 'Much as we may want to. Palantia needs you.'

'Don't,' said Sara, releasing the scholar's hand and rolling away from him.

Jehn stared sadly at Sara's back. Tension was apparent in the stiffness of her neck and shoulders, and he longed to comfort her. *But what could I say? Her world has been turned over yet again. I can't offer her any solution.* 'I'm sorry—'

'We can stay here as long as we like,' said Sara, sitting up, her face turned to the sea. 'You said it yourself, time moves differently. Honeysuckle wouldn't have put us here if it meant I was going to miss the Trial or not get inducted before the Dreamer wakes up.' She shrugged. 'As far as I see it, it's really up to me when we leave.'

'Honeysuckle is a wise creature, that's true. But she can't predict the Awakening. I think you're reaching, Sara.'

Sara snorted. 'What do you know? The last Awakening was a thousand years ago.'

'Yes, that's true, but I've studied the Dreamer for much of my adult life. And besides, there's more at play here than a simple Awakening—that we both know. The Sluagh is working at something that affects the Dreamer. Who knows what its plan is? If the Dreamer were to die... there would be far-reaching ramifications for both my world and yours. Are you really comfortable assuming that everything is fine, while we lay about enjoying a perpetual summer's day?'

Sara shook her head, rolling her eyes, 'I know, I know. I can't argue with your rationale. Beauty and brains. That's a dangerous combination, Jehn.'

Jehn laughed, 'Tell me about it.' He stared into her eyes, relishing the skipping of his heartbeat when she smiled. 'We'll work this out, Sara. We've been brought together for a reason, I'm sure of it.'

'The Universe moves in mysterious ways.'

'The Dreamer does, that's a certainty.'

* * *

'So now that we've agreed we should be getting back... just how do we do that exactly?' Sara twisted a lock of hair around her finger, inspecting the split ends with disgust. *I need a haircut. Not that it really matters, I suppose.*

'I suspect the answer lies within your own powers. We just need to work out what that might be.'

'Very helpful, thanks,' said Sara, giving Jehn a wry grin.

Jehn laughed, 'Sorry. That was a little recursive.'

'To understand recursion, you must first understand recursion.'

'What?'

'Just something a professor told me once.'

'You're a fascinating woman, Sara,' said Jehn, 'As long as we're stuck here, maybe I can ask you some questions about your world.'

Sara didn't know if she should be flattered or offended. 'Um... okay?'

Jehn ploughed on, ignorant to her hesitation. 'I'm curious about your daily life. Do you have a profession? How do you spend your free time?'

'I do have a job, yes, but it's not what you'd call a profession. It's also probably something you wouldn't know or understand.'

'Try me.'

'I'm an IT Support Officer. I help when people have problems with their computers.'

Jehn's eyes lit up. 'Ahh, you're a technologist! How intriguing. I've read much in the histories about the Technology Era. Three Dreamers ago, if I recall correctly.'

'But...' Sara's head spun, remembering what Terentius had said about the non-linearity of time in Palantia. 'Ah, never mind. Time is weird.'

Jehn laughed. 'That it is! So, tell me more about your technologist profession. It must be a source of constant enjoyment.'

Sara pursed her lips. 'Oh Jehn, you think *I'm* fascinating.' She laughed at his puzzled expression. 'Look, being an IT Support Officer isn't that exciting in my world. Lots of people do it, many probably enjoy it, but for me it's just a way to pay the bills. I don't love it, and I don't really like the people I have to work with, either. Being a Dreamer is probably much more to my liking.' She sighed. 'Even if I won't know I'm doing it.'

Jehn smiled. 'That's not quite accurate,' he said. 'Did

Terentius not explain? Dreamers may sleep during their tenure, but they do retain a degree of consciousnesses. It's necessary so they may direct their thoughts and feelings into Palantia, to influence and create. Whilst your body will be asleep, your mind is free to wander as you see fit.'

'So, I can visit you and Terentius and the others in my dreams?'

'Yes, but I don't believe you can interact with us in any real sense.'

'That's almost worse than going to sleep and never seeing you again!'

Jehn pressed his lips together. 'I suppose you're right.'

'And we're back to the stark reality of what being a Dreamer really means. Sacrifice. I didn't think it was so bad when I didn't know anyone here. When I didn't know you.'

A low rumble broke the stillness. Sara and Jehn looked up in surprise. Out of nowhere, clouds were building into towering thunderheads. Lightning slashed across the sky, leaving a silver after-image superimposed upon the horizon.

'Oh geez,' said Sara, 'That's my fault.' Jehn looked at her quizzically. 'Apparently my mood can affect the weather. Don't ask. I can't explain it.'

Heavy raindrops began to patter on the water as the storm moved closer. In seconds, the drops were a wall chasing up the beach, and the pair turned tail and ran for shelter.

'There's nowhere to go!' Jehn shouted over the noise of the thunder and crashing waves. Sara looked over her shoulder. The sea was churning to a froth beneath the storm's onslaught.

Lightning forked, and the air crackled with electricity. The lightning sparked towards the ground, making contact with the beach not far from their location. Sand flew into the air, melting and moulding into twisted stalagmites. Sara and Jehn drew back in terror, their hearts racing.

Sara's breath came in short, sharp huffs as fear threatened to overwhelm her. *Think!*

There came a rush of cold, wet air from behind, and Sara turned back in horror. The sea rose above in a huge cresting wave, and with no time to react, the pair were enveloped in the briny embrace and pulled out to sea.

CHAPTER 30

Thorn stole a glance at the unicorn. Terentius hadn't spoken a word—verbal or otherwise—for two days now. Nothing seemed to stir him from his fugue, not even when they'd happened upon the spectacular sight of a glittering blue fern glen. The place was a sweet and grateful sanctuary amid the thick foreboding of the 'Shadowing.

'Tell me the colour, Ander,' said Belina, her white eyes casting around the clearing.

'Blue, my love,' he said, 'with a touch of purple, like the gemstone necklace you wore on our wedding day.'

Belina sighed, smiling. 'Iolite.'

'That's the one! It looks just like that.'

'I can feel it,' said Belina, touching her hand to her throat. 'I can sense the hue, feel its shimmer. What miracle is this?'

'Her manifestation powers are greater than I first thought,' the unicorn said, breaking his long silence.

'Terry! You've come back to us!' Ander slapped the unicorn on the shoulder, drawing a stern glance from both Thorn and Senna, but Terentius appeared not to notice.

'Are you hale, old friend?' said Thorn, his searching gaze sweeping the unicorn's face. 'What do you mean?' Terentius' eyes remained distant, and he did not reply.

'What's wrong with him?' Ander whispered.

'Grief. Denial. Apathy,' said Senna, 'All the hallmarks of the Malaise.'

'The Malaise! No, can't be,' Ander shook his head. 'Not old Terry. He's too tough for that.'

'It doesn't work like that, Ander,' said Senna, 'I've read about it. It can strike anyone. Young or old, weak or strong. The Malaise does not discriminate. It is a disease of the mind, brought on by a traumatic event.'

They turned as one to watch the unicorn. Terentius stood in the centre of the glen, staring at nothing. 'What can we do?' said Ander. 'We have to snap him out of this!'

'Patience, *am Mathan Mòr*,' said Thorn, grasping the big man's arm, 'He may come out of it in his own time. But we must hope to reunite him with Sara as soon as possible. He blames himself for losing his charge—such blame is folly, yet none of us can help how we feel. The burden of responsibility is a heavy one. I know it well.' He glanced around at the group. 'Perhaps we should take this opportunity to rest. With luck, we will break from the 'Shadowing tomorrow. The Great City is not much further beyond.'

They set their sleeping rolls upon the soft undergrowth. None saw the grey shape swirling overhead, the dust from its wings camouflaged against the glittering ferns. The powder fell silently upon the companions, and within moments, each was yawning, their eyelids drooping.

'I should take first watch,' Thorn mumbled, but there was no reply. The others were already asleep, and a great weariness washed over the Aes-Sidhe, too. He tried to rally, but slumber overtook him, and his eyes finally closed.

The unicorn's head dropped, his horn grazing the ground.

He vaguely noticed a shape flutter towards him, but the Malaise had him in its grip, and so he did not turn to watch the movement. His thoughts wandered, full of regret and self-flagellation. An unwitting but ideal target.

The giant moth moved lazily through the glen, alighted on the unicorn's horn, and spread its wings to reveal the hypnotic pulsing within. Terentius jerked, resisting the moth's spell, but the creature released a cloud of dust into the unicorn's eyes. Terentius blinked frantically but could do nothing to clear his vision. A wave of exhaustion flooded through his mind.

The moth seized this opportunity. It crawled down the horn onto the unicorn's forehead, its barbed feet digging beneath the fur to scratch the flesh below. The vile insect crept higher, its noxious body shrinking as it eased towards its destination, savouring the mix of panic and confusion arising from its victim.

The moth's antennae brushed the hairs within the unicorn's ear, and Terentius' eyes widened in panic. All sound was silenced but a soft scratching within the unicorn's ear canal. A shiver ran through his body and then Terentius' eyes finally closed.

The moth, now a tiny thing, settled into its new home and began to absorb the terrified thoughts hurtling around the unicorn's mind.

* * *

Thorn woke first, jolting upright in shock. His heart drummed against his chest and he sucked in a slow breath to ease his panic. His companions were as he'd left them the night before, still sleeping soundly. Even Terentius appeared to be at rest—an unusual thing for a unicorn, but not so surprising, given his ordeal and current state of mind.

Thorn rose to his feet and began to gently shake the others from their slumber. Despite groggy mutterings, the Aes-Sidhe soon had the party fully awake. The unicorn, however, merely opened his eyes and raised his noble head—again, Terentius remained mute. *Come back to us, old friend*, thought Thorn, hoping to break through the unicorn's mental wall. He sighed when his efforts were in vain.

'Ahh, that was some sleep!' said Ander, running his fingers through his hair. His hands came away covered in grey dust, 'Hah! I need a bath, and soon. I've got dirt all over me!'

Thorn's eyes narrowed and he touched his own hands to his hair and face. His hands, too, were dusted with the grey powder. 'What—?'

'What is it?' said Senna, 'Is something wrong?'

Thorn wiped his hands on his pants. 'I don't think this is dirt. It feels different.'

Belina rubbed some of the dust between her fingers. 'It's very fine, like a powder. Or pollen. Something natural, but not dirt or sand. It makes me feel strange.'

'Some odd 'Shadowing thing, no doubt,' said Ander, 'Doesn't seem to have done any harm though, so probably not worth worrying about.'

'Perhaps,' said Thorn. He frowned, not comfortable with dismissing it so easily.

'Come on, Thorn,' said Ander, laughing at the other's seriousness, 'let's just take it on face value. We all needed a decent sleep, and now we've had one. We can power on to Thalanthas at a good clip. Maybe cut down on our rest breaks and make it in what… a couple of days? Seems like a bonus, if you ask me. Nothing's wrong, I'm sure of it.' He pulled out his whittling knife and deftly cut a starfruit into quadrants, passing a piece to Thorn. The Aes-Sidhe shook his head. Ander shrugged and ate the proffered slice straight from the blade.

Senna watched the exchange, his brow furrowing with the infuriating itch of a not-quite-remembered piece of information. 'I may have read something—'

'Bah!' said Ander. 'You scholarly types and your facts and trivia. I'm telling you, it's nothing! Let's just go. No point hanging around talking about something that doesn't mean anything. It's no wonder you lot never get anything done.'

Senna's face fell.

'Ander! That's enough!' said Belina. The big man ducked his head and quickly set about packing up, avoiding eye contact with his wife.

'I'm sorry, Senna,' said Belina, 'I don't know what's put him in this mood, but he shouldn't take it out on you.'

'It's fine,' said the attendant. 'We're all a little on edge, I suppose. Once we get to the Great City, maybe things will be better.' Senna glanced at the unicorn to find Terentius looking straight at him. He started. 'Terentius?'

'He's not really looking at you,' said Thorn, 'he's lost in his thoughts.' Thorn hoisted his pack. 'Everyone ready to go?'

Senna nodded. As he turned to collect his belongings, he saw a shimmer in the unicorn's eye. A tiny crystal lingered on his lashes before dropping and disappearing into the ferny undergrowth. With a stiff gait, the unicorn moved to follow the group, and they started off again as dawn kissed the land, turning it golden.

CHAPTER 31

The hummingcat sparkled back into existence upon the beach. The waves had subsided, and the air was calm and still once more.

She looked up and down the shore, searching for Jehn and Sara. She'd given them ample time to themselves, and the threat from the 'Shadowing had well passed. It was time to go.

The hummingcat let out a questioning trill, repeating the sound when there was no answer. Concerned, Honeysuckle flew across the sand, seeking a sign of the pair. There was none. Honeysuckle was alone. She blinked in confusion. ♪ *Where?* ♪

She spied something glistening, the small shape rolling over with the gentle lapping of the sea. She ran to it and pulled it from the sea's grasp.

It was a small glass receptacle, tied on a leather thong. She knew this thing. A single whisker—hers—lay within. Jehn would not part with this if he had a choice. Honeysuckle's pulse quickened, and static flickered from the tips of her ears. ♪ *Where?* ♪

CHAPTER 32

Thorn leapt upon a fallen tree and peered into the distance. Ducking this way and that, he soon made out what he was searching for and, with a grin, flew back to the others.

'Not much further,' he said, his fine features awash with gladness. 'I can see a break up ahead.'

'All right!' said Ander. He grabbed Belina by the hand and took off, not waiting for anyone else.

'Ander, wait!' Thorn frowned at the big man's recklessness, and hastily followed after him. The Aes-Sidhe looked back over his shoulder and called, 'Senna, please see to Terentius. I'll make sure there's nothing to surprise us.'

Senna eyed the unicorn. Terentius remained silent as ever, but Senna felt sure the unicorn wanted to speak. The boy walked up to Terentius, who stood with stiff legs, seemingly waiting for instruction. Senna put his hands on either side of the unicorn's head and looked into his eyes. 'Terentius. Can you hear me? Please talk to me. I'm worried about you.'

A shimmer; then another crystal crusted upon the unicorn's midnight lashes. Senna reached up and touched his finger to the tiny stone. 'What is this?' The boy held the crystal up to the light. Something sparked and danced within, but it was so minute, Senna couldn't make it out. He pocketed the crystal and rubbed the unicorn's cheek. 'I'll ask Thorn to take a look,' he said. 'We should catch up with the others, Terentius. Here, I'll guide you.'

With gentle pressure upon the unicorn's flank, Senna turned Terentius towards the path and ushered him along. The two walked side-by-side into the trees.

Before long, the vista opened, and soon they found themselves facing a wide-ranging grassland, dotted with wildflowers. Daisies, poppies, and cornflowers swayed in the stiff breeze. Specks of pollen filled the air, causing Ander to let loose a roaring sneeze. Belina's laughter rang out across the meadow.

Thorn joined Senna and the unicorn, and they stood together, staring out across the open landscape, as the sun's yellow disc sunk beneath the horizon, leaving streaks of orange across the purpling sky. Ander and Belina danced together among the flowers, glad to be free of the oppressive forest.

* * *

Senna produced the crystal from his tunic and handed it to Thorn. The Aes-Sidhe took it and squinted at the tiny stone. 'It's a diamond,' he said. 'Where did you find this?'

'On Terentius' eyelash,' said Senna.

'What? His eyelash, you say? Then this is a unicorn tear. Legend holds that a unicorn's tear can store the dreams and memories of its owner. As you can imagine, such a gem is very rare. There are few unicorns in Palantia, and Terentius is the only one on this continent. I wonder what it contains.'

'I saw something moving,' said the attendant. 'But it is too small for me to make out.'

'Indeed?' The Aes-Sidhe looked to the western sky, and fixed his gaze on the rising moon. It was waxing gibbous, nearly full, and shining brightly. The meadow glowed in its silver light. Thorn raised the crystallised tear to the moon and peered inside. The moonlight refracted upon the tear, setting forth tiny coruscations. There was indeed motion within. Thorn steadied his breath and looked deeper, his fae senses heightened, his vision sharpening.

A scene played out in miniature: the party sleeping, a shape hovering, dust falling. Darkness shrouding the unicorn's face. The scene repeated over and over, and Thorn watched carefully, hoping the tear would reveal something more.

'What do you see?' said Senna.

'Us, at the fern glen. Something definitely happened while we were sleeping, but I don't understand what.'

'What have you got there, Thorn?' Ander arrived behind them, causing Senna to start in surprise. He stepped away from the big man, still leery from his verbal assault earlier on. Ander shifted awkwardly, but said nothing.

Belina stood apart, head cocked slightly as she listened to the ambient sounds of the meadow. A cricket chirped far in the distance, its call echoed from a place close by.

Thorn shook his head, and began pacing back and forth, stopping to spy within the tear again and again.

'What is it, man! What's got you so riled up?' Ander grasped the Aes-Sidhe's forearm, pulling Thorn to a stop as he passed by.

'I should've known this was more than the Malaise!' Thorn's face was stricken, and he tugged his arm free. Terentius stood a small way from the group among a clump of dandelions. Thorn rushed to his friend and peered into the unicorn's eyes, searching for some sign, some explanation. Terentius remained passive.

'The dust.'

Thorn spun round to face the speaker. Belina picked her way towards him, her white eyes tracking over his face, seeing him in a way beyond earthly vision.

'It felt strange. And we slept so soundly,' she said. 'Don't you agree? It wasn't a natural rest. Something put us to sleep.'

'Of course,' said Thorn, nodding. 'To get us out of the way? But to what end?'

Belina stared sightlessly at Terentius, her head tilting. The sounds of the meadow faded away as she reached out with her newly enhanced senses. 'Listen.' She gestured at the unicorn, 'Can you hear it?'

Thorn frowned, 'I hear nothing.'

'Listen closer. There is something.'

Thorn focused, straining to hear what Belina could sense. He closed his eyes, blocking out the other sounds—insects whirring and chirping, the rush of wind rattling dry seed pods, Ander's harsh breathing, his own rapidly beating heart. He slowed its pulse, concentrating, breathing deeply. *Skkrrrttch.* Thorn's eyes flew open.

Belina faced him, her expression knowing. 'You hear it.'

Faint. A tiny sound. *Ssskkrttch.* 'Where is it coming from?'

Belina nodded at Terentius. 'Him.'

It was then that Thorn noticed Terentius' mane was no longer adorned with its usual array of gem beetles. *How long have they been gone? It's not yet the season...*

'Something shrouding his face...' Thorn hastily searched

the unicorn's mane, then ran his hands over the unicorn's neck, mumbling an apology as he gently pulled Terentius' head lower. Terentius' eyes shifted to meet his gaze, and the unicorn stamped a hoof deep into the soil beneath. Thorn kept up his inspection, and felt carefully around the horn, moving past the spiral to the top the unicorn's forehead. His fingers probed, searching for an explanation to the strange sound. A bump, then another. Thorn looked closer to find scabbed flesh, the injuries small but deep.

'Ander,' he called, 'look here, what do you make of this?'

The big man hurried over and peered at the marks. 'Scratches. Healed for a couple of days, by the look. Probably from when we were pushing through the scrub. Some of those branches were wicked. I have a few scratches of my own.'

Senna's face went suddenly pale and Thorn's stomach dropped. 'What is it, Senna?'

'I remember now,' said the boy. He looked at each one in turn. 'I remember what I'd read.'

'Tell us.'

'The dust. Sleeping poison. His listlessness. You are right, Thorn. This is not just the Malaise, though perhaps that made things easier...'

'What are you talking about, boy! Finish your sentence! What's wrong with Terry?' Ander's tone rose in pitch and Belina went to him, hushing him with a quiet word.

'It was just a story. Or I thought it was,' Senna's gaze grew distant as he brought the tale back to his mind. 'It was in a book called *Things from the Stitch*. My sister used to read it. She loved stories of dark things; something about the horror and excitement made her feel alive, she said. I was too young, of course, but I insisted she read me one. Mother and Father were away and Delma was meant to be looking after me.

'Each story was about a creature that supposedly lived within the Stitch, slithering out at night to prey on hapless travellers—or naughty children. I had convinced myself them all fancy, but was intrigued, nonetheless. The author called this particular creature a void creeper.

'The creeper could put its victim to sleep and crawl inside them...'

'That's disturbing,' said Thorn, 'But it's just a story. I don't know of any such creature in Palantia.'

'It's not from Palantia. Not technically. It's a Stitch creature. Or so the story said.' Senna rubbed his bare arms, feeling a chill not entirely from the cool evening air. 'What if it's real?'

'How do we get it out of him?' Ander retrieved a blade from the brace across his chest. 'How do we kill it?'

A patch of dandelions shimmered. Honeysuckle appeared, sneezing as puffs of seeds flew into the air at her arrival. The group spun round in surprise.

'The cat!' Ander knelt down and patted the ground, trying to coax Honeysuckle to him. Her eyes were wide, the pupils nearly fully dilated, and her whiskers twitched reflexively. 'She's scared! Cat, where's Jehn?'

'Her name is Honeysuckle.' Senna picked up the humming-cat and smoothed her fur. 'It's all right, little one. You're safe.'

Honeysuckle surveyed the group from the safety of Senna's arms. She locked eyes on Terentius. Senna felt a low vibration from the hummingcat's stomach, and then the cat was a ball of tension and sinew. She hissed, bunching back against Senna's chest.

Terentius approached haltingly, his legs stiff, his hooves dragging through the grass. It was as if he pushed against a terrible force. His eyes rolled as he struggled forward. The hummingcat's growls reverberated with a low frequency tone. It was all Senna could do to hold her.

The unicorn staggered, going down onto one foreleg. His horn scraped the ground, and Honeysuckle took the opportunity to launch from Senna's arms, leaving an array of scratches in her wake. Senna yelped, rubbing his injured skin.

Honeysuckle leapt at the unicorn, a terrible growl emanating from her small throat. The sound magnified, and the air seemed to shiver. Terentius closed his eyes and whimpered in pain. Honeysuckle had her paws upon his face, and he relented, dropping his chin to the ground. The hummingcat's vibrating attack slammed into Terentius over and over.

The others stood in shock, uncertain how to react to this strange violence. 'Thorn, do something!' said Ander.

'Wait,' the Aes-Sidhe replied. 'Look!'

Terentius ear quivered against the sonic assault. He let out a blood-curdling cry. Something small and dark emerged from the unicorn's ear and fell to the ground. Without hesitation, the hummingcat pounced, slamming her paw down upon the tiny thing. It grew beneath her claws, and she dug in deeper as the moth resumed its natural size.

Senna gagged at the sight of the vile thing. The very shape of it made his stomach turn over in disgust. Thorn stepped forward, whistled once, and, in a single motion, took the knife from Ander's hand and threw the blade into the creature's thorax as Honeysuckle leapt aside. The moth twitched once and became still.

Heavy breathing broke their trance, and Terentius huffed

as he lifted from the ground. 'Ah,' he sighed, 'Leandra Lus-a'-chraois, you save the day again.' Honeysuckle bounded over to Terentius and wound about his legs, rubbing her face against him. 'Thank you, little one. Yes, thank you.' He touched his nose to the hummingcat's. 'Now, what have you done with Sara?!'

CHAPTER 33

The Sluagh screeched in fury and threw the empty essence bottle at the wall of the cellar. The glass smashed, the tiny shards tinkling to the ground.

Footsteps paused at the cellar door and the Sluagh narrowed its eyes, but the King did not enter. Some shred of self-preservation stayed Uinnseann's hand as his fingers strayed to the door's bronze handle.

The footsteps slowly disappeared down the hall, and the Sluagh was left alone with its impotent rage. Hot breath seethed through sharp teeth, and it gripped the edge of the shelf, talons clacking against the wood.

Gone. Dead! Before it gave me ANYTHING! Foiled by a motley crew of pathetic lesser beings. What a waste! The Sluagh paced the length of the cellar, fuming. It was fortunate indeed that Uinnseann had not come down to investigate the clamour. The Sluagh would not have controlled its wrath, and that would have been disastrous.

No more games, then. I shall end this and take what is rightfully mine. Power belongs with those willing to wield it, not a pack of miserable weaklings. I'll take the Candidate, and then the Dreamer, and then all of Palantia. I'll tear the Stitch apart with the strength of their essence, and no further human influence will corrupt this world with its filth. The Sluagh's emerald eyes flashed. Then I will rule.

CHAPTER 34

The sun rose upon a fine, cool morning, spreading its golden light across the meadow. The sunlight sparkled upon a small lake in the distance; clumps of glossy-leaved canna lilies marched towards the small water source. Blades of grass peeked up from within the lilies, swaying gently in the breeze. It was a peaceful setting; serene and beautiful.

Terentius stamped his hooves upon the ground. 'I'm just in utter disbelief. Taking Sara so she could, what... canoodle? I was beginning to think you had some sense, cat, but I was clearly mistaken!'

'Please, *mo chara*, we've gone over this,' said Thorn, attempting to placate the unicorn's stunningly long-lived anger and frustration. 'She did what she thought best at the time. She meant no harm, you know that. She is Jehn's friend, and has bonded also with Sara. This is just an unlucky happenstance.' The unicorn's dark mood showed no sign of lifting. Thorn sighed softly. 'We'll find them, Terentius,' he said. 'Honeysuckle will keep searching. There's no one better placed to track them.'

Terentius tossed his head and snorted. 'No one better but the one who put them in that situation in the first place!'

Honeysuckle trilled a small note, as contrite a sound as a cat was wont to make. She sparked and disappeared for a moment, reappearing with the thong of the glass whisker bottle in her mouth. She blinked her amethyst eyes sadly. Senna lifted the tube from her. 'What's this?' he said.

'A trinket of Jehn's,' said Terentius. 'It's why she's so upset. She says he wouldn't just leave it, though in all honesty I wouldn't be surprised if he was sick of carrying it around and just tossed it away.' The hummingcat hissed at this hurtful remark. 'Pah! You brought it on yourself.'

'Is he normally this mean?' Senna whispered to Ander and Belina. 'Honeysuckle is scared and worried, and he's not sympathetic at all!'

'He's worried too,' said Belina. 'Before there was hope that the hummingcat had Jehn and Sara in a safe place. But now that sliver of hope is lost. We are fortunate, perhaps, that Terentius is feeling his anger and not his despondency. Otherwise, the Malaise may have gripped him once more.'

'What are we going to do?' said the boy. 'We will be at the Great City in a day or so.'

'We can't very well present a Candidate when we don't have one, now can we?' Terentius said sharply, 'And don't bother whispering about me. I can hear you with more than my ears.'

Senna blushed. 'I'm sorry,' he mumbled.

'We are all on edge,' said Thorn, 'It's understandable. But we should continue on to Thalanthas, and hope to come up with a plan by the time we reach the city gates. You never know, we might be granted a miracle!' He smiled, but his attempt at levity fell flat.

'Very well,' said Terentius, 'Let's away. There's no point standing here any longer. We may as well be moving.' He stalked off towards the lake.

* * *

They reached the shore of the small lake by mid-morning, and despite the protestations of Terentius, stopped for a small rest. The hummingcat had been zipping in and out of the Stitch every quarter hour or so, which was quite unsettling to Senna, whom she had chosen to be her carrier.

The attendant sat on a small boulder upon the shore, trailing his fingers in the cool, clear water. Honeysuckle materialised on his lap, and Senna leapt up in surprise. The hummingcat tumbled from his grasp and splashed into the lake. It was only a few inches deep here, but the little cat went right under. Senna gasped and reached down to pull her out. His hands closed on nothing but a clump of water grass. 'Honeysuckle!'

Senna waded into the water, casting about with eyes and hands, but the cat was nowhere to be found, despite the water being clear as glass. 'Honeysuckle!'

Ander rushed to the boy's side, 'What is it?' The big man had not yet apologised for his mean attitude earlier, but for now that was forgotten.

'Honeysuckle... she fell in. But I can't find her!'

Ander waded out deeper and ducked beneath. The water clarity was incredible; he could see all the way out to the middle of the lake. Ander resurfaced, pointing. 'There's something in the middle. Like a whirlpool underneath. I need to get closer.'

He took off, his broad strokes eating up the distance. Senna looked back to see Thorn, Belina and Terentius waiting on the shore.

Ander swam a few more lengths, then ducked under again. A shape was emerging from the swirling vortex, and Ander immediately rose to the surface. He trod water, and loosed a blade from his chest, as yet unable to determine if the shape was a threat.

A boom sounded from the lake's depths, and the shape catapulted out of the water, splashing back down in a fit of spluttering coughs. Jehn bobbed on the surface, water streaming off him, with Honeysuckle poised upon his back—somehow, perfectly dry.

Ander gasped. 'Jehn!' He swam towards the scholar. As he reached his friend, a second shape flew from the lake, and now Sara was gasping for breath beside the pair.

'Sara!' Terentius' voice rang out across the lake and the unicorn galloped into the water, carving an impressive wake. Sara spat out a piece of water weed and awkwardly swam to Terentius, flopping onto his back. Ander took Jehn's arm and pulled him close, swimming a strong sidestroke to shore. Honeysuckle rematerialised on the boulder and shook a few droplets off her paw.

A soggy trio of humans and one waterlogged unicorn emerged from the waters to a laughing Thorn and Belina. Thorn threw his arms around first Jehn, then Sara. 'Welcome back, friends! It seems you've had quite the adventure without us!'

'You could say that,' said Jehn. He and Sara locked eyes and grinned.

* * *

Sara fidgeted at the sleeves of the tunic that Belina had lent her while her own clothes were set out to dry by the fire. It had seemed prudent to have a rest and meal while everyone caught each other up on what had happened since they'd seen each other last, but Sara was restless. She stood apart with Jehn, he in silence beside her, respecting her need for stillness. They stared out at the lake, watching a red-crested moor hen picking in the reeds for tiny insects.

Time *had* moved differently, as Sara suspected, but not the way she'd expected. Several days had passed in Palantia while she and Jehn were held in the Stitch. She realised now that it wasn't just the hummingcat's doing, but rather her own, subconsciously manifesting and holding her and Jehn in time. *Even in a magical world, my superpower is avoidance!*

A hoof scraping on gravel announced the unicorn's arrival. He tilted his head and blinked, and Jehn took the not-so-subtle hint. The scholar broke away, his hand lightly touching Sara's as he went to join Senna in the middle of the group.

'It seems I let my emotions get the better of me,' said Sara, sheepishly glancing up at the unicorn. 'It's like you warned me, Terentius. The storm...' she trailed off. 'But never mind, we're safe, you're all safe. We're back together again.' She looked away to hide her mixed feelings, even knowing that Terentius would sense them.

The unicorn's gaze tracked the moor hen, not speaking as he watched the water fowl pounce on a diving beetle that had surfaced in the shallows. 'Much has happened, Sara,' he said, finally, 'With much yet to come. Despite our own personal challenges of late, the Trial of the Dreamer still lies ahead. It will be demanding indeed. We have lost significant time in your training, and I, too, am inadequately prepared. We must hope the Council acts favourably.'

The moor hen dashed the diving beetle on a rock, splitting its shell like a walnut.

'We'll do our best, Terentius,' said Sara, feeling as exposed and vulnerable as the beetle, which waved its legs impotently. 'I know we could've done more training, but you've taught me heaps. I understand my role much better. I know what it means.' She sighed softly. 'And anyway, there's only so much preparation we could do. I think we just have to leave it up to fate now and see what happens.'

'That is a very mature attitude, Sara,' Terentius turned to face her. His starry, midnight eyes shone brightly. 'I want you to know I am proud of you,' he said. 'I have absolute confidence in you.'

'Ha! Do you, now?' Sara laughed and patted the unicorn's shoulder. He glared at her a moment, but could not hold in his own mirth, and musical laughter erupted from deep in his throat. Sara doubled over, holding her stomach as she alternately laughed and gasped for breath. On a whim, she threw her arms around the unicorn's neck. His mane was soft as down and smelled of sunshine and comfort. She buried her face in it and breathed in his scent. 'I'm so glad we met, Terentius,' she said, her voice muffled by the thick mane. 'You've changed my life in so many ways. Thank you.'

He whickered, and the soft affectionate sound made Sara's heart full. She pulled away and reached to put her hand on his nose, staring deep into his soulful eyes.

The unicorn blinked rapidly. 'Uh... you're welcome. Now excuse me, there's something in my eye.' He trotted away, his head turned from her. Sara smiled.

CHAPTER 35

They reached the first outlying homesteads of the great Aes-Sidhe city of Thalanthas mid-morning, and by early afternoon had traded the soft ground for the cobblestoned streets of the lower town. Sara and Senna stared in wonder at the beauty and elegance of the stunning capital.

The modest homes and storefronts of the lower town were crafted from wood, many with arches and beams bent and hewn from living trees. Soft, rounded edges were a popular choice of architecture, and it was rare to spot a sharp angle. Each house included a garden celebrating a full vigorous and various range of plant life; fruits, flowers, vegetables and bushes of all sorts made up a patchwork of verdure against the brown buildings.

A crystalline river wound through the city, so intensely clear, Sara could almost count the scales on the many small trout that skimmed upon its sandy bed. The wide main road took them over small wood and stone bridges, decorated with intricate carvings of ivy and nasturtium all along their length. Weeping willows lined the road between the buildings, long trailing branches bending to brush the ground.

As they reached the city proper, Sara could not help but notice the people coming out of their homes and stores to watch as they passed by. Unfailingly, each person wore an expression of gladness.

'People are happy to see us,' Sara said to Jehn, as they walked side by side. Each time their fingers touched, a thrill jolted in Sara's stomach. Internally, she felt a certain melancholy, knowing this would soon pass, but her heart wanted what it wanted, so she leaned into the experience. *Why not allow myself this small moment of happiness before it's all over?*

'Terentius' arrival is one of great fortune,' said Thorn, grinning. 'He is well-loved by the people of Thalanthas.'

'Do they know him?' said Sara, deadpan but with a teasing sparkle to her eyes.

The unicorn ignored her remark and trotted away, tossing his head so his magnificent mane flew in waves. The beetles had returned throughout the day, in twos and threes until the whole swarm had eventually settled within, and now they sparkled iridescence with every catch of the light.

'Hah!' Sara giggled mercilessly. 'Vain, too!'

Ander roared with laughter. 'Tell the story, Thorn!'

'What story?' said Sara, intrigued.

'A story from my childhood. I'm sure you will enjoy it,' said Thorn, grinning. He ran his fingers through his raven hair. 'Many, many decades past—the Aes-Sidhe are quite long-lived, you know—I was playing in the rose garden near the Council building while my father was in session at Court. King Kirwyn often met with Terentius on matters of state, and so the unicorn was a frequent visitor to Thalanthas in those days.

'Terentius liked to wander the grounds before an audience, and this day was no exception. I was a young boy, and like most boys, was fond of exploring and getting up to mischief. I thought it would be fun to follow Terentius and see if I could sneak up on him.'

'Oh dear, I dread to think where this is going,' said Sara.

Thorn laughed. 'I followed Terentius as he strolled down the narrow path of the rose garden, surreptitiously nibbling a rosebud here or there, and thoroughly enjoying the solitude. He—and me, his silent shadow—meandered down the spiralling path towards the pond at the middle of the garden. The pond was overgrown with a thick covering of lily pads. I remember the pale pink flower spikes were just starting to open. Terentius had paused here, to take in the beautiful surroundings no doubt, and that was when I chose my moment. I sprung out from my hiding place among the roses and smacked Terentius fair on the rump!'

'You didn't!'

'I did! But that's not the worst part. So surprised was Terentius that he shied to one side, caught his hooves on the lip of the pool and toppled over, completely disappearing from view. In seconds, he found his feet and burst out of the pond, but he was covered from tail to ears in mud and lily pads. I will never forget how the pondweed hung in strands from his mane. But the best part? There was a frog on his horn! Terentius shook his head, and the frog plopped back into the pond, swimming away as fast as its froggy legs would take it. I have to say, things were starting to sink in by that stage, and my childish giggling faded.'

'What happened then?'

'Ah well,' said Thorn, 'Terentius is very proud of his glorious mane, and with a public appearance looming, he was beside himself. A fast gallop to the nearest stream for an emergency bath was the least he could do before being seen in such filthy raiment!'

Sara couldn't imagine Terentius looking anything but per-fect, but the thought of him covered in mud was absolutely hilarious. 'So, you're the reason he was such an old codger when I met him.' She burst into gales of laughter.

'You're all the reason,' the unicorn shouted back at them, 'imps and children, every one!'

* * *

Thorn stopped at the gate of a white-washed double-storey building that was crisscrossed with decorative wooden beams. Shuttered windows dotted the second floor, and each sill was covered in an array of colourful flowers. Smoke curled from twin chimneys at either end of the building's roof. The path up to the door was clear of weeds, and had recently been swept of debris. An arrangement of stiff bristled brushes provided a station for cleaning one's boots before entering. Two broad stone steps lead up to a wide, dark redwood door that was inset with four contrasting pine panels. Each panel depicted scenes representing the four seasons. A painted sign swung above the entrance, depicting the silver disc of a full moon. Ornate script announced the place as *The Moon's Fancy*.

'We should take lodging here,' said Thorn, indicating the sign. 'It is a well-respected establishment, with comfortable beds and hot baths. The food is excellent, and the wine is plentiful. It will serve us well after a long trek through the wilderness!'

He made to walk the path, but Sara stopped him. 'Don't you want to stay with your brother, Thorn?'

'I think it's best I remain away for now,' said Thorn. 'I will see Uinnseann at Council.' He nodded at the others, then strode down the path. He wiped his boots on the brush contraption before leaning on the heavy door to enter. With a last backward glance, he disappeared inside.

The aroma of cooking wafted out to reach them, and Ander breathed in deeply. 'Ahh, something smells delicious!' Taking Belina by the hand, he strode down the path and headed within.

Jehn turned to Sara and Senna. 'Thorn has an uneasy relationship with the King. He usually prefers to minimise the disruption his appearance has to the Court. Though this visit is a special one with your Candidacy, Sara.'

'Hang on,' said Sara, 'His brother is the King here? I thought he was a High Counsellor.'

'Uinnseann Elised is both,' said Jehn. 'The Court is separate to the regency of Thalanthas. If you like, we can talk more about it over our dinner. Perhaps Thorn will be more open about his family once he's been in his cups a little while. You can always ask.'

'I'm not sure I should.' Sara turned to the unicorn. 'What about you, Terentius? Is there a… um… stable?'

The unicorn rolled his eyes witheringly. 'Do you think me so lowly to spend my evening amid the straw and filth with the livestock?'

Sara's hands flew to her mouth in embarrassment. 'Oh gods, no, I'm sorry!'

'I have my own quarters within the Court grounds. I will retire there for the evening after I see about making arrangements for an audience with the Council. I will send the hummingcat for you in the morning.'

He began to trot up the road, but Sara ran after him. 'Wait!

267

Shouldn't I stay with you?'

'Do you want to?' the unicorn asked. 'I had thought you might like to spend some time with your new friends. Perhaps one in particular,' he finished, speaking softly so that the others could not hear.

'Oh, well, um,' Sara stammered, and gave a quick nod. 'Yes. That would be nice.'

The unicorn smiled. 'Then the matter is settled. I shall see you again in the morning. Have a pleasant evening.'

Sara re-joined Jehn and Senna, and they marched down the path, keen to join their friends inside and fill their bellies with food that did not consist solely of trail rations or fruit. Jehn held the door open as Sara passed over the threshold. Feeling uncharacteristically bold, she grinned back and said, formally, 'Why, thank you, kind sir!' Jehn laughed and swept his arm across in a low bow.

The tavern interior was as elegant and fine as the rest of the town suggested, but still retained a comfortable and welcoming ambiance. The walls bore exquisite tapestries and artworks depicting fine figures, many of whom were posed with musical instruments. The spacious room was filled with people of all sorts, joined in friendly conversation and banter. Food and drink flowed freely, and yet all were well-behaved and seemed to be having a wonderful time. A pile of flaming logs crackled in the fireplace, fine tendrils of smoke exuding a delicate, sweet fragrance. In one corner, a group of youths were in healthy competition over a game of darts, throwing the tiny feathered bolts at an intricate wooden target, and laughing happily as they made (or failed to make) each shot.

Ander stood at the far end of a long trestle table. It was impossible to miss him. The big man waved enthusiastically.

'Friends!' he shouted, 'over here! We saved you a seat!' The trio wended their way through the thronging crowd of people and chairs until they reached their companions. 'Sit, sit! I'll get us more drinks!'

'And something to eat, too, please,' said Jehn. He pulled out a chair and offered Sara a seat. She sat down, trying not to blush as Thorn watched on, his mouth pulled up on one side with a knowing smirk. Jehn took a seat beside her, and Senna the next one over, settling in beside Ander's empty chair.

'Terentius has gone ahead to his own place,' said Sara. 'He said he'll meet us tomorrow. Honeysuckle will let us know when he's ready. Actually, where is Honeysuckle?'

'She's fine,' said Jehn. 'Once we were all back together, she disappeared into the Stitch. Cat business!' He fingered the leather thong at his throat, glad to be reunited with the precious whisker bottle.

Ander returned with a tray, effortlessly carrying it above the heads of the other patrons, despite it being overladen with pitchers of beer and bottles of wine. He placed the tray on the table. 'Food is on the way.' He grabbed a pitcher of beer and didn't even bother to pour a glass, but instead drank straight from the jug.

Belina shook her head. 'Ander, please mind your manners.'

Ander wiped his frothy mouth on his arm, 'Sorry. I was hoping you wouldn't notice.'

'I may be blind, but I know you. Use a glass.'

Everyone shared an amused glance as Ander sheepishly poured his beer as neatly as possible.

'Sara, would you like some wine?' said Belina, holding up a crystal decanter.

'Oh yes, please,' said Sara, 'Can I give you a hand?'

'No need.' Belina deftly poured first one glass, then another, and another, to the perfect amount without spilling a drop.

'That's amazing! How can you do that when you can't see?'

Jehn nudged Sara, trying to silently note her insensitivity.

'Oh Jehn, it's perfectly all right,' Belina said, sensing the scholar's subtle motion. 'I can see, in a way,' she went on, wonderment colouring her voice. 'I had hoped my other senses would improve, but they have heightened beyond my wildest hopes. An effect of your powers, Terentius explained. Did he not tell you?'

'No, he didn't.' Sara thought back to that moment in the forest where she had wished so hard, hoping against all odds that the unicorn could bring back Belina's sight. *I should be careful. These powers are strong and unpredictable.* She made a mental note to talk to Terentius about how this might help during the Trial.

'You have my eternal gratitude, Sara,' said Belina, raising her glass.

'Hear hear!' said Ander. 'To your health, Sara! May your time in Palantia be long and prosperous!' The others lifted their drinks and toasted. Sara smiled awkwardly, her eyes flicking to Jehn. He pressed his lips together. They had chosen not to share Sara's revelation about the role of the Dreamer being a death sentence for their budding relationship. Sara drained her wine glass, and took the carafe, pouring the red fluid right to the brim.

The food arrived then, and Sara dove straight in, suddenly starving. The meal was spent in relative silence, except for satisfied sounds and the clinking of cutlery.

The evening continued in a pleasant fashion with Ander and Thorn sharing increasingly grandiose stories of their adventures. Belina chimed in here and there with a correction to Ander's recollections.

'This has been an amazing adventure,' said Senna, 'But I admit I am eager to return to the Grove, and to Meryn. I feel a longing to get back to my old routine.'

'Homesickness,' said Ander, 'I don't really get that anymore. Belina is my home, and as long as we're together, that's all we need.'

'Relationship goals,' said Sara.

Senna cocked his head in confusion. 'What's that, Sara?'

'Oh, nothing,' she said, shrugging, 'It's just a saying from my world. Used for when a couple seems to have it all worked out. Something you might aspire to if you were in a relationship.'

'That's interesting. I like it! I'll have to tell Meryn when I get home. I'm sure she'll find it amusing, especially if she ever gets to meet Ander.'

'Hey!' the big man pouted, but it was all in jest, and they all laughed together. 'At any rate,' said Ander, 'I'm a great house guest, and Belina and I would love to meet your sweetheart, Senna.'

Senna grinned. 'I'll hold you to that, Ander.'

The night went on. Jehn talked a little about his studies into the Dreamer histories, and while Sara found this interesting, she was distracted often when his hand brushed hers. They stole small secret looks as the evening drew on, and Ander and Thorn's tales became more and more unbelievable.

Eventually Thorn stood, swaying a little, and bade them a temporary farewell as he went to mingle with the youths still playing their target game on the other side of the tavern.

Sara watched his interactions with interest. Thorn's arrival was well-received by the young men, as were his casual flirtations—a hand touching an arm here, a whisper in an ear there. 'Uh, Jehn,' she said, leaning over and speaking in a low voice, 'is that why Thorn and his brother don't get along?'

Jehn was very confused. 'What do you mean?' he said, his brow crinkling in puzzlement.

Sara gestured at Thorn and the youths. 'That. He likes men?'

'What would that have to do with anything?' Jehn was utterly befuddled. Sara blushed, realisation dawning that she was making a fool of herself. *Oh gods, why. Why do I say these things!*

'Not everyone agrees with that where I'm from,' she said. *If the floor opened up and swallowed me now, that would be a good thing.* She gulped at the thought. *I don't mean that literally, Dreamer powers!*

'Truly? How very strange!' said Jehn, his curiosity piqued. 'What a mystifying world you must live in where people agree or disagree over who is attracted to whom. This is quite fascinating, Sara. Is it part of your culture? Is there a law? Who decides this?'

Sara shook her head, not sure what to say.

'In any case,' Belina interjected, saving Sara from further embarrassment, 'Thorn's issues with his brother do not relate to any personal situation, but rather the matter of familial hierarchy. Thorn is the eldest, and therefore should be King by hereditary rank, but he declined that role in favour of a life on the road. He always had a wanderer's spirit. King Kirwyn was a doting and lenient father who encouraged his sons to live the lives they chose. Thorn's younger brother, Uinnseann, was always more interested in history, politics, and building the Aes-Sidhe community, so he took up the mantle when King Kirwyn passed away. The people of Thalanthas love and respect Uinnseann, and he is a just and kind ruler, like his father. But whenever Thorn returns to the Great City, the people remember that their King is not the true heir, and it raises old tensions again.'

'Well, that makes more sense,' said Sara, still inwardly cringing at her social *faux pas*. 'Thorn doesn't strike me as the kind of person who would enjoy sitting in state all day long and dealing with all the troubles of running a city, especially not one of this size!'

'Right you are,' said Thorn, grinning as he returned to the table and poured himself another glass of wine. 'A life of adventure and freedom is what I dream of. My brother is welcome to the fine particulars of government and politics. I wish him all the best!' Ander raised his glass and yelled another 'hear hear', happy for another excuse to toast, whatever the celebration.

They continued their merriment long into the night. Perhaps due to having many wines under her belt, Sara felt an urge to voice her feelings. She stood up, and without warning or preamble, opened her mouth and began to sing. It wasn't a tune she knew or had heard before; the music simply burst forth from within. All of Sara's tumultuous emotions culminated into a melancholy, almost painful strain. The minor notes lifted and fell like a bird on the wing; the song was yearning, sadness, resolution. Sara let it flow, unimpeded:

Let blessed sleep consume me now,
My tired limbs concede.
This soul to rest, this mind to ease,
Oh, into dreams I flee.
The heart which bleeds, beats slowing down.
The tears dry on my cheek.

273

My thoughts fly free upon the night,
To search for whom I seek.
Sleep comes slow to those who Dream,
Whose thoughts are wrought with what might be.
And thus, I sing this mournful theme,
A Dream be but another dream.
I roam the night, and see you now,
Within your dreams, I creep.
With dawning sun, the memory fades,
And I return to weep.
Our love is past, gone by my vow,
To stand between the Trees.
I yearn to touch your hand once more,
Oh, someone save me please.
Sleep comes slow to those who Dream,
Whose thoughts are wrought with what might be.
And thus I sing this mournful theme,
A Dream be but another dream.

As the final lyric faded away, there was a brief pause where the entire room was utterly still, eyes riveted on the singer. Not a sound broke the silence until Ander leapt up, clapping enthusiastically. The whole tavern filled with applause, patrons rising in a standing ovation. Sara slumped back in her seat, unsure what had come over her.

'Sara! That was incredible!' said Thorn. 'What a voice!'

Sara smiled weakly, mumbling a thank you. Ander poured her another glass of wine. She took it, but did not drink, instead frowning and shifting around in her seat. She could not bear to look at Jehn. He would have known. There's no way he couldn't. *What am I doing?*

She rubbed her face and tossed back the wine, concentrating

on the burn as it slid down her throat. She glanced at Belina. The woman sat tense and upright, her head cocked to the side as if straining to hear something beyond the sounds of the crowd. A rush of shame ran through Sara, and she pushed away from the table, darting into the throng of tavern patrons.

'Sara! Where are you going?' said Jehn, his voice coloured with concern. She shook her head, tears threatening, and fled from view.

No one noticed a shadow detach from the darkest corner and melt away.

CHAPTER 36

The Sluagh slipped down the cobblestone street, unseen by the few people still outside at this late hour. Its face was set with a malevolent smirk and it rubbed its hands together as it melded from shadow to shadow.

Despite its few setbacks, the Sluagh was pleased. Tonight had given the opportunity to observe its prey, and what it had learned was useful indeed. *Uncertainty, insecurity, sadness. A desire to flee her destiny. All feelings I can take advantage of.*

The Sluagh passed a white cat sitting by a house's gate. The cat met the Sluagh's gaze and hissed, the hackles rising on the animal's back. The Sluagh hissed back, sending the cat fleeing down the path to its home. *Cats. Pah! Even the non-magical ones are pests.*

The Sluagh entered the home of Uinnseann Elised by its secret doorway, melting into the stone and emerging within the cellar below. It stood at the small window, gazing at the street and the smattering of stars just visible in the distant sky.

They will want the Trial to take place tomorrow. The unicorn will insist. But the Candidate is so unsure of herself, her confidence so tenuous. That insecurity will aid my plan. And at any rate, the Sluagh licked its lips, sucking air through its sharp teeth, *the essence tastes better with fear. Stronger too. All that self-preservation, all that concern, wrapped up into a delicious sup of power. Ah.* The creature smiled unpleasantly. *And then, when the Trial goes ahead, I will be there to harvest.*

* * *

Well before the rising of the sun, while the Great City of Thalanthas still slept, its citizens tucked up and dreaming in their beds, the Sluagh crept into Uinnseann's chamber. The creature leaned over the sleeping Aes-Sidhe. 'King,' it said, the word shivering with a discomfiting sibilance.

Uinnseann sat bolt upright in his bed, eyes darting with fear as his gaze landed on the shrouded figure at his bedside.

The creature's viridian eyes flashed, and a pulse of cold terror shot down the King's spine. 'She is here,' the Sluagh said. 'The unicorn will want the Trial to proceed as soon as possible.'

The King wiped the sweat from his face with the back of one hand, rubbing it dry with the bedclothes. 'Terentius Aodhfin has requested an audience with the Council for the morning,' he said. 'Should I decline?'

'No. Take the audience.'

The King's brow furrowed in confusion. 'But won't that risk revealing your presence? My brother is here also. If he speaks to the Council as well...'

'It is no matter. All they have are suspicions. None but you have seen me,' the Sluagh's tone grew deep and menacing. 'And if you were to tell them... well, no one will believe you. No evidence, no proof. You've been acting strangely, of late.

277

The King is tired, they will say. He is not in his right mind. Under so much pressure. Not as young as he once was. Not as worthy as his brother.'

The Sluagh's wheedling sing-song voice penetrated deep into Uinnseann's psyche, its words like arrows hitting their target. Uinnseann found himself nodding in agreement, his hands slick with sweat.

'Agree for the Trial to go ahead.'

'But...' the King's eyes blinked rapidly. 'Won't that unlock her full power?'

The Sluagh laughed softly. 'Oh yes! Oh yes, indeed. The Dreamer will reach her full potential. And who will be there to wrest that power from her while she is at her most vulnerable? Why, none other than I!' The Sluagh's mouth stretched into a triumphant grin, its yellowed teeth gleaming dully in the pre-dawn light.

Uinnseann recoiled at the malevolence in that grim smile, but the creature ignored the King, continuing its declamation as if he were not there at all.

'Yes, yes! I will take her power and make it my own,' the Sluagh said, eyes no longer focused on its terrified audience, instead looking to a future only it could see, 'Such power I shall possess! With control over the old Dreamer and the new, none will be my equal. None will possess the force to stop me!' The creature's cackling laugh assaulted the near-maddened King, and his eyes flew about the room, desperate to escape.

The Sluagh's voice reached a shrill pitch. 'The world will be mine. No longer will I need to slink and slither in the cellars of pitiable filth such as you!' The Sluagh drew its face close to Uinnseann's, and he felt its hot breath upon his cheek. He gulped and tried not to breathe in the foetid smell.

The creature drew a long nasal breath, and laughed low and guttural. 'I smell your fear, little King. It is hot and thick like an arterial clot. Perhaps a taste is in order. To celebrate!'

The Sluagh made a twisted gesture with one hand. Uinnseann drew back in horror, pulling the bed covers with him as he scrambled away from the dark creature. The Sluagh let out a wicked laugh and disappeared with a flickering of shadow, leaving the King gasping and sobbing at the far corner of the bed.

CHAPTER 37

Sara was Dreaming. She hadn't meant to, but the combination of alcohol and high emotions created a fertile ground within Sara's already full and turbulent mind. Once her head hit the pillow, Sara's imagination broke loose.

She sat on the sill of a large, round window in the tower of a tall building—a castle, it seemed, from the stone walls and floor—looking out upon a long, clear lake that mirrored the sky. Willows surrounded the lake, their slender branches kissing the water. A pair of white swans sent vee-shaped ripples in their wake as they paddled by. Near the shore, a tall stilted white crane with black wing tips took flight to swirl in the air. A second crane joined the first, and the pair twisted in an elaborate choreography. Sara watched as sparkling blue mist coalesced around the dancing birds, forming into the shape of a beautiful grey horse. The horse galloped upon the air among the cranes. Sara's heart pulled tightly at the inexplicable symphony of movement.

The dance continued, intensifying, and further shapes formed. Other animals joined the frenzy of activity, swirling amongst the mist. Sara tore her gaze away from the window, and looking down, saw a young woman seated on the floor below her. The girl sat upon a thick woven carpet that was stitched with silver and gold stars. It was almost like she sat within a galaxy.

The girl was slowly brushing her long, lustrous hair, her face hidden by the frame of golden tresses. Sara put the girl's age at mid-teens, perhaps seventeen at the oldest.

The girl spoke in a singsong voice. 'Love is the essence of all things.'

Sara tried to turn away, but the movement was slow and sticky like wading in honey. The girl drew the brush through her hair several more times, before carefully placing it upon the thick embroidered rug. She hummed a few notes in a running scale, then took up a thin stick, swirling it on a palette which held a soft but pliable material. Sara frowned, confused. The substance looked like fondant. The girl sang a clear note, and the colours of the palette changed, flickering with each part of the girl's magical song.

Finally, Sara found her voice. 'What are you doing?'

The girl stopped her ministrations and met Sara's gaze, her golden hair falling away to reveal her face. The girl's face held a wisdom far beyond her apparent years. She reached out to touch Sara's hand. 'I am forming worlds. Let me show you how.'

* * *

Sara woke with a start. She lay still, the blankets heavy and overly warm. She calmed her breath and tried to ignore her parched throat and throbbing temples. She glanced around the shared quarters, seeking the water pitcher she'd noticed the night before, when she'd stumbled in and hidden beneath the bed clothes, embarrassed and shaken. She pulled back the blankets now, quietly, not wanting to disturb her companions.

The first grey streaks of dawn were chasing away the darkness, and she could just make out the shapes of the furniture, and her friends, still sleeping peacefully in their beds. Except for one. She scanned the room, but the Aes-Sidhe was nowhere to be seen. She felt a nervous flutter in the pit of her stomach, and rose in silence, slipping on her shoes in the gloom. She crept across the room, past the water pitcher on the small table, freezing as she stepped on a creaky floorboard. No one stirred, however, so Sara eased her way out the door and made her way down the stairs. She paused at the landing.

Thorn sat in front of the fire, stoking the coals with a poker. Another man sat beside him, raven-haired like Thorn, but without his silver-shot strands. The strange man wore a sleeping robe, and his face was so pale as to be almost translucent. Dark circles smudged the hollows of the stranger's eyes, and he fidgeted and picked at his clothing, fingers shaking as he did so. Thorn laid a hand over the other man's, and spoke to him in low, reassuring tones. Sara couldn't make out what he was saying, but the other man nodded, his cheeks wet with tears. Without making a sound, she turned and crept back up the stairs.

* * *

Jehn was sitting at the small table in the living area, idly tracing a water stain with his finger, when Sara returned to the room. She met the scholar's questioning gaze and hastened over, whispering what she'd witnessed.

'The man you describe sounds like Thorn's brother, the King,' said Jehn, 'But why would he be here under such clandestine circumstances?'

'I don't know,' said Sara. 'It's very strange. Do you think Terry has spoken with the Court already?'

Jehn's expression softened. 'You really shouldn't call him that, Sara. Terentius takes true names very seriously. But no,' he continued, 'I don't think there has yet been time for that. Terentius promised us he would send the hummingcat, and it is not yet dawn. This is something else. Thorn will reveal the matter to us if it requires our involvement. It may be a family matter.'

'It looked pretty serious to me,' said Sara. 'Maybe we should—'

They heard the creak of the doorknob turning. Thorn slipped through the doorway. 'Ah, you're already up,' he said. 'Let's wake the others and go downstairs. I've ordered us some breakfast.'

Jehn and Sara shared a glance, but did not comment, going instead to rouse their friends. Ander protested fiercely when Jehn opened the curtains, letting the morning sun stream across the big man's face. He threw his arm across his eyes and moaned. 'I'm sorry,' said Jehn, suppressing a smile, glad that his own head was clear, 'but breakfast will help nurse your hangover.'

There was no time for Sara to share her suspicions, and so once up and dressed, the party followed Thorn down to the main room, where a delicious array of morning meal foodstuffs awaited. They dug in, pulling apart fresh warm bread and smothering it with creamy butter, and pouring frothy milk on full bowls of fruit and cereal. There was a vat of steaming porridge, and a thick, dark brew which reminded Sara very much of black coffee. She had two cups, with dollops of cream to cut the bitterness.

'I had a visit from my brother this morning,' said Thorn, after finishing his plate. 'He told me something very concerning.' Sara caught Jehn's eye and raised an eyebrow. The Aes-Sidhe continued. 'Once you have all finished eating, you should meet Terentius straight away. Don't wait for his call; instead, make haste to the Council chambers.'

He stood up, brushing crumbs from his lap. 'I will go on ahead now and see you shortly.' He left the table and headed out the tavern door, fingering the pommel of his sword as he passed outside.

'What could be the matter?' said Senna, sipping at his glass of apple juice and eating the last few bites of his porridge.

Sara told the others what she had told Jehn, how she had witnessed part of the meeting between the two brothers, but could not overhear their conversation. 'The King looked exhausted,' she said. 'Maybe he's sick.'

'I don't know,' said Senna, 'the Aes-Sidhe are extremely robust of constitution, and at any rate, I should think Thorn would tell us. He said the King had conveyed something concerning to him. That doesn't sound like a personal illness. It sounds much more serious.'

'I agree,' said Belina, her milky eyes moving back and forth between the speakers, 'Thorn is not one to react so without good reason. For him to go against Terentius' instructions suggests a matter of some seriousness. Perhaps it relates to the Dreamer. Another attack, maybe?'

'That seems possible,' said Jehn thoughtfully, 'Or a development from the Grove that we are yet to hear. The Dreamer may be closer to Awakening than we first thought.'

'Whatever it is, we should finish up here,' said Sara, her stomach fluttering at the prospect of facing the Trial. She plucked up a final piece of toast. 'It's going to be a big day.' She eyed Jehn, nervously.

He gave a reassuring smile and stood up, neatly pushing in his chair. 'You will be fine, Sara,' he said, 'I believe in you. We all do.'

'That's part of the problem,' Sara muttered under her breath.

Ander grabbed one last pastry from the platter, and then they all filed out the door into the early morning air.

* * *

The hummingcat sat atop a stone wall next to the gate of the Council grounds as the companions arrived. The little creature was still as a statue, but for the hypnotic swishing of her tail. She greeted them with a lilting run of notes, rising at the end as if a question. The gate swung open and Terentius trotted down the wide path, Thorn at his side. Their expressions were grave.

'What's going on?' said Sara, running up. Jehn swept the hummingcat into his arms, and he and the rest of the party joined their friends.

'Not here,' said the Aes-Sidhe. He led them at a brisk pace through the gate and down a side path lined with a spiky hedgerow bright with ruby red berries. They followed his direction and trailed along in silence. Soon they passed into a wide grassed lawn. The blades were trimmed to perfection, forming a lush cushion beneath their feet.

'We can talk freely here,' he said.

'Really?' said Sara, in disbelief. 'We are right out in the open!'

'Exactly, Sara,' said Terentius, 'there is no place for a spy to hide that would put him near enough to hear us.'

'All right, I see,' she said, 'Well, will you tell us what's the matter?'

'I will allow Anwyl Orinthorn to explain,' the unicorn said, gesturing for the Aes-Sidhe to speak.

Thorn ran his fingers through his silver shot hair, pulling loose the band that held his ponytail. He smoothed back the strands and deftly re-tied his hair. 'I apologise for the secrecy. Its necessity will soon become clear.'

The Aes-Sidhe explained how his brother had arrived in a panic at the tavern in the early hours of that morning, waking the establishment's poor proprietor before even the hint of the dawn. Uinnseann Elised had struggled to speak while Thorn waited, patient despite his concern at the King's sudden arrival at such a strange time. 'I was struck by his appearance. He was oddly *thin*—not as if he had lost weight, but rather as if his very essence was diminished, as if he was only halfway in this world. It was an alarming thing to see one's brother in such a state.' Thorn closed his eyes for a long moment. When he opened them again, they shone with tears. 'He could not put words together, and instead uttered nothing more than animalistic moans. My heart broke for him.'

Jehn reached for his friend, putting his arm around the Aes-Sidhe. 'That must have been terrible, Thorn. I'm so sorry.'

Thorn nodded, 'Thank you, *mo chara*. I tried my best to calm him, but as you can imagine, it took some time before he could gather himself enough to string a sentence together. When he finally did, the words tumbled out in a flurry. My brother wept as he told me what had happened to him these past months. He has been a prisoner.'

The companions burst into a mess of questions and exclamations. 'A prisoner? Where? How!' Ander fingered the brace of blades across his chest menacingly. 'Who do I need to have words with?'

'Please, calm yourselves,' said Terentius, his sombre tone low and soothing. 'Orinthorn will explain.'

'A creature,' said Thorn, breaking away from Jehn and pacing back and forth across the soft grass. 'He called it the Caccinae, though I don't know of such a thing, nor does Terentius. My brother described it as an Unseelie manipulator—the creature tortured him with its mental incursions, beating down his confidence and will until he felt he was nothing. I can barely imagine it. My brother is—was—a force to be reckoned with. None matched him at the game of diplomacy. To see him brought so low...'

'It seems,' said Terentius, tossing his mane, 'that this creature—whatever it may be—preys on those tiny insecurities that all people have. Uinnseann Elised described it as constantly whispering at him, taunting and teasing until his mental defences chipped apart and fell away.'

Sara frowned. 'That's... unpleasant. Terrifying, actually. So now we have two creatures to deal with. The Sluagh and this Caccinae thing. Great. As if this wasn't going to be trouble enough.'

'Unless it's one and the same,' said Jehn, rubbing his chin, thoughtfully, 'Attacking the Dreamer, manipulating my imagination, maybe even sending that void moth... Whatever has held Uinnseann Elised thrall—it's not a stretch to consider one fae doing all these things. It has proved already to be a formidable enemy.'

'I believe you are right, *mo chara*,' said Thorn. 'From what my brother told me, this creature's attacks started small, almost unnoticeable at first. He believes it started with a simple seed sown. He can recall how one day, he became uneasy at the laughter of someone walking by. He said he felt a sinking sensation in the pit of his stomach, and he was certain they were laughing at him. This small paranoia persisted, until, little by little, it overcame him. He found himself unable to trust his fellow counsellors, or any of his staff and advisers. For a long while, he did not realise he was being manipulated.'

'How horrible,' said Sara, 'I can see how effective that could be, especially if the King is anything like me and always worrying about what people are thinking...' She trailed off, embarrassed to reveal herself so.

Terentius smiled kindly. 'Please don't be ashamed, Sara. That feeling is normal. We all care what others think of us. Even I.'

'I get that this thing was manipulating your brother, Thorn,' said Ander, 'but I don't see how no one noticed!'

'The creature kept its ministrations to itself for some time,' said Terentius, 'I expect that Uinnseann's behaviour changes were gradual to those around him. Inexorably, the creature eroded the King's self-belief such that he became crippled by insecurity. Once it revealed itself to him, the thrall was complete.'

The group listened in horror as Thorn continued. 'My brother felt there was no escape. His councillors knew something was wrong, but struggled to help—especially when my brother's insecurities lead to... aggressive, out of character, conduct. Internally, he was ashamed, but the

Caccinae—Sluagh, whatever it is—continued to play on that feeling, used it to drive a further wedge and keep him isolated.'

'Classic abuser,' muttered Sara. 'This thing needs to be stopped.'

'Indeed, Sara,' said Thorn. 'Last night, the creature came to my brother in his bedchamber, gloating and boasting about its plans to steal the new Dreamer's powers. It revealed its plan to wield this stolen power and become an unstoppable evil.'

'Then that seals it,' said Sara, 'it's the same thing. The Sluagh.'

Terentius nodded. 'We are forewarned now. Some small part of Uinnsean's soul rallied after his fear subsided, and a semblance of his former self returned. His love of Palantia and its people would not let this happen without his intervention, however small that may be.'

Uinnseann had fled to the inn and begged Thorn to ensure the Trial of the Dreamer not go ahead, explaining this would be where the creature would strike. Thorn assured his brother he would notify Terentius and the others before their audience, so that they may advise the Council of the true extent of the threat.

'I sent him on to stay at his Court offices,' said Thorn. 'At least there, he will not be alone and isolated at his home, where the creature rather may appear and discover the truth.'

'Anwyl Orinthorn and I conferred on the matter this morning, and we have agreed,' said Terentius. 'We shall defer the Trial until the Sluagh threat is neutralised. Once we have completed our audience with the Council, I suggest we return here to discuss a plan of attack. The creature is clever and sly, and its ability to manipulate the Stitch will make it difficult to trap.' He turned to Sara. 'I will go over this more after the meeting, but I'm afraid you will need to play the role of bait.'

Sara scrunched up her face. 'Gee, what could possibly go wrong?' She looked to Jehn, hoping he would protest, but the scholar just gave a narrow smile and shrugged his shoulders, deferring to the unicorn.

'I have a bad feeling about this,' said Ander, his usual merry tone now turned serious, 'We don't know enough about this Sluagh thing. As Jehn said, it seems pretty formidable. And it can move through the Stitch. It could be anywhere, at any time. We should be prepared, just in case.'

'I understand your concern, Ander,' said Thorn, 'But the Sluagh is unlikely to attack in the middle of the Court with the entire Council, and all of us there. The meeting shouldn't take long, and we will soon after have the full resources of the Council to assist us. The Aes-Sidhe will rally its guard—magical and military—and we will capture this rogue fae and bring it to justice.'

Ander frowned and shook his head. 'Look, Thorn, I get that there is protocol and all that, special processes and steps to follow with this whole politics thing, but surely you can see the risk here. It's not like you to go in unprepared.'

Terentius shuffled his hooves impatiently. 'Everything we know about the creature's mode of attack points to stealth and patience. It is cunning and intelligent. It will not be hasty.'

Sara sighed. *I have to trust he knows what he's doing.* 'All right,' she said, 'We'll make our plans after. Ander, you'll be with me. Belina, you too. I'm sure I'll be fine.' Sara felt a cold spot flare in her gut at those words, but she pushed the feeling away.

Ander shook his head again. 'We hardly know anything, Terry! We are just guessing! I don't get this at all.' His voice rose and his ears grew red. 'Did that moth thing addle your senses?' Belina touched his arm, whispering something in his ear that Sara could not hear.

'Someone comes,' said Senna, pointing at a young man dressed in blue and purple robes who was hurrying towards them over the grass.

The young man huffed, trying to catch his breath. 'Honoured guests, Court will be in session in a few minutes. If you wish to make a petition, please follow me immediately.' He waited a few seconds, drawing in a handful of ragged breaths, and then turned on his heel and sped away. Glancing around at each other, Sara, the unicorn and the rest of the party followed briskly after.

* * *

The Court officer took them into a waiting area, saying they would be called shortly. He left through an archway to the left.

Sara looked at her surroundings. She and her friends sat on marble benches in a stunning open-air courtyard with a tiered stone fountain in the centre. Water burst in a shower of sparkles from the spout at the top and cascaded down into a series of basins, each overflowing into the next. The effect was calming and peaceful. Exotic tropical plants filled the courtyard: prehistoric-looking bromeliads, delicate lilies and hibiscus in a profusion of vivid colours. The air was fresh and cool thanks to the abundance of plant life; Sara breathed deeply of its richness.

The tinkling chime of bells rang out above the trickling of the fountain, and a set of double doors in the far wall swung open. A different Court officer entered, bowed, and gestured for them to follow.

The officer stood at stiff attention and proclaimed, 'Protocol dictates one petitioner may speak per audience. Whom shall address the Council?'

'I,' said the unicorn, equally formal, 'Terentius Aodhfin, wish to address the Council on a matter most grave.'

Ander rolled his eyes at the pomp and circumstance, and Belina lightly punched his arm in response.

'Very well,' said the officer, who thankfully had not noticed. 'Your associates may accompany you into the chamber, but they are to remain in the gallery. Please enter now.'

Sara met Jehn's eye, and he shuffled closer, his hand grazing hers as they filed into a large antechamber, with the unicorn in the lead. The circular room was decorated with just a few urns and potted plants. A second set of double doors on the far side opened inward and the clerk stood to one side, allowing the party to pass through.

The Court chamber was imposing and intimidating despite the smooth curvature of the Council table, and the pleasing natural elements that formed the structure of the room: ivy and trailing creepers rambled over the walls, and wisteria in full flower dangled from the rafters, wafting its sweet fragrance on the air. Terentius parted from the group and entered the centre of the circular table, stepping atop the raised dais without hesitation, his hooves clacking on the stone surface.

The clerk ushered the rest of their group into the gallery lined with wooden pews, each with plump velvet cushions trimmed in gold rope. Besides themselves, the benches were empty, which Sara thought rather strange. 'Where—'

'Please take your seats,' said the clerk, officiously, 'and

remain quiet through the proceedings unless addressed by the Court.'

Sara's mouth snapped shut. She lowered her chin and stared at the floor. Jehn settled beside her, with Ander and Belina on her left. Senna hastily filed in next to Jehn and the party sat in silence.

The deep tone of a gong rang out, and Sara glanced to the ceiling, noticing a large golden disc suspended above. The padded mallet was connected to a rope that disappeared into the eaves; Sara was not sure if it was automated, or if some poor soul was up there in the rafters. The sound made her heart flutter.

Across from the dais, another set of double doors opened, and in marched two pairs of guards, who took up station on either side of the doorway. Then came the Counsellors, one at a time, dressed in their finest clothes, faces serious. At last, came the High Counsellor. *Thorn's brother*, thought Sara. *Thorn was right, he looks strange, like he's partway between life and death.* She looked away, disturbed and uncomfortable. The guards bowed stiffly and marched out again, closing the door behind them.

Terentius swung around on the dais, pivoting to meet the gaze of the Counsellors as they settled into their seats. Each nodded graciously at the unicorn. The same gladness of the townsfolk was reflected in the faces here. Finally, Terentius turned to the High Counsellor, ruler of the Great City of Thalanthas, King Uinnseann Elised. The unicorn bowed his head, bending his front legs so low that his spiralled horn nearly scraped the floor, 'Your Grace and Honour,' he said, 'Noble members of the Court and Council, my heartfelt gratitude for allowing me this audience.'

The King raised his hand, palm up. 'At ease and good greetings, Terentius Aodhfin. We welcome you to our fair city. You honour us all. It has been too long.'

'Indeed it has, Your Honour, Counsellors,' said the unicorn. He raised his chin and stared hard at each of them. 'And now I must request we refrain from any further courtesies and get right to the matter at hand.' Without waiting, the unicorn forged ahead, 'The source of the Dreamer's malady has been discovered, and it seems that it is one of our very own. A fae. Corrupted. Unseelie.'

Gasps and cries of disbelief rang out. The King rapped his gavel on the sounding block, the harsh sound echoing around the large chamber. 'Order, order! Explain your words, sir Terentius. What do you mean by this?' *He plays his part,* thought Sara, *despite knowing this creature could be anywhere—perhaps even in this room.* Sara tensed, and Jehn squeezed her hand, offering silent reassurance.

'I have come, with my friends here in the gallery,' said the unicorn, his voice low and urgent, 'from the Dreamer's Grove, through the unpredictable 'Shadowing… some of us even through the Stitch itself. We have travelled to plead the Council for immediate action.' All eyes turned to the gallery, and upon seeing Thorn, a babbling of whispering chatter began. Thorn sighed and crossed his arms.

Terentius coughed, loudly and pointedly. 'Through our own experiences,' he said sternly, 'We have come to the strong belief that a rogue Sluagh is the cause of the many troublesome and downright dangerous circumstances happening across Palantia.'

One of the Counsellors, a white-haired man far older than any of his fellows, interrupted, shaking his head. 'No, no, no.

You have it askew. Sluagh are dark fae, that's correct, but they are harmless. They play an integral part in sustaining the Dreamer. To do harm to one such as she would be antithesis to their race. You must be mistaken.'

'I am not,' said Terentius, as he turned his head to glare at the man, 'And it is a sad state of affairs, Einion Abhainn, that you should doubt the veracity of my words.' The white-haired Counsellor snapped his mouth shut and stared down at the table without saying anything further. It was clear to Sara that Terentius was held in extremely high regard here in Thalanthas. She longed to ask Jehn about the unicorn's history, as the scholar would surely know, but feared the reprisal of being caught whispering during this important audience.

'As I was saying,' the unicorn continued, sweeping his gaze across the faces before him, 'We believe this rogue Sluagh is siphoning off the Dreamer's essence, causing the paroxysms witnessed by attendants and scholars alike.' He glanced to the gallery, and nodded at Jehn and Senna. 'My friends here can attest, and we have seen other disturbing examples that point to Sluagh interference. The creature collects power, and what it chooses to do with that power is something we would not have come to pass.'

'Could this Unseelie Sluagh be among us now?' The tremulous voice belonged to Silvana Verdantine. She remained nonplussed from the King's outburst the previous session. Her hands shook slightly as she lifted a crystal glass of clear wine to her lips. She was careful to avoid looking in Uinnseann's direction as she waited for the unicorn to respond.

Instead, the King himself stood slowly to his feet. The susurration of cloth against furniture belied the tension that instantly ran through the chamber, with Counsellors shifting uncomfortable and casting furtive glances at each other. Uinnseann took a long, deep breath, and sighed heavily. 'I do not think so, Silvana,' he said, softly, his eyes downcast with regret, 'But Terentius Aodhfin speaks words of truth about this dark fae.' He leaned upon the table, and his knuckles whitened. 'The creature has been here, in these very chambers, within these walls.'

Silvana gasped. 'What? How do you know this?'

'I have seen it.'

'No, your Honour,' said Silvana, 'it cannot be!'

The King's calm composure faltered. Uinnseann banged his hands on the table, and Silvana flinched, cringing back in her chair. 'It comes to me in the night,' said the King, his voice rising, 'Whispers lies in my ear... or half-truths. I cannot tell the difference. So cruel, it is. So sly...' He tapered off, muttering as the paranoia rose to overwhelm him. The Sluagh's hold over the King was still strong; despite his valiant efforts to remain in control, his confidence had begun to fray.

The Council members whispered to each other, staring at the King as he wrung his hands, blinking frenetically as if trying to clear his vision. 'Your Honour,' said Terentius, sharply, commanding the other's attention and snapping him out of his strange trance.

The King dropped his hands and sat down heavily. He blinked a few more times, and then, taking a long, deep breath, raised his gaze to the unicorn. His expression was calm once more, and when he spoke, his voice was clear and strong, 'I apologise, honoured Counsellors and guests. I have not been well, as you are no doubt aware. Please, sir Terentius, tell us what you need from the Council.'

The rumblings and whispers stilled, and the unicorn began.

'Before I speak to my request, I have other tidings, welcome news during this time of strife. As you may be aware, the Dreamer has been on the verge of waking for a short time now. As is our custom, a new potential Dreamer is selected prior to the Awakening so that they may be trained and prepared for their new role. We are most fortunate that a strong Candidate has been located and has already been brought to Palantia.'

The Council erupted into a storm of questions and exclamations. One Counsellor stood. His blonde hair was cropped short at the sides and swept into a quiff on top. He wore a small pointed goatee and a sharp moustache. 'We must conduct the Trial immediately!'

The room rang out with echoing sentiment. Silvana pointed a finely manicured finger directly at Sara. 'Is that her?' The Counsellors in front of the gallery twisted around to better inspect the human who slumped in her seat, trying to make herself invisible. 'She's rather... mature for a Dreamer.' Sara sunk lower, her face bright red.

The resounding strike of the King's gavel silenced the rowdy discussion. His expression was dark, and his eyes wild. 'There shall be no Trial! It is too dangerous! That's what it wants! The Caccinae... I mean, the Sluagh. The creature wants to steal another Dreamer. It wants her power! It will drain their essence and then we will not stand a chance! We can't allow it, I won't allow it!' Uinnseann was screaming now, his face red and blotchy, slick with sweat. 'It eats and eats, and it won't stop. It won't stop until it eats the world, and it won't stop even then. The Stitch! The other world! It will sneak and steal and *feed*! And then there will be nothing. NOTHING!' He clawed at his face, blood beading upon the welts left by his fingernails. A strangled mewling burst from his throat and

297

the King slumped forward, twitching and seizing.

Thorn leapt up from the gallery and vaulted over the barrier, knocking aside Counsellors and furniture alike as he sprinted towards his brother. Terentius reared in surprise, and Ander sprang out of his seat, dashing across the room to aid his friend. Senna, Jehn and Sara leaned forward on the gallery bar, mouths open in shock at this bizarre turn of events.

The Council erupted into chaos, the chamber ringing with shouts and screams. The double doors burst open and a cadre of Court clerks swept inside, the two pairs of armoured guardsmen at their heels.

'What's happening?' Belina's eyes were closed, a frown on her face as she listened to the hubbub around her. She clenched her hands at the bar, knuckles white, body stiff with tension, 'I can't make it out from all the noise!'

The guardsmen cut a path directly to the centre of the crowd, pushing Thorn aside without even looking at him, to get to their King. Uinnseann's eyes rolled back and his head lolled around as if his neck were broken. The guardsmen started in shock and Thorn shouldered them away to reach his brother. 'Seann! Seann!' Thorn shook the catatonic King in a desperate attempt to rouse him.

One of the guardsmen realised who he had shunted away and tried to apologise in a stammering rush, 'M-my lord Orinthorn, f-forgive me.'

'Don't worry about that now,' said Thorn, 'Help me!'

'Make way!' shouted Terentius. He leapt off the plinth and soared over the table to land sprightly on the far floor. 'Lift him up! Hold him!'

Thorn swept the table free of encumbrances and Ander hoisted the King bodily onto the now-empty table surface.

Thorn laid his hands on his brother's head to stop it moving back and forth. The guardsmen held back the Counsellors who were straining to watch as Ander pinned the King's jerking legs.

Terentius leaned forward and laid his horn across the King's forehead. Uinnseann's eyes were unnaturally wide, staring at a fixed spot on the ceiling. His mouth gaped, encrusted with spittle. The unicorn concentrated hard, an auroral light flaring within his spiralled horn.

Sara's nails dug into Jehn's hand, and he winced. She glanced over, saw his pained expression, and hastily released her hold. He nodded at the apology that fell from her lips.

Anxious moments passed, and the unicorn laboured for breath—so hard he fought to quell the King's convulsions. Time stretched and warped, and it felt to Sara that an age had passed. Finally, the King's eyes mercifully closed. A peaceful sigh issued from his cracked lips, and Uinnseann's body stilled.

Thorn stared at the unicorn in alarm, tears pricking at the corners of his eyes and threatening to spill over. 'Is he dead?'

'No, my friend,' said the unicorn wearily. 'He sleeps, and will for some time now. The seizure is over.' Terentius turned to the guardsmen. 'The King will need to be cared for, please take him to the infirmary at once, and ensure he is made comfortable. Do not leave his side.'

'Yes, sir,' said one of the guardsmen, saluting. He laid aside his weapon, and his fellows followed suit, hurrying to lift the King and ease him into a nearby chair.

A sudden shout rang out, harsh against the shocked stillness of the chamber. 'This is outrageous!' said the blonde Counsellor with the goatee, 'The King in clearly unhinged! All this talk of Unseelie Sluagh, and Dreamer attacks, it's just the nonsensical ramblings of a man gone mad. The King is unfit to hold his position. He must be made to secede immediately!' A ripple ran through the throng of Counsellors and clerks, murmurs of assent mixed with angry muttering.

Thorn wheeled around to fix his steely gaze on the bearded Counsellor, 'My brother is not insane! No more than you or I, Moryn Sionnach.' Thorn kicked aside a fallen chair as he marched up to the man. He stared down the Counsellor, fear and fury conflicting his handsome features, 'This creature, this rogue Sluagh, has spent months—months!—playing on my brother's fears and worries. It has picked and prodded and tormented him until he broke. And none of you did a thing to help him! He is an honourable leader who loves his people. We should give him our support and compassion, not call for his downfall!'

Belina felt a prickling across her scalp. She stood up, pushing the wooden pew back with a screech. 'Something—'

Suddenly the hummingcat materialised in mid-air, her luxurious fur crackling with energy. The little creature hissed and spat as if possessed. Honeysuckle launched straight at Sara, who, out of sheer instinct, thrust up her hands to protect her face from the furious ball of tooth and claw.

As Jehn and Senna looked on in horror, a black shadow coalesced above Sara, inky tendrils unfurling to wrap around her. The hummingcat flew into the tenebrous blackness, screaming in rage. The darkness tightened and the humming-cat screamed again, now a cry of intense pain, and the small furry body was flung outward, smashing against the gallery railing and crumpling to the ground like a wet sack. Jehn let out a strangled shout of horror.

Sara struggled to move, but her efforts were in vain. The

twisting black coils had her firmly grasped, and in front of the eyes of her terrified friends, she was pulled backwards across the pews. With a violent crash against the rear barrier, she was drawn into a vortex on the chamber's far wall.

'Sara!'

The unicorn sped towards her and Sara reached out her hands, crying his name, but despite all his magic and mastery, despair overcame her. Terentius wouldn't get to her in time. The blackness spread and melted and was gone in the blink of an eye, all trace of Sara gone with it.

CHAPTER 38

'You think the world revolves around you,' a voice rang out, dripping with spite, 'Like you are the centre of the universe, and everything and everyone is just a player to your stage...'

Her mind was thick as if it were stuffed with cotton wool. Foggy. Sluggish. *Who is that?* The voice was familiar, almost recognisable. *Like it belongs to someone I know, but just can't place.* It seemed like several different voices all rolled up into one hateful package.

'...Why are you even here? What does your presence achieve?'

It made her hurt inside, this voice, like part of her was dying, or worse: that she hadn't even been alive to begin with. Her voice croaked as she choked out a question. 'Who am I?'

'You?' the voice spat, derision an acid that burned her. 'You are nothing. Unimportant. Inconsequential.'

The voice was convincing. Confident. It knew her, knew what she was inside: nothing.

'Completely and utterly forgettable. Just a tiny speck to be brushed away and never thought of again...'

Her sense of self, all that she was and had hoped to be, seemed distant and hazy. Maybe the voice was right. She was no one, nothing. A speck.

'...Old and useless. Amounted to nothing. Accomplished nothing.'

It's all true. What have I done with my life? Nothing to speak of. Nothing to celebrate. I don't even know who I am.

'You lack passion. Always have. Lack commitment. I expected more. You are a disappointment.'

She cringed at the words, slicing to the bone with their truth. *I've just been coasting... not settling on anything to achieve. Not trying. Will I just keep coasting until I die? Will I make any difference on the world?* She laid her hands over her face, touching the wetness of her silent tears.

The voice scoffed. 'And how could one such as you make a difference to anything? You are dull. Boring. Nothing you say is of any interest. No one cares about you. No one cares about a speck.'

A speck. Dust on a lens. An irritation. *I'm just a waste of space.*

'Ugly. Plain. They point and stare. Turn away at the ugly girl.'

The words cut deep. Opened up old memories. Of being young and excluded. *Unwanted.*

'You aren't even worthy of a second glance.'

Not worth a second glance... She stopped, realising she was parroting back the words in her head. A face flashed across the back of her eyelids. Kind, with piercing blue eyes. *But he did. This man. And the others, too. They saw me.*

The voice broke into a mocking laugh. 'Saw you, did they? Had no choice. You forced yourself into their midst. Like you always do. Pretender. Only care about what you want. What you feel.'

No. That's not right.

'Always wanting to wear the spotlight, to have every eye on you, and why should you? What makes you so special? You're not special...'

Her hands fell to her lap and she opened her eyes to the blackness of the void. Her heart began to race in a familiar way. Her mouth became dry; her face, hot. 'Not special,' she said, nodding, 'But is it really so bad, this accusation of narcissism, of seeing yourself at the middle of everything? That's how you experience life, from inside your own head, from your own central perspective. How else can you see the world? You can't experience anyone else's life, only your own. Everybody else is doing just the same. So, no. I'm not special.'

She smirked. 'It's kind of a redundant insult. You should try harder.'

The voice hissed angrily, and a rushing of air washed over her. She closed her eyes.

* * *

She stood in the ruins of a stone city. The air was still and dry, but despite the arid surroundings, she felt neither cool nor warm. She scanned the ruins, trying to find something or someone to guide her out of this maze.

The ruined city was vast, stretching out in all directions. All that remained of its former glory were square pillars, their surfaces sheer and smooth. The pillars varied in height, some at waist or chest height, others towering above her head. Curiously, wooden posts radiated out from some pillars, and as she walked slowly towards the nearest, she noted that these were marked with a series of numbers. Not one sequence was the same.

She heard a small sound—the scrape of movement on stone—and looked up. A boy dressed in a cloak of grey feathers stood upon the tallest stone column, glaring down at her, his expression one of utter disdain. He held a white candle in his cupped hands. The tiny flame flickered and changed colours: orange, then blue, then green.

She placed a hand upon the boy's pedestal and traced the numbers with her finger. It was a puzzle. Unconsciously, dreamlike, she reached up to touch the wooden post. Curling her hand around it, she twisted it forward and back in an odd rhythm. A mechanical grinding sounded within and the pillar began to sink into the ground.

The boy's mouth twisted into a torturous leer, and with a cracking of bone and a contorting of limbs, he transformed into a great horned owl. Spreading its vast wings, the enormous bird unclenched its talons and dropped the candle to her waiting hands. Letting out a terrible screech, the owl beat its wings over and over, buffeting her with its wind and raising up a fierce dust storm. She squeezed her eyes shut and shielded her face against the rising debris.

With a final shriek, the owl fled, and the onslaught was over. She cracked open her eyelids and saw that the candle's flame had been extinguished. For reasons she couldn't fathom, this filled her with despair—as if a last crucial hope had died with the tiny fire.

In the distance, she heard someone crying.

The world shifted.

The stone city was gone, and she found herself at a doorway hewn into the rock of a cliff. She did not question this change in scenery, did not ask why she was now inexplicably

305

somewhere else. It made sense. It was just... right.

The outcrop thrust from the earth in defiance of the flattened plain of its surroundings. She pushed on the stone door, anxious to find the source of such sorrow. The door slid easily inward, allowing her to slip within the darkened hollow.

Inside, she inched her way forward, one hand trailing along the damp, rocky wall, the other gripping the smothered candle, wishing for the comfort of its feeble flame. The crying became a low wail, fraught with the agony of a thousand loves lost.

The passage opened, and in the centre of the grotto, she saw someone hunched on the floor, their silver-grey hair long and matted in tangled clumps. As she approached, they stood up, joints popping and creaking. With agonising slowness, the grey-haired figure turned around and raised his head. The old man's face was lined and gaunt, but still his piercing blue eyes were clear. She recognised him instantly. The man from before. But ancient now, worn down by life and sorrow.

'I know you,' she said, her heart breaking at the sight of him, one so full of life, now humbled by time.

He shuffled forward, voice cracking like his old bones, anguish dripping like tallow. 'It doesn't matter. Nothing matters. All lies, and sadness. And disappointment. You left me.'

His words were a wave crashing against a rocky shore. Constant, inexorable and true. Her breath hitched in her throat, choking her with guilt. 'I didn't mean to. I didn't—'

He coughed, his hand clutching his throat. She reached for him, and he flinched, drawing away, pulling his shredded robes to his bony chest. 'Why even bother? It's done. It's over. Just go to sleep and don't wake. It's not worth the effort, not worth caring. Everything hurts too much.'

A flood of despair washed over her, and she struggled to breathe. Tears pricked at her, and she sunk against the wall, the bone-chilling stone digging into her back.

'What's the point in caring? It doesn't amount to anything.' His voice grew softer, barely more than a whisper, 'Just lay down and shut your eyes. Let it all go away.'

I am very tired, she conceded, exhaustion threatening to drown her. *It is hard, this life—and living. A constant battle over can and can't, should and should not. It would be easy, so easy, to just... let go.*

She released a slow, long breath, and closed her eyes. She just needed a rest, a little one, not long. Just a few moments.

'What's the harm? Why fight it? Why fight at all? Rest now. Give over to sleep. It will keep you.'

A small voice scratched at her behind her eyes, and she screwed up her face trying to ignore it. *I am so tired*, she thought, *go away and let me rest.*

Fight! said the small voice, its insistence vexing her exhausted mind.

She wrinkled her forehead, confused as to who that voice belonged to. *There is no one here but the two of us. Me. And him. Oh, him.* Her heart ached.

Fight! The voice was a little louder, as if strengthened by her notice.

The old man eyed her suspiciously. The silver strands of his hair began darkening to ebony, his tattered robes smoothing. 'Don't you just want to let it all go?' he said, fixing her with his brilliant blue eyes, 'Didn't you just say it would be easy? Just surrender.'

She breathed in sharply, and clenched her fists, nails biting into the soft flesh of her palms. The pain brought her back to herself. 'Surrender? That's not what I meant.'

Sara! the inner voice was more than a whisper now. It was gaining in strength.

Sara, she thought, *who is this Sara?* She squeezed her eyes shut, trying to clear her muddled mind. 'Who am I? Am I Sara?'

The old man straightened, his hunched back merely an affectation. His sibilant voice hissed with barely contained anger. 'No one, nothing. There is no Sara. Sara does not exist.'

No, that doesn't sound right, she thought. *None of this is real!*

A grey fog swirled through the cavern, shrouding the old man, who looked less human now. His face sharpened, the skin rippling, and his eyes shifted from that beautiful blue to glittering green. She turned away, in fear and disgust. The hissing voice continued, its wheedling persistence worming at her resistance, seeking to break it down. 'You are nothing.'

She shook her head. 'No, you're wrong. I am someone.'

SARA! the inner voice screamed in her mind.

'I AM someone!'

'Pah!' said the hissing voice, 'A speck, a meaningless thing!'

But the creature's confidence was wavering, and she drew courage from that. She lifted her chin in defiance. 'I am needed. I'm loved!'

'No!'

She squeezed her eyes shut, wishing with all her heart. 'Love forms the world.'

Her pulse skipped, and she opened her eyes.

* * *

Unicorns filled the room. Figurines and soft toys lined the shelves on every wall, and unicorn mobiles dangled from hooks in the ceiling. A unicorn wind chime hung in the open window, tinkling a sweet cadence with the slight breeze. A rampant unicorn reared upon a large rug placed in the centre of the floor.

Sara remembered this place. It had been hers when she was small; a wonderful sanctuary in her childhood that remained so until she moved out of home. It was there she ran to in her mind when everything seemed dark and she needed to work out who she was and where she was going. This time, she was not alone.

A dark, shapeless form hunched in the open closet, far at the back amid a pile of dusty, faded shoe boxes and tattered, well-read books. Sara crept forward upon the unicorn rug, her fingers digging deep into the plush carpet. She crouched in front of the closet and peered inside. Black fabric draped a skeletal frame, and a thick cowl hid the other's face. She kept her voice gentle as she asked, 'Who are you? What are you doing back there?'

The robed form quivered, then turned to her, and Sara scrambled back in shock, remembering. She could see its face this time, vaguely reptilian, but with intense green eyes. 'I know you!'

Tiny flecks of grey spittle emitted from its thin black lips as it hissed its fury. 'Release me.'

'I am not holding you.'

The creature's face wrinkled in fury. 'You are. Give me my freedom!'

'Freedom is a strange concept,' said Sara, staring up at the ceiling and watching the motion of a unicorn mobile slowly turning. 'I think we are only truly free in our own minds.'

'Enough of this! You bind me to this place, this infantile corner of your consciousness. Let me out!'

Sara got to her knees and raised her chin, undaunted, her sanctuary imbuing her with confidence. 'If that is true, then I will not,' she said, shaking her head. 'I know what you are. You must face justice for your wrongs. You hurt people. Killed people.'

Sara stood, arms at her side, fists clenched as she held back her anger. 'You murdered Honeysuckle.'

The Sluagh snorted. 'A hummingcat is worth nothing.'

'Nothing! Are you so callous to care so little for life? You conspired to enslave Dreamers, and sought to tear the very fabric of the two worlds apart, and for what? Greed? The attainment of power? Did you ever think what you would do when there was nothing left?'

The Sluagh snarled and spat on the floor. 'Why should I care? Your world is dying anyway,' it said. 'You—your kind—you are killing it. Once upon a time, your world was wild. Nature and all its children ruled and danced and fought and loved and slept. But man grew and spread and developed and *never slept*, and soon there was almost nothing left. Your kind disregard the magic in your world, you ignore it as you scurry around like ants, burning and building and killing, caring about nothing but your own gain. I have seen it. I have looked into the dreams of your kind and seen your desires—to conquer, to steal, to bring violence to one another, to fill the earth with more of your senseless kind. You are a scourge. Don't preach to me about caring for life.'

The Sluagh broke off its tirade, chest heaving as it caught its ragged breath. Its glare upon Sara was filled with a dark fury.

Sara eyed the dark creature, her gaze roaming its reptilian features, searching for a sign of regret or remorse. There was none. She sighed, her own anger dissipated, replaced with a dull, numbing pity.

She spread her hands and shrugged. 'You are right. Humans are awful, they do all the horrible things that you say. Our history is fraught with war, torture, merciless slaughter. We have inflicted unspeakable evils upon each other for greed and power.' Sara's eyes shone brightly, lit by some inner spark. 'But you are also wrong. Humans laugh, they love, they feel, they want to do better, to *be* better. They believe in something more, in something greater. They give so that others may live. They care for those less fortunate than themselves. They believe in a higher power. Some even still believe in unicorns.'

Sara searched the other's eyes, and, seeing a tiny spark of its former self, her expression settled into a gentle smile, 'You were not always this way, so broken and jaded,' she said, kindly. 'You had a purpose, a reason for being, and somehow that was taken from you. I am sorry. This is not all that you are. You are young, and have a full life ahead of you.' She reached out. 'I can give you back what you've lost. Just take my hand.'

CHAPTER 39

J ehn held the hummingcat in his arms, his face stained
with tears. She was so tiny and her fur so soft, even now.
He sobbed as he stroked her poor, broken body, 'Oh, my
little Honeysuckle.'

Senna hugged an arm around the scholar's shoulder, his
own eyes glistening wetly. Terentius stood apart from the
others, head bowed and coat ashen with grief, eyes closed
to shut out the reality of his failure. He had saved the King,
but could not save the hummingcat, and now Sara was lost
too. Never in his long life had he felt so powerless. He stared
blankly at the floor below him, his reflection mirroring his
despair.

Thorn had taken charge. He dismissed the Council, sending
them back to their homes with promises of news when it
came. The chamber was silent, but for the small sounds of
grief and the soft chattering of sparrows nesting in the rafters.

Ander paced back and forth, unable to sit still. Now he came
to a sudden stop, his frustration evident on his face. 'We have
to do something!' He dragged his hands roughly through his
shaggy mane. 'We have to help her!'

Belina placed her hand on his chest and stared at his face
with sightless eyes. 'They could be anywhere, Ander. Where

would we start?'

Ander pushed her hand away. 'I don't care! She's our friend! We can't let that thing have her!' He swung on his heel and returned to pacing up and down the chamber, fists clenching in frustration.

'It is lost,' said the unicorn, sounding older and more tired than they had ever heard. 'They are no longer in this world. The Sluagh has taken her through the Stitch. They are Betwixt, between this world and the other. I cannot reach her. The only one who could was Leandra Lus-a'-chraois.' Terentius gazed sadly at the hummingcat's prone form. He felt a wave of despair wash over him, and closed his eyes, sorely tempted to slip back in and let the Malaise take him once more.

'What about another hummingcat?' said Ander, desperation overcoming any idea of sensitivity. 'Where can we find one? Jehn, do you know?'

'Ander, please,' said Belina, shaking her head, 'not now. It's far too soon.' She gestured to the scholar, who was sobbing silently. 'He needs to grieve. He has lost much this day. We all have.'

Thorn leaned his head against Terentius' side, trying to offer some comfort to the distraught unicorn. 'There is still hope, my friend,' he said, his finger and thumb rubbing nervously together, betraying his true feelings. 'She is strong, and you have taught her well. Don't give up.' Terentius eyed the Aes-Sidhe doubtfully.

Jehn rose, holding the hummingcat like a precious thing, his tears dropping on her fur where they settled like dewdrops. 'She should be in the sun. I will take her.'

'We will accompany you, Jehn,' said Belina. 'You shall not be alone in your grief.'

313

Through shimmering eyes, the scholar gave a small nod. Together they left the Council chambers behind, walking reverently, in utter silence, out into the midday warmth.

The sky was bright cerulean with whips of cloud high above the horizon. Such a clear and beautiful day as this seemed wrong, and it jarred Jehn's heart anew. *Mine Milis, my little flower. Gone.*

The procession made its way through the outer grounds, past the rose garden, into an area that resembled a wildflower meadow. It was hedged with neatly trimmed box, but the grass was long and wild. A papery white tree with brilliant orange teardrop leaves stood in the centre of the place, its foliage rustling and trembling against the caressing wind.

With delicate care, Jehn placed the hummingcat upon the soft grass beneath the tree. He lay beside her, staring at the little cat's bewhiskered face. Her eyes were closed, and Jehn wished with all his heart she were just sleeping. He reached out and gently stroked her velvet nose, drinking in the look of her so he would not forget his friend's sweet grace. *Her sacrifice.*

Terentius bowed his head and knelt beside the scholar, leaning his flank against the other's shoulder, two beings twinned in their sadness at such terrible loss.

* * *

A leaf fell from the tree and landed on the hummingcat's still form. Jehn carefully picked it up and twirled it in his fingers. *Aspen, like at the Dreamer's Grove.* His heart panged anew, thinking of Sara. He resolved to come up with a plan once Honeysuckle was laid to rest. *I can't leave Sara with that creature.* A sudden gust of wind blew, and the branches above shimmered, dropping more leaves.

The merest hint of blue mist hazed across the meadow, a glimmer of sparkle here, a flash of glitter there. The unicorn's head slowly rose, and he looked up at the leaves that were now falling faster above them. The leaves were a blaze of gold as they danced and fell. Music swirled on the wind, and a bright point of light sparked within the tree's branches. The beam expanded, coruscating outward in blinding white pulses. Ander and Senna shielded their eyes with their hands, but the others turned their faces upwards and stared right into the dazzling light.

The shining glow gave way to a woman's form, and to their astonishment, Sara floated within the cloud, her eyes closed, her expression peaceful. She held the hand of a small black-haired boy. Together, the pair descended and alighted upon the ground. Sara opened her eyes. They were filled with stars. She looked at each and every one of her friends, holding their eyes with her own a moment, until at last, her gaze fell upon the hummingcat's small, still body.

A small frown played on her lips, marring the peace there, and she turned to the boy. His emerald eyes welled with tears and he ducked his head against Sara's side. She let go of the boy's hand and touched his face, nodding at him to stand aside. The boy did as he was asked, hands clasped behind his back, young face full of remorse.

Sara knelt and laid her face ever-so-lightly against the hummingcat's own. She gazed into Jehn's eyes as he lay on the ground, watching her in awe. Her lips turned upwards in a smile, and she pressed them against the scholar's. He responded instantly, kissing her back, desperately, as if he might die without her.

She broke away, and breathed onto the hummingcat's face, a low hum sounding as she exhaled. The air thrummed and the swirling leaves shuddered, flying up and away against the vibration.

And then, Leandra Lus-a'-chraois, the Brave Honeysuckle, the smallest hero, opened her amethyst eyes and *sang*.

* * *

A late afternoon breeze whispered through the Dreamer's Grove, setting the burnished leaves of the aspen trees dancing. Mist swirled, and out of it came Sara and the dark-haired boy. He clutched an ornate silver bottle in his small fist, and he shuffled his feet as he looked up at Sara next to him. She released his other hand and knelt down in front of him, smoothing a strand of hair from his cheek.

'It's all right, Neese,' said Sara, her face serene, 'You go on now.'

With gentle care, she pushed him towards the dais. He hesitated, but with her urging, he climbed the wooden step left there by an attendant. The boy looked down at the Dreamer, whose face was ashen and still. Her chest rose and fell, but there were long moments between her breaths. The boy unstoppered the bottle and held it near the Dreamer's mouth.

In a barely discernible voice, he spoke an arcane phrase: 'Bí saor.'

The Dreamer's lips parted and she inhaled deeply, drawing the whole of the silvery essence into herself in one long breath. Her cheeks flushed with life, and she smiled. The boy gasped, staggering backward off the step. The entire forest shimmered, the paper-white bark of the aspen trees darkening. The Dreamer opened her eyes, and the Grove exploded in a rain of cherry blossom.

Sara's gaze briefly met that of the Dreamer, and then she slowly dropped to the ground. The cherry trees shimmered, shifting back to their former aspen, which let loose their golden tears. The leaves cascaded to mingle with the pink petals and shroud Sara like a veil.

The Dreamer rose, taking the dark-haired boy's hand as she stepped off the dais, and walked lightly to Sara's sleeping form.

Using the remaining petals of her magic, the Dreamer lifted Sara and placed her on the dais, smoothing her hair and gently plucking away the aspen leaves there. She placed a kiss upon Sara's forehead, and then disappeared with a flare of silver light, boy in tow.

Epilogue

'You passed the Trial, such as it was, Sara,' said Terentius, his tone a mixture of pride and sadness. 'I wonder if you even realised?'

Jehn rubbed his arms, trying in vain to massage some life back into them after the long night's vigil. 'I think she did,' he said. 'She is special. Extraordinary. I wish I had known her longer.'

A few attendants wandered nearby, giving the pair their space, but staying close enough to hear and record the first words of the new Dreamer. The first strains of dawn chorus had begun, and as the sun peeked above the horizon, the birdsong continued in earnest.

The hummingcat trilled and leapt upon the dais, settling down next to the sleeping woman, her purring a loud rumble. Jehn leaned down and brushed Sara's lips with his own. 'Love really was the answer. It's so simple.'

'Compassion,' said Terentius. 'Despite all that she had been through, she remained hopeful and optimistic about the goodness in everyone. Even a corrupted fae. Even a sullen old thing like me.' He sighed, and shook his mane. 'The Council could not but agree. It was hard for them to deny her, she demonstrated it in so many ways.'

Jehn patted the unicorn's shoulder, 'She was—is—kind and true. She will be a wonderful Dreamer. Just what Palantia needs.'

Sara sighed in her sleep, and murmured, 'I have this for you.'

The attendants perked up, one scribbling the phrase into his journal. They clustered in a small group, whispering to each other.

Jehn stared at Sara's face, searching for some sign or meaning of her first Dreaming words. Eyes still firmly closed, she raised her hand to the scholar. He started in shock. *Dreamers don't move.* Terentius quickly shifted his stance, shielding the view of the dais.

Sara opened her fingers. Nestled within her palm was a glass cube. Jehn took it tentatively, turning it over in his palm.

'What is it?' Terentius whispered to the scholar, his midnight eyes flashing with curiosity.

Jehn held the cube up to the light, peering into its centre. Inside was a tiny room full of unicorns. He grinned. 'A part of her. A special place.' He laughed. 'Take a look.'

Terentius peeked inside. He saw his own image reflected there.

The sun stretched fingers of golden dawn, beaming across the dais to light up Sara's face. The Dreamer's laughter rippled, flooding the Grove and rolling out to touch the whole of Palantia with its joyful sound.

The unicorn snorted. 'She made me into a rug.'

The End

Glossary

Some of the words and phrases used in this novel are derived from our world. Pieces of our many languages filtered through into Palantia over the centuries, with their origin in Dreamers past. Here are the meanings of a few key ones:

a*m Mathan Mòr* – the Great Bear (constellation) (Scottish Gaelic origin)

bi saor - 'be free' (Gaelic origin)

ifrinn – hell (expletive) (Irish origin)

mine Milis – little sweet (Irish origin)

mo chara – my friend (Irish origin)

plentyn – child (Welsh origin)

Acknowledgements

Thanks to my friends and family for their unwavering support over the far too may years it took to finally publish this book. I hope you enjoy it. It has been an amazing journey from that first silly idea, to a crazy month of NaNoWriMo, to a proper couple of years of honing my craft and constantly learning.

This book is dedicated to my brother, Steven, who passed away in 1999. I truly feel he would be a wildly famous comedian by now if he hadn't been taken too soon. I know you would be proud to see me put this creation into the world, brother. I love you.

I also dedicate the world of Palantia to my wonderful, magical friend of twenty years, Sara. You taught me so much about faeries and magic and trusting in signs from the Universe. I'm so thankful we met that fateful Christmas Day. Who could've predicted that little chat window would be the start of a lifetime of imagination together. To my Faery, I remain forever and always, your Unicorn.

About the Author

Born and raised in Tasmania, Australia, N E Absolom lives with her husband and their herd of overly spoiled indoor felines. She loves good stories, snacks, and sleeping in late. When not writing, she moonlights as a very normal office worker, and when she's not doing that, she's battling her way through an extensive video game collection.

N E Absolom is truly convinced that unicorns exist, and if she can't meet one, she can at least write about them.

Seek the magic in the mundane, and never stop believing.

You can connect with me on:

 https://neabsolom.com

www.ingramcontent.com/pod-product-compliance
Lightning Source LLC
Chambersburg PA
CBHW050132120726
47903CB00002B/320